TRIGGER
BRATVA BODYGUARDS #1

JAX KNIGHT

Trigger
Bratva Bodyguards #1
Copyright © 2025 Jax Knight
Published by Hudson Indie Ink
www.hudsonindieink.com

Jax Knight has asserted her right under the Copyright, Designs and Patents Act 1988, to be identified as Author of this work.

All rights reserved.

No part of this publication may be reproduced or transmitted in any form or by any means, electronic or mechanical, including photocopying, record, or any information storage or retrieval system, without prior permission in writing from the publisher.

Thank you for respecting the hard work of this author.

This is a work of fiction. Names, characters, places, brands, media, and incidents are either the product of the authors imagination or are used fictitiously. The author acknowledges the trademark status and trademark owners of various products referred to in this work of fiction, which have been used without permission. The publication/use of these trademarks is not authorised, associated with, or sponsored by the trademark owners.

Trigger/Jax Knight – 1st ed.
ISBN

PROLOGUE
HUGH "TRIGGER" SCOTT

LONDON - HAUNTED AND HOMELESS

Damp jeans clung to my legs, the chill seeping deep into my bones. My body ached and my drenched hair dripped water into my eyes as I shifted to ease the stiffness from sitting too long. The city sprawled out before me, cold and uncaring, its streets a maze of concrete and glass that swallowed up the lives of everyone caught in its grip. The wind howled, pushing against me like it had a score to settle, but I didn't care. I was just another lost soul, slumped on the pavement with a sign scrawled on the back of a cereal box, begging for scraps to ease the hunger gnawing at my gut.

God, I hated what I'd become. But I was too far gone to do anything about it, and too messed up to even try. Nobody gave a shit anyway, so why should I? I f was drifting, unseen, untethered, numb to everything around me.

The crowd surged past, heads down, ignoring me, their lives moving forward while mine stayed stuck in the gutter. Then, from the sea of indifferent faces, one guy caught my eye—Marko Rominov. A young man, dressed casually but with clothes that spoke of money, and a subtle confidence in his every step. Even through the haze of my apathy, I couldn't help but watch him. Something about him intrigued me—the way he moved, purposeful, like he knew exactly who he was and where he fit into the world.

He reminded me of the person I used to be, before everything fell apart, before the army spat me out as a broken man with a head full of demons. Only a year had passed, but already it felt like a lifetime ago.

I hadn't seen him in a while, probably because I wasn't at my usual spot. A twisted ankle had forced me to find a new corner to occupy. When our gazes locked, I almost said something—he'd been decent to me before, tossing a few notes my way and even stopping to chat—but I couldn't be bothered. On my better days, I appreciated the effort, but on days like today, I'd rather he just kept walking. I looked away, hoping he'd take the hint. But he didn't. Instead, he crouched down beside me, heedless of the rain soaking through his jacket.

"Hey there, it's been a while," he said, his voice clear above the steady patter of the downpour. His gaze flicked over me, pausing on my bandaged ankle and the bruise around my eye from a run-in with two arseholes a few nights ago. Feeling worse than usual, I'd decided to bury my troubles in some cheap gin, got drunk, let my guard down, and paid for it.

"You doing okay?" he asked, his tone curious but direct. That was something I respected about him—he always seemed to see me, not just my situation. Most people, they either looked through me or tossed a few coins in my cup without a second thought. They didn't care about the man underneath the rags, the guy who used to be something more.

But Marko... Marko actually looked at me, like he saw the person I once was and still might be, if I could just find a way out of this mess.

I shrugged, too drained to respond. Marko didn't seem bothered by my silence. He reached into his pocket and pulled out a handful of notes and coins, dropping them into the empty coffee cup at my feet with an easy flick of his wrist.

"Here you go. Get yourself somewhere warm tonight," he said, his smile genuine. "I'll see you around."

And just like that, he was gone, disappearing into the crowd as quickly as he'd appeared.

Thunder cracked overhead as I grabbed my battered backpack—the last remnant of my old army kit—and hobbled off. Most nights, I'd find a shopfront or a derelict building to curl up in, but tonight, I decided to take Marko's advice. The rain and cold had worn me down, and for once, I was sick of sleeping on the ground.

Maybe it was his words, or maybe it was the faint spark of dignity I'd felt when he looked at me like a man, not a wreck. Either way, I decided—I deserved at least one night off the pavement.

The walk to the shabby little hotel, where I knew I'd find a place for the night, was slow and painful, and it was dark by the time I got there. Inside, the reception area was as grim as ever. A single flickering bulb lit the space, casting shadows on the dreary walls. Joe, the old man who ran the place, sat slouched behind the counter, smoking defiantly despite the 'no-smoking' signs, and looking as grumpy as ever.

"A room for the night," I said, sliding over enough cash to cover it.

Joe grunted, taking the money and handing me a key with a hefty wooden tag. No sleek keycards here.

"Haven't seen you in a while," he said, his voice rough, like gravel in a tin can.

"Been keeping my head down," I replied.

"Aren't we all," he muttered, leaning back in his chair with a creak. "You have a good night now."

The stairs groaned with every step I took, the smell of dampness and stale cigarettes lingering in the air, seeping into the walls and floors. The room was exactly as I remembered: peeling wallpaper, a lumpy mattress, and a radiator that barely sputtered out warmth. But it was dry, and it was mine for the night.

My soaked clothes clung to me, uncomfortable and heavy, so I quickly peeled them off, leaving them in a heap by the door. I caught my reflection in the cracked mirror and barely recognised the bedraggled man staring back at me. The long hair, the overgrown beard—he was a far cry from Warrant Officer Hugh 'Trigger' Scott, the man who once wore his uniform with pride, commanded respect, and stayed sharp and focused. Staring at myself now, it was hard to believe I'd ever been that person. But maybe that was for the best. If I didn't look like him, I could fool myself, if only for a moment, into thinking I wasn't. And that helped keep the ghosts at bay, at least for a while.

The shower was basic—a narrow cubicle with lime-scale-stained tiles and weak, trickling water—but it was enough. I stood there for a moment, letting the pathetic flow run over me, but it didn't take long before the temperature dropped. Shivering, I turned it off, grabbed the threadbare towel, and dried off.

Naked, I collapsed on the lumpy bed, completely exhausted. The rain battered the window, the sound a constant pulse that finally dragged me into sleep.

"Move! Move! Get down!"

Sweat soaked my skin as I ran, the oppressive heat making it harder to breathe.

"Take cover!"

I dropped behind a boulder, my back scraping against the rough stone. The air was thick with dust and the sharp bite of burning debris. Gunfire cracked around me, sharp and close, but I focused, blocking out everything but the pounding of my heart.

"Get that fucking sniper, Trigger!" the Lieutenant, Alan Jackson, barked through my radio.

"Looking, Sir," I replied.

Sighting my rifle, I scanned the horizon, every muscle wound tight, every nerve on edge. Nothing.

Where is he? Where the hell is he? There!

A quick squeeze of the trigger, and the bastard went down.

"Hell yeah," Langton shouted nearby, and I smiled. They didn't call me Trigger for nothing. One pull was all it ever took.

"Fall in. Let's regroup and get the fuck out of here," the Lieutenant called.

Still scanning, I made my way toward the rest of my patrol.

The whizz of a bullet sent the Lieutenant to his knees, falling forward onto what looked like a pile of rubble.

A deafening roar split the air, hurling me backward. The ground rushed up to meet me—the impact jarring every bone in my body. Dust clogged my throat, the bitter grit choking me as I struggled to breathe. A second blast tore through the air, and I groaned. I'd fucking missed one!

Sweat ran into my eyes, stinging and blurring my vision. The air tasted of metal and smoke, thick with the acrid burn of diesel fuel. My chest heaved, my heart pounding loud enough to drown out the turmoil around me.

When my vision cleared, I saw them—scattered like broken dolls in the sand. Their faces stared back at me, eyes glassy and lifeless. Every one of them dead, except me. The silence that followed was crushing.

I jerked awake. My chest tight, my heart thundering in my ears. I shot up in bed, heart pounding, gasping for air. The room was dark, only the faint glow of a streetlamp cutting through the curtains. My hands trembled as I rubbed my face, trying to remind myself I wasn't there anymore.

The familiar ache of guilt and loss settled in my chest, and I stared at the ceiling, exhausted, waiting for sleep to claim me again and at the same time hoping it wouldn't.

The remnants of the nightmare still clung to me the following morning, despite a few hours of peace, a constant presence that never fully lifted. But at least I moved a little easier. The money Marko had given me covered one night at the hotel and a few more at the local shelter. With rest and decent food, my ankle healed quickly, but the rest—my mind—wasn't so easy to fix.

Returning to my usual spot a few days later, I watched the traffic on the street while keeping an eye on the door of the building where I usually saw Marko. I hadn't been at my best when we last crossed paths, so I wanted to thank him properly.

When Marko finally stepped out, he was with another man I didn't recognise, but I summoned the courage to approach, anyway. "Hey, uh, thanks for helping me the other night," I said, my voice hoarse, hesitant.

His smile was friendly, but his eyes held curiosity. "Don't mention it. You're looking better," he said.

Before I could respond, Marko nodded toward the man standing beside him, who had yet to speak. "Trigger, this is my brother, Miki." I nodded to the guy, unsure of what to make of him.

Miki didn't say anything, just studied me, his gaze unwavering, as though he was searching for something beneath the surface. His posture was controlled, almost predatory, the stillness hiding a lethal edge beneath—something I recognised all too well.

"You served in the military, didn't you?" Marko asked.

I nodded, surprised by the question but not bothered—I guessed the backpack was a giveaway. "Yeah. Sniper. Served in the Parachute Regiment with the British Army in Syria. Medically discharged after an IED wiped out my team. Left me with a head full of shit I can't shake."

Marko smiled ironically, his gaze flicking toward Miki. "That explains the edge," he said, more to him than to me.

"Which is the reason we want to offer you a job," Miki said, finally speaking. His expression remained unreadable, yet there was an undeniable precision in the way he moved, as though every word and glance was carefully considered, each action deliberate. This was a man used to power.

I glanced at Marko, searching his face for clues, but his expression gave nothing away. Whatever this was, it wasn't a casual offer. For the first time in months, my mind perked up.

"You interested?" Marko asked.

"Depends on what it is. And I'm not sure I'm the right person. I'm not exactly at my best."

They exchanged a glance, then turned to me and grinned. That should have made me wary, but instead, it was intriguing, sparking an excitement inside me that I hadn't felt since before my discharge, and I smiled back.

"We've been watching you, Trigger," Miki said, his voice

steady, measured. "We need someone with your skills, and we think you might be exactly who we are looking for. Let's talk."

And with those words, I knew my life would never be the same again.

CHAPTER 1
SARA CUNNINGHAM

MANCHESTER – LEAVING THE PAST BEHIND

The house was still dark as I packed our bags, my hands shaking from a mixture of fear and resolve. Everything had been building up to this moment, but now that it was here, I couldn't help but second-guess myself. Could I really do this? Leave him behind for good and start over on my own? Would he let me? What would I do if he came after me?

He was away on another business trip. Still, I'd been tiptoeing around for so long that I couldn't stop, as though he might suddenly appear and catch me in the act of leaving. My chest tightened at the thought and I clutched the strap of the bag in my hand, its edges biting into my palm. Every little noise seemed louder in the silence—my breath, the rustle of clothes, the soft thud of shoes against the floor. The reality of what I was doing felt overwhelming, each decision echoing louder than the sounds around me.

I glanced at my two young daughters, fast asleep in their beds, blissfully unaware of the storm inside me. For a moment, I lingered, taking in the small, cherished pieces of their world: Lily's stuffed rabbit, its fur worn thin from countless hugs, their Disney princess bedding, and Emily's crayon drawings of animals taped haphazardly to the walls. This room wasn't perfect—far from it—but it was all they knew. A pang of worry gripped me, sharp and unrelenting, threatening to shatter my resolve. What if I was making the wrong choice?

My breath wavered, but I forced it steady, straightening my spine as determination pushed back the doubt. No, I wouldn't let fear win. This was it. There was no going back now. Memories surged forward—bruises, broken promises, the relentless cycle of abuse. I couldn't stay. Not if I wanted my daughters to grow up safe, happy, and free of fear.

When I first met Adam Carruthers, he seemed perfect. He swept me off my feet, charming and attentive in a way that felt like a fairy tale. After a whirlwind romance, we married, and I was too young and naïve to see the cracks in his carefully crafted facade. Beneath the charm lay insecurities he couldn't confront, ones that slowly seeped into every corner of our lives.

Adam was a liar and a cheat, with a gambling problem that had been getting worse lately. His business acumen never matched the grandiosity of his ego, and I'd lost count of how many of his schemes crumbled, leaving me to pick up the pieces. His failures were always someone else's fault—usually mine.

Seven years of marriage had worn me down, hollowing out the parts of me that once believed in him. But my daughters' love remained my anchor, their innocent affection the only thing that made it bearable. That was, until the day he broke Lily's arm.

A sob threatened to break free, but I bit it back, clenching my fists to stem the tide of memories. The hurts he'd begged me to forgive. The accusations whispered in the dark. The nights I cried silently, terrified the girls would wake and see. I'd convinced myself I could shield them from it, protect them from the worst of him. But I'd been wrong—so terribly wrong—and it nearly cost Lily her life.

The memory clawed at me. Lily, crying out in pain as Adam shoved her off the slide. Her small body hitting the ground with a sickening thud, her arm bending unnaturally. He'd tried to pass it off as an accident, but I saw the truth. I saw him. The anger in his eyes, the lack of remorse. Adam had hurt her on purpose—his own daughter.

My stomach twisted painfully as my gaze swept over her small body, finally landing on the cast on her arm. This time, it had been her arm—but it could have been so much worse. I couldn't let it happen again. Lying to the doctor had been difficult, but I knew that Adam's lies were always so convincing to others. They believed him when he'd said it was an accident. If I had tried to contradict him, he'd have made it seem like I was being a hysterical woman. Then he'd have made me pay for daring to speak up. So, I stuck to the accident story and bit my tongue.

Since then, he'd acted like nothing had happened. The incident was over for him. But not for me. That was a few days ago. It had been the final straw. I'd been planning to leave ever since.

My girls deserved better than this. Better than fear and uncertainty. Better than him. I had promised myself I would protect them, no matter what it took. And now, it was time to keep that promise.

With one last glance around the house, my heart ached. These walls had seen too much—lies and pain were woven into every corner. This house had defined our lives for too long, but it wouldn't anymore.

Taking a deep breath, I turned and walked to the door.

Clara, my neighbour and one of my closest friends and the only person I could trust, stood waiting outside with the car idling. She gave me a quick hug and handed over a bag.

"Here's everything you'll need—train tickets to London, the details of where to go, and a bit of extra cash," she said.

"Thank you." My voice trembled with emotion. "I really don't know how to repay you."

"My cousin Lolita's got a flat ready for you. It's small, but it's a fresh start. She's got a little girl around Emily's age, so she'll help you get sorted, finding a school and nursery. You know where I am if you need me." Clara handed me a phone. "This is for you. Just a cheap one, but you can upgrade when you're back on your feet. My number's already saved. Call me when you get settled."

"You've been such an incredible friend," I said, my voice cracking. I hugged her tightly, trying to hold back the tears threatening to spill. "I'll miss you so much."

"Likewise. Better get going before we both start bawling," she replied, her voice steady, though the sadness in her words was unmistakable.

I nodded, quickly wiping my eyes. She was right. We needed to leave before the goodbye became unbearable.

After loading the luggage into the car, I returned inside for the girls.

"Mummy?" Emily's sleepy voice called out, her sister Lily stirring beside her.

"It's time to go, sweetheart," I whispered, my voice thick with emotion. Kneeling beside their beds, I tried to steady my breath. "We're going on an adventure."

The girls blinked at me, their confusion melting into quiet excitement. I dressed them quickly, bundling them into their warmest clothes and coats, taking care not to jar Lily's arm.

"Are we leaving Daddy?" Lily asked, her wide eyes searching mine.

"Yes, darling," I replied, my heart breaking at the simplicity of her question.

"Where are we going?" Emily asked. As the oldest, at five, she'd seen more than she should, and it tugged at my heart that her eyes were no longer quite as innocent as they should have been.

"We're going to our new home. A flat. Aunt Clara's cousin will be our neighbour and she has a little girl your age. Everything is going to be okay. I promise," I reassured them softly.

With one last look around, I took their small hands in mine and led them outside. My own hands shook as I closed the door on the place that had been both a home and a hell. As the lock clicked in place, I realised the finality of it and relief surged through me. That life was over.

We were never going back.

Clara opened the car door without a word and ushered us inside. The engine rumbled to life, and we pulled away from the curb.

At the train station, Lily's eyes sparkled with excitement, her little body practically vibrating with energy as she hugged her stuffed rabbit tightly. Are we really going on a train, Mummy?" she asked, her voice filled with wonder.

I smiled and nodded, brushing a strand of hair from her face. "Yes, sweetheart."

"Yes, an adventure!" Lily squealed in delight.

We climbed aboard, settling into our seats as the train began to move. The rhythmic clatter of the tracks soon became a comforting background noise, a steady beat in the quiet of the compartment. As the train sped along, the tight knot in my chest began to loosen. I looked at my daughters. Emily stared out of the window, a smile on her face as Lily bounced eagerly in her seat, pointing out the passing scenery. They were so full of life, so excited about what the future held. For them, this was exciting and fun. For me, it was scary and uncertain, but necessary.

With every passing mile, my certainty grew. We were leaving everything behind, but it didn't matter. This was the right decision. A new chapter was unfolding. The thought of him, of what he might do if he found us, crept in like a shadow. But I refused to give it space. There was no room for that now. We were leaving the past behind us, and there was only one direction left to go. Forward.

It was time to start over. I had no idea what lay ahead, but it didn't matter. Whatever it took, I would make it work.

CHAPTER 2
TRIGGER
SEVEN YEARS LATER – PRESENT DAY – A SENSE OF BELONGING

The clank of iron resonated through the gym as I hoisted another set of weights over my head. My muscles burned, but I ignored them. The pain was familiar, and in some twisted way, it felt good—a reminder that I was still alive.

The gym was a large, modern space, fully equipped with everything we could need—rows of free weights, cardio machines, punch bags, and even a proper boxing ring. I loved the smell of sweat and leather that clung to the place, familiar and grounding.

I wasn't who I'd been before. Not by a long shot. Seven years ago, I was a broken man—alone, lost in the fog of PTSD. I didn't know what was left for me, not until the Rominovs dragged me off the streets and into their world.

Now I was here, in a different place, surrounded by brothers—Marko, Vlad, Boris—and Miki. Miki Rominov. When he'd offered me a role in the Bratva, I hadn't hesitated to accept. Of course, I'd asked a few questions first, but when I learned of their code, I felt a shift in my world—like I had finally found my place, a reason to get up in the morning and do more than just exist.

Now, years later, I was a loyal Bratva soldier.

Marko stood over me, spotting as I pushed the bar up again. His hands hovered steady beneath it, his sharp eyes focused on my form. "Come on, Trigger. Push it," he said, a smirk tugging at the corner of his mouth. "Or is that all you've got?"

I gritted my teeth, shoving the bar upwards with all the force I could muster. "Mate, I'll show you what I've got," I shot back, my breath ragged but my tone laced with defiance.

Marko chuckled, his grip steady. "Don't make me have to scrape you off the floor, Trigger."

I shot him a grin through gritted teeth. "That ain't happening. Been there, done that."

We both chuckled, but there was more behind those words for me than banter. Marko had been the first to give me a shot when I was nothing but a down-and-out veteran with a chip on my shoulder. We weren't just colleagues or mates; we were brothers now. No question about it.

"Come on, old man, time to prove you've still got it!"

"Fuck you, kid," I shot back with a grin. I might be thirty-six today, but I wasn't going to let any of the younger guys think I couldn't keep up with them. Hell, I could out-lift them all. Well, except maybe Miki… or Vlad.

The rhythmic *thud-thud-thud* of fists meeting leather caught my attention, pulling my gaze across the gym.

Vlad worked the heavy bag with the kind of laser focus that could cut glass. Each punch landed with a powerful thump, his movements precise, controlled. Training with Vlad was an exercise in intensity; he wasn't one for idle chatter, especially during sessions. I couldn't help but smirk as I watched him—unshakable, relentless, the complete opposite of Marko, whose dry humour kept the mood light. Vlad was all business—a fortress of quiet determination.

He carried that same unwavering focus into everything he did. But behind that serious exterior was a sharp, playful wit. He wasn't afraid to flirt with the Rominov women or crack a joke when the moment called for it. In the rare times he let his guard down, Vlad could have everyone laughing—or rolling their eyes.

He'd been with the Rominovs for years—long before I showed up—and that kind of loyalty wasn't given lightly. I'd earned my place beside him over time, and while Vlad didn't say much, his actions told me everything I needed to know. He had my back, just like I had his.

"Oi, Trigger, you gonna lie there all day or actually lift something?" Marko's voice cut through my thoughts.

Huffing, I pressed the heavier barbell above me, sweat trickling down my face. The strain in my arms sharpened my senses, each rep testing my limits. It wasn't easy, but that's what I liked about it—fighting through the discomfort, pushing myself further.

Marko slapped me on the back as I set the barbell down. "Right, I'm off. Miki's got me buried in some IT mess."

"IT mess, eh?" I shot him a grin, catching my breath. "What, someone forget their password again? You're the only guy I know who needs a degree to fix a printer."

Marko grabbed his towel, shaking his head with a grin. "You keep this up, Trigger, and I'll be the one fixing your back when you throw it out."

"Throw my back out?" I snorted, shaking my head. "I'll throw you across the room, you little shit," I chuckled, tossing my towel at him.

Marko laughed softly, his wink quick. "Don't hurt yourself, old man." He waved over at Boris, who was working the bags. "Oi, Boris, make sure Trigger doesn't put his back out, yeah?"

"Shut it!" I shouted and Marko laughed as Boris chuckled.

"See you later for that celebratory drink, old man," the little fucker stuck his head back in to shout.

"Yeah, and the first round's on you for your cheek," I replied, laughing.

"Want me to spot you, Trigger?" Boris asked.

"Nah, I'm done lifting, mate. I'm going to head for a shower," I replied as I racked the barbell, wiping the sweat off my brow as I stood up.

"Okay, well don't slip. If you fall and put your back out in there, I'd not coming to rescue you," he sniggered. His voice was rough, but it had a playful edge, the kind of tone that suggested he was just as likely to throw a joke as he was to land a punch.

"What is it with you little shits today and this obsession with my back? I'll show you who's got the edge around here," I growled, smirking as I grabbed my towel.

Boris was a blur of motion at the heavy bag, his fists landing with precision as he worked through a series of sharp jabs. He wasn't as stoic as Vlad, but there was a quiet intensity in the way he moved, the rhythm of his strikes as fluid as a fighter who knew exactly what he was doing. His eyes flicked around the room, taking everything in, though he wasn't distracted—just always alert, always ready.

He paused for a moment, wiping the sweat off his brow, and caught my eye with a smirk. "You wanting to spar, Trigger?"

"Maybe—"

"Oi, Trigger!" Miki's voice cut through my reply, sharp and commanding.

"Yeah boss?" I asked, approaching him.

He nodded toward the weights I'd just used. "You're slacking."

I raised an eyebrow and grinned. "You see me slacking? Mate, I just hit my max."

"Next time, go heavier. Unless you're getting too old?" Miki didn't smile, but I caught the flicker of amusement in his eyes.

"Very funny, arsehole. I'm only a few years older than you. You too," I shouted at Vlad when he snorted and chuckled at the ribbing I was getting.

Just because it was my birthday, everyone thought it was a great day for ageist jokes.

"So, what have you got for me, boss?" I asked, eager to get a task to do.

"Nothing. Get yourself home and relax a bit before your celebration tonight. It's your day off; I don't want you working."

I frowned. "Are you sure you don't need me for anything?"

"No. Go do something fun with your day and we'll see you tonight. Vlad is going to pick you up so you can have a drink for once," he said.

"Whatever you say, boss," I told him with a cheeky salute.

"Beat it, fucker," he laughed. "See you tonight, bro."

His words sent a warmth through me, a sense of belonging I badly needed. After leaving the forces, I'd been alone and floundering, with no family to turn to. Not anymore. Miki wasn't just my boss, and these guys weren't just mates—they were my family, and I'd do anything for them.

Unsure what to do with myself, I headed home for a

shower, spending a bit longer than usual under the steady stream of hot water. The sensation worked its way into my muscles, soothing the dull ache that always seemed to settle in my shoulders and lower back. My hands braced against the tiles, head bowed as steam curled around me, and I let the rhythm of the droplets hitting the floor drown out the noise in my mind. It was a small comfort, but one I'd learned to cling to over the years.

Today marked another year I'd lived where others hadn't. The ever-present guilt threatened to consume me again, but I refused to let it. I'd been holding it back for too long to allow it to take over now. Images of Syria, of the lads, Alan, the blast, flickered like the afterimage of a camera flash when I closed my eyes. Therapy helped. God knows, I'd resisted it at first. The stubborn, proud part of me had scoffed at the idea. But the Rominovs had insisted, footing the bill without blinking.

"You can't take care of us if you're not taking care of yourself," Miki had said, his voice firm but kind.

I'd hated how exposed it made me feel initially, talking to some stranger about the darkness crawling through my head. But slowly, brick by brick, I'd started tearing down the walls I'd built around my pain. The counselling hadn't erased it, but it had given me the tools to cope—to keep moving forward despite it. Tools that helped me when I woke up sweating in the middle of the night, gripped by panic. I'd learned to count my breaths, to feel the ground beneath me, to focus on the present, rather than letting the past swallow me whole.

Now, I used the breathing technique to settle me. My hands were steady as I turned off the water, grabbing a towel to dry off. The smell of fresh laundry on the fabric reminded me that small, normal routines had become anchors for me. I pulled on a pair of joggers and an old band T-shirt before making my way into the living room, where my guitar waited propped in its stand.

Music had always been my escape as a kid growing up with just my grandad. Long before the army, I'd spent hours in my bedroom with my first guitar, a battered second-hand Stratocaster, teaching myself riffs from my favourite rock bands. It wasn't just a hobby; it was therapy in its own right. The feel of the strings vibrating under my fingers, the way a melody could take shape and fill the space around me, it was soothing in a way words could never quite capture. I'd had to sell my old guitar when I'd first ended up on the streets but now I had a brand spanking new, custom made, Gibson Les Paul.

Just looking at its sleek lines made me smile. I picked up the guitar, settling onto the comfortable leather couch. My fingers moved almost automatically, tuning the strings by ear. A few strums filled the room with a warm, resonant hum. The opening chords of "Stairway to Heaven" by Led Zeppelin came unbidden, and I let the melody flow, the familiar notes wrapping around me like a shield.

Somewhere in the middle of playing, the tension in my chest eased, just a little. My breathing slowed, the jagged edges of my thoughts smoothed out by the music. I closed my eyes, letting the sound carry me to a place where memories couldn't reach. Not entirely, anyway.

A knock on the door pulled me out of the reverie. I set the guitar aside and crossed the room, peeking through the peephole. Vlad stood on the other side, a bag of takeout in hand and an easy grin on his face.

"Thought you might need some company," he said when I opened the door, holding up the bag. The smell of fish and chips wafted through the air, making my stomach rumble.

"You're a lifesaver," I said, stepping aside to let him in. Vlad knew that unless I kept my mind busy, usually with work, it would take me to the dark place I'd fought so hard to get out of.

We settled at the small kitchen table, digging into the food with the kind of appetite only a day's workout could produce. Vlad kept the conversation light, talking about the gym, some new Netflix series he'd been binging, and a prank Marko had pulled on one of the new recruits. I laughed, the sound genuine, lifting my spirits in the way I needed.

"I heard you playing when I arrived. You've come a long way, you know," Vlad said suddenly, his tone shifting. He gestured at the guitar still resting on the couch. "I remember when the therapist wanted you to start playing again, but you wouldn't. Said you didn't have it in you anymore."

I shrugged, wiping my hands on a napkin. "Yeah, well, I didn't think I'd have a lot of things in me anymore. Turns out, I was wrong."

Vlad nodded, his expression thoughtful. "Miki was right to bring you into the Brotherhood. You've been a great asset, and you're part of the family now."

His words filled me with pride. "Yeah, Miki, offering me a role was the best thing that could have happened. I was on a slippery slope to destruction, but being with you guys has given me a place in life again."

"You deserve it, Trigger. You deserve to live. There's a reason you survived. It might be to have our backs, or it might be something else. You'll figure it out eventually," he said, his voice as calm and steady as always. His words carried a deep understanding of my struggles, and I knew why. Everyone in the Brotherhood knew Vlad's past—how he'd lost his family, except for a sister, and been taken in by Maxim Rominov. He didn't talk about it much, but the parallels were clear. If anyone understood what it was like to rebuild after losing everything, it was Vlad.

I nodded, not quite sure how to respond. Survivor's guilt had almost ruined me. I still couldn't shake the feeling that I didn't deserve to be here sometimes, but Vlad was right—I had made progress. The funny thing was, I hadn't really noticed how far I'd come until he pointed it out. The past didn't have the same grip on me that it once did.

"Come on, let's go get you drunk and celebrate your special day."

As we walked to the door, something shifted inside me. I wasn't as tethered to the past as I used to be. For the first time in years, I wasn't thinking about what had been taken from me or wondering how much longer I could keep pushing forward. I was thinking about what came next, about the future. I was learning to live in the present, to embrace it. And that, I realised, was worth celebrating.

I was finally living again. And it felt damn good.

CHAPTER 3
SARA
PRESENT DAY – SIMPLY SARA

The bell above the shop door jingled, breaking my concentration as I pushed the final pin into a client's evening gown, ready for me to sew. I glanced up, half-expecting a new customer, but it was just Lolita returning from her coffee run. Her usual bounce was unmistakable—a sure sign the morning's tasks, taking the kids to school, a run to the bank, and picking up dry cleaning, had gone smoothly. She juggled two steaming cups on a tray, a brown paper in hand, and a dry cleaning bag tucked under her arm, and grinned at me as she entered.

"Your lifeline, madam," she said, setting a paper coffee cup down with a flourish in front of me on the counter. "And mine, though I'll take credit for keeping us both caffeinated."

"You're a saint," I replied, sliding the pin cushion off my wrist and finally breathing a sigh of relief as I took my first sip of the sweet nectar that masqueraded as a Mocha.

"What's in the bag?" I asked, glancing at the bulging paper sack.

"Croissants, because someone forgot to eat," she chided, raising an eyebrow.

"Thanks, Lola, but I just need a few sips of coffee, I'll get the pastry when I'm done with this dress," I said, brushing off her concern, but Lolita's raised brow told me I wasn't about to get away with it.

"Uh uh, I know you, Saz," she said, shaking her head, her tone light but firm. "It's mid-morning, time for your sugar boost. Now stop what you are doing and eat," she ordered, crossing her arms as she eyed me, her stance making it clear there was no debate.

With a sigh, I set the gown aside and unwrapped the flaky croissant she handed me. The chocolaty smell filled the air as I took a bite, and I closed my eyes briefly, savouring the warm, crisp layers.

She gave me a sharp nod of satisfaction, the corners of her lips curling upward. "We need to keep your energy up to keep those creative juices flowing," she said with a grin.

I returned her smile, grateful to have someone who cared enough to remind me to look after myself. Not something I'd known much before. We might have met through her cousin, Clara, but it wasn't long before we forged our own friendship. Lolita had been a godsend when I'd first arrived in London, helping me find the flat next door to hers, and providing a lifeline during my darkest days. As single mothers, navigating the difficulties of raising kids on our own while balancing work, we'd become each other's support system. Her daughter, Cammy, was now best friends with my girls, and the three of them were inseparable.

It was Lolita who'd pushed me to take the job at the bridal shop doing alterations. I'd studied fashion and design before meeting Adam and becoming a stay at home mum, so it was a good fit for me. I worked there for a couple of years. Then I got a job with a major fashion label as a low level assistant, doing freelance alterations on the side. When I was made redundant last year, I finally took the plunge and rented this small shop. At first, I floundered under the mountain of paperwork required to run a business, but Lolita had stepped up, giving up her cleaning job to help me manage it all.

Lolita sipped her coffee as she leaned against the counter. "Marcie Matthews rang earlier. She'll be in tomorrow to try on her dress."

"Okay, I'll make sure it's done by the end of the day," I told her with a nod, my fingers already itching to get back to the gown I'd been working on. My gaze went to it. "This needs to be finished first, it's being picked up later. And there are two more dresses for alteration as well."

"You're a machine, woman," she said, flashing a grin.

"There's no choice, we have commitments, mouths to feed and bills to pay," I said, feeling the familiar pressure of my responsibilities.

"Yeah, business is really picking up now, though. We're doing alright," she responded. "Don't worry so much."

"Marcie's been amazing with the referrals," I admitted.

"She has indeed, but it's your sewing skills and designs that are winning you the clients, Saz, not just Marcie's recommendation. Remember that. She's been great, but you need to take credit for yourself and be proud of all you've achieved."

I met her gaze, my throat tightening as I swallowed hard. "I know, Lola. It's been difficult believing in myself after all those years with Adam putting me down. But with your and Marcie's help, I'm starting to get there."

Marcie Matthews, the event planner who'd first walked into the shop needing alterations, was one of my biggest supporters. The day she commissioned a design for herself had been a turning point, a high that still lingered in my chest —the idea that someone not only liked my designs but was willing to wear and pay for them. That excitement still sent little happy shivers through me whenever I thought about it. Marcie's referrals had given my business the boost it needed, transforming it, within a few months of opening, from *Sara's Alterations* to *Simply Sara*—a shop now offering bespoke designer outfits.

"I'm off to get some work done," Lolita said, heading toward the back office. The shop was small—just enough space to be practical, with the work area neatly organised to keep things running smoothly. At the back, there was a tiny kitchen, a toilet, a cramped office, and a larger storage space. My workspace took up most of the main shop, with a fitting room tucked to the side and a small counter at the front. It wasn't big, but it suited my purpose for now.

My eyes flicked to the window, where sunlight streamed through the glass, casting golden patches across the polished wooden floor. The sign depicting my new business was stencilled in delicate script on the window, and each time I saw the words, my chest swelled with pride. It had taken years of doubts and late nights stitching by lamplight to get here, and every small step forward felt like a victory. Lolita was right—I should be proud.

The quiet buzz of her voice as she spoke on the phone to a client was followed by an unmistakable whoop of excitement. I couldn't help but smile. Every time Lolita made a booking, she'd either do a little dance or a celebratory shout. Sometimes, I couldn't decide who was more excited about this business—her or me.

"That's another two people booked in for design consultations next week. They're looking for mother-of-the-bride and mother-of-the-groom outfits. That makes ten, on top of your usual alterations, and another four consultations for the following week," Lolita called.

As my assistant, she was nothing short of invaluable, freeing me up to manage the creative work, while she took care of the business. Lolita's transition from cleaner to full-time assistant had given her newfound confidence, and her sharp eye had made her an integral part of this venture.

"If this keeps up, we might even be able to get out of these shoebox flats we call home," I said, glancing up as she returned to the shop floor.

A gentle smile spread across Lolita's face. "You're doing great, Sara. Better than great. And when the time comes, we'll both pack up and find somewhere with actual storage and a garden. I believe in you."

I returned her smile, feeling a surge of warmth. "In us. I couldn't run this place without you," I said sincerely.

"Oh, please. Of course, you could. You're the design genius. I'm just the assistant," she teased, but her eyes gleamed with affection. "Though, I'll admit, my daily coffee runs are definitely a major contributor to your success."

"I think I'll keep you around for that," I said with a grin.

She laughed, heading over to one of the racks. "So, what happened at the lawyers' this morning?"

I hesitated, fiddling with the dress in my hand. "They sent the papers to him. We just need to wait for the response."

"I'm glad you're finally taking this step," she said, her voice soft with understanding.

"Yeah," I nodded, letting out a slow breath. "It's been almost five years since I left. I thought he'd try to find us, but he never bothered. And from what the lawyer said, he's found another poor fool to latch on to. All these years, I've been so worried. I should have filed long ago."

"You should have, but you weren't ready. Now you are," she said, her voice full of quiet strength. "Once he signs the papers, you'll finally be able to put him and that part of your life behind you for good."

I nodded. "Let's hope so. I don't want him dragging this out just to make things difficult."

Lolita's expression darkened. "He'd better not. And he'd better not come near you or the girls again. Ever. Or he'll have me to deal with."

The venom behind her words made me grin. It really was good to have a friend I could rely on so much. "I don't think he will," I said, the certainty in my voice surprising even me. "Adam hasn't even bothered trying to find us. With any luck, he'll just sign the papers and be done with it. Then we can all move on once and for all. The girls hardly ever mention him anymore. I think Lily's forgotten about him entirely. Emily hasn't, of course, but even she doesn't bring him up much now." The fear that had once shadowed our every step had begun to fade over the years and now it was almost a distant memory.

"How long will it take?" Lolita asked.

"That depends on Adam. The sooner he signs, the sooner it'll be done."

"It's a waiting game, then?"

"Yeah," I said, sighing. "But when it's over, I'll finally be… really free." My voice wavered unexpectedly, the emotion catching me off guard. There were times I'd doubted I'd ever get to this point, but now, for the first time, it felt within reach.

Lolita gave my arm a reassuring squeeze. "You deserve it, Saz—your freedom, the shop, your success, your designs. It's all coming together for you. This is your time to step out of his shadow and shine. I know it."

"Thanks to you and Marcie," I said, my chest tightening with gratitude.

"Well, like I said, Marcie's been amazing," Lolita agreed. "And I may have helped a little." I opened my mouth to protest, to tell her she'd done more than just a little, but she silenced me with a raised finger. "But the real credit is yours alone. That said, as your friend and assistant, I fully intend to bask in your glory right along with you," she added, her eyes sparkling.

Her confidence in me was infectious, and a smile tugged at my lips. We worked side by side for the rest of the morning, the easy rhythm of our friendship making even the busiest of days feel manageable. Lolita's quick wit and sharp eye were invaluable, and her laughter filled the shop with a warmth that lingered long after the customers had come and gone.

By mid-afternoon, the rack of alterations was nearly empty. Lolita glanced at the clock. "Time for the school run. I'll grab the girls and see you back home later."

"Thanks," I said. "Tell Emily and Lily I'll be home by dinnertime."

She nodded, grabbing her coat and bag, and I waved goodbye. As the door swung shut behind her, the shop fell quiet once more.

I turned my attention back to Marcie's dress. With a soft tug, the last thread slid through the fabric, and I tied off the end with care, before removing it from the sewing machine.

Placing it on the mannequin, I stepped back to admire the work. The material perfectly brought to life my 1930s-inspired design. The silk flowed like water through my hands, its deep emerald hue and beaded embroidery gleaming in the light. The dress was long, and fitted, reaching just above the floor at the front, with a gentle train at the back that would sway subtly with each movement. Its sleeveless cut, with layers of beads in place of short sleeves, would accentuate the graceful curve of Marcie's shoulders, adding an elegant touch of vintage charm. The neckline dipped into a soft V, highlighting the décolletage. It was a testament to the timeless glamour of the era, but with a modern twist, and I couldn't help but smile at how beautifully it had all come together.

Marcie would be here to collect it tomorrow, and I knew she'd expect to pay me then. But I smiled to myself—this one was on the house. It was the least I could do for all her support.

When my divorce came through, I was going to reward Lolita for hers by making her a full partner in the business. I would have done it sooner, but with Adam still in the picture, I worried that if he found out about the shop and how my designs were starting to bring in money, he might try to cause problems. He'd always been an entitled prick, and I wouldn't put it past him to try to take me for all I was worth.

That was why I hadn't waited any longer to file for divorce. The sooner it was final, the sooner I could move on—without worrying about Adam's shadow hanging over me. I was on the verge of creating a legacy for my girls, showing them that a woman could rise above hardship and succeed on her own.

The first step was clearing out Adam. Once he was gone, I'd give Lolita her partnership, and together, we'd build something that mattered.

Before placing Marcie's dress in a garment bag, I ran my hands over it once more. It was beautiful, and more than that, it was mine. A symbol of how far I'd come—and how far I could still go.

As I cleared everything up, my thoughts drifted to the future. My heart raced, a wave of excitement flooding through me. If things continued to grow like this, we might even be able to expand—hire more help, maybe move to a bigger shop. My mind raced with possibilities, and though the familiar voice of doubt still lingered at the edges, it was quieter now, overshadowed by hope.

Right at that moment, life felt thrilling, as if I were rushing headlong towards my dreams—and I couldn't wait to see just how great they could be.

CHAPTER 4
TRIGGER
SEVERAL WEEKS LATER – THE GHOSTS STILL LINGERED

My phone vibrated in my pocket as I pulled on my jacket after working out with Armen and Rolan, two of the other bodyguards.

"Trigger," Marko's voice came through the line as I wiped sweat from my forehead and stepped outside for better reception.

"What's happening, boss?"

"I'm at the flat with Melissa Martin. Turns out we were right—Mathieson wasn't working alone. His half-brother, Timothy Evans-Hughes, is also involved."

"Timothy Evans-Hughes, the MP? The bloody Foreign Secretary for the UK?" I asked, incredulous.

"The very same," Marko confirmed grimly. "And it gets worse. Mathieson left letters for Melissa. According to him, Evans-Hughes runs hunts where the wealthy pay to torture and kill innocent people. He wants Melissa to gather evidence to bring him down."

Aiden Mathieson. The name stirred up familiar anger. The Glasgow lawyer had used the Malia Boys and Broxys—two local gangs—to attack Bratva and Polish Mafia businesses, trying to fracture the alliance between us and Glowacki. All of it was part of his grand plan to destroy us. Mathieson had used Nigel Simpson, a slimy London lawyer, as his go-between.

We'd crushed the gangs and killed Mathieson, but we'd always suspected he wasn't the only one pulling the strings. Marko had been keeping tabs on one of Mathieson's bank accounts. Six months after his death, activity in the account had led us to Melissa—his biological daughter, though she hadn't known it until she'd inherited his money. And now it turned out the Foreign Secretary himself was tangled up in this mess. The list of enemies just kept growing.

"How the fuck is she supposed to pull that off?" I demanded.

"She has skills," Marko admitted, sounding reluctant, before explaining how her stepdad had been a cat burglar who'd taught her everything he knew.

I let out a low whistle. "So it's likely Evans-Hughes was behind the attacks on her, then?"

"I believe so. Either way, she's under my protection now. I won't let that fuck or anyone else touch her," Marko said, venom lacing his tone.

"You've got a soft spot for this woman?" I asked, amused at his intensity.

"Yeah, so treat her like she's already mine," he replied firmly.

"You got it, baby boss," I teased. Marko hated that nickname, but I used it occasionally, especially when he needed winding up. Ever since he dragged me out of the gutter, I'd called him my baby boss due to his youth. He'd grown into a man who could hold his own against any of us, but I wasn't about to let him forget his roots.

"Enough of that shit, Trigger. I'm no baby; I can wipe the floor with you any day, old man," he said with a chuckle.

"You could try, you mean. If I'm feeling generous, I might even let you, just to boost your confidence," I fired back.

"Shut the fuck up!" Marko said, but his good-natured chuckle lightened his tone.

"Seriously, Trigger, I need you to take care of Melissa," he added.

"You know I will," I assured him.

"Good. Get over here. We're heading into town so she can pick up clothes and stuff. After that, I'm taking her to dinner. I need you to drive us around and keep watch."

"Be there soon. I'll get Boris to take over from me here first," I said.

"Great. And don't bloody call me baby boss in front of her, or I'll gut you in your sleep," he warned.

I chuckled. "Got it, Boss! No calling you baby in front of your woman. Only Melissa gets to call you that now, right?"

"Fuck you!" he laughed. "Just get your arse here and leave the cheek at the gym."

I waved goodbye to Armen and Rolan, then got into my car and dialled Boris. "I need you to take over tailing Nigel Simpson today," I told him. "Marko needs me elsewhere for now."

"On it," he assured me before hanging up.

Within twenty minutes, I was sitting outside the flat, waiting for Marko and his new lady to emerge.

They strode out hand in hand, and I couldn't help but smile.

Marko was a great guy, and I'd seen how he looked at his brothers and their partners. He'd never admit it, but he wanted what they had, and I couldn't blame him. Being around them, seeing how much they'd changed since finding their partners, made me realise how much love could anchor a person.

Not that I was relationship material. Not with my baggage. But Marko? He was. And seeing the way this woman looked at him gave me hope.

"Melissa, this is Trigger. He'll be driving us today," Marko said.

"Hi," she said, offering a tentative smile.

"Nice to meet you," I replied with one of my own.

―――

Hours later, I was parked outside a restaurant, waiting for them to finish their meal so I could take them back to the flat and get some rest. I was bloody knackered after working the night shift watching Simpson, then squeezing in a workout before Marko's call. It was catching up with me.

Not that I was going soft. I'd just been pulling double shifts lately to cover for one of the guys who was sick, and I was looking forward to some shut-eye.

When Marko and Melissa emerged, they looked totally wrapped up in each other, and I felt a small pang of longing. Before I could dwell on it, movement in the rear-view mirror caught my attention.

A car was speeding towards them.

"Marko!" I shouted, snapping him out of his bubble.

"Down!" he yelled at Melissa, shoving them both into a doorway as the vehicle veered onto the pavement and hurtled past them.

I jumped out of the car, gun drawn. "Fucking bastards!" I shouted, firing at the speeding vehicle. The rear window shattered, but the car kept going.

Marko and Melissa bolted across the road.

"Let's get out of here," Marko ordered and clambered into the back of my car as I slid into the driver's seat.

"I can't believe some asshole tried to run us over," Melissa blurted out as I quickly spun the car around and sped off.

After a few blocks when I was sure the car wasn't going to turn around and follow us, I slowed down, determined to avoid any unwanted police attention.

"Where to?" I called back.

"To the Estate," Marko replied, holding Melissa close.

"Whoever was shooting at us knew where we were and must have been following us, waiting for an opportunity to attack. Whether they were after you, me, or both of us, it doesn't matter. We are going to stay with my family where it will be safer."

Melissa's voice trembled as she protested. "Are you sure we can't return to the apartment and go to see your family tomorrow as planned?"

"The apartment's not safe, Melissa," he said firmly.

"We don't know that!" she shot back, pulling away from him.

I couldn't stop the smirk that tugged at my lips. It looked like Marko had found himself another strong-willed woman, just like his brothers. Hitting the button for the dividing screen, I gave him a pointed look in the rear-view mirror before letting it rise. He could convince her about the Estate on his own. I wasn't getting involved in that.

Not long after, I pulled up outside the Rominov family home. The welcome party was already waiting.

"Melissa, these are my brothers, Miki and Ash, my cousin, Romi, and our good friend, Miki's bodyguard, Vlad," Marko introduced them as I grabbed Melissa's shopping bags from the boot. "You've already met my bodyguard, Trigger," he added, gesturing to me.

I gave her a smile and noticed the rest of the guys do the same. Despite the imposing lineup of Bratva men, Melissa seemed to relax as Marko guided her inside.

I handed the bags off to Vlad. "I'm heading home to get some rest," I said.

Vlad smirked. "Good. You look like shit."

"Feel like it too," I muttered, giving a snort.

He chuckled and nodded goodbye as I drove off. By the time I reached my apartment, my eyelids felt like lead, the adrenaline had faded, leaving only a deep weariness in its wake. I stumbled inside and collapsed onto my bed.

But despite the fatigue, sleep didn't come easily. The events of the night looped in my head, a constant string of what-ifs. What if I hadn't seen the car in time? What if Marko hadn't reacted fast enough? My mind buzzed with unanswered questions. The near-miss churned my gut, feeding that familiar fear—that one day, like before, I wouldn't spot the danger until it was too late.

Eventually, exhaustion dragged me under, but the past refused to stay quiet.

I was back in the desert, crouched behind a crumbling wall under the punishing sun. My rifle was steady in my grip, but the stench of death clung to the air, and gunfire crackled in the distance.

Without warning, the world erupted. Bullets screamed past, explosions fractured the earth, and everything spun into a blur of noise and terror. My body betrayed me, locking in place, paralysed by fear.

A scream tore from my throat, unheard beneath the thunderous barrage. Then the darkness came, consuming everything.

I jolted awake, drenched in sweat, breath coming in sharp gasps, my heart hammering against my ribs. The flat slowly came into focus, but it didn't bring relief. The nightmare was always there, an old enemy, never far behind—sometimes a repeat of that terrible day, other times the details shifted, but the result was always the same: only me left.

No matter the years or the therapy, the memories remained a relentless tide, rising to drown me when I least expected it. Alan's death always hit the hardest. My best mate since the first day of training, he'd soared through the ranks with ease, a born leader. Married with kids, he was the kind of man people looked up to, the kind who made the world better just by being in it. Why had fate chosen him that day and not me? He'd left behind a wife and two little boys, their lives shattered in an instant. I'd had nobody waiting, no one to grieve me. It never made sense—why his story ended and mine dragged on. Time had stopped me blaming myself for missing that sniper, but it hadn't erased the survivor's guilt. That's why I split the money I received when I was discharged among the families of those who were killed. I hadn't wanted to profit off their loss, even if losing them had fucked me up.

Sitting up, I ran a trembling hand through my damp hair. The motion did little to ground me. My thoughts still swirled, fragments of faces and voices from the past refusing to quiet. Once, they had found me in every moment of silence; now they came only when my emotions were heightened. Fear and worry seemed to summon them. I was fractured—not quite as broken as I'd been, but still like a vase that had been shattered and painstakingly pieced back together. The cracks were still there, visible if you knew where to look. And something was missing. Maybe, one day, I'd feel whole again.

Tonight—Marko, Melissa… it had been too close. It reminded me how fragile safety was, how easily something critical could slip past unnoticed. The ghosts of my past weren't done with me yet. They waited in the shadows, always ready to strike when I was at my weakest.

As the silence settled, all I could think was: would they ever go? And could I stop adding more names to the list of those who haunted me?

CHAPTER 5
SARA
A FEW WEEKS LATER – DESIGNS ON TRIGGER

The soft hum of the sewing machine was a steady comfort as I worked. This dress was a short, delicate thing—simple but elegant—the satin fabric smooth under my fingers. I should have been concentrating solely on it, but my mind wandered. I gnawed on my lip, brows furrowed, and a tightness settled in my chest as the worry returned. Adam still hadn't signed the divorce papers.

It had been weeks since he was served the paperwork, and after hearing nothing from him, my lawyer had sent someone to the house yesterday. They found it had been sold—no forwarding address, no trace of Adam. At first, I thought he was just stalling, avoiding the inevitable, but now, with no word from him, I was concerned there was more to it.

Clara had told me she'd seen him a few days ago, walking around the local area with another woman, so he clearly hadn't disappeared. That should've put my mind at ease, but instead, it only raised more questions. What was he up to? And why couldn't he just sign the papers and move on?

I shook my head, pushing the thoughts aside. It wasn't worth worrying about right now. I had enough on my plate.

The dress needed finishing. Still, the tightness remained in my chest, a vague unease I couldn't seem to quiet.

The door clicked open, and a breath of cool air swept through the shop as my next client, Melissa Martin, stepped inside, a little flustered. She looked up, offering a quick, apologetic smile.

"Sorry I'm late, Sara. Traffic was a nightmare," she said, brushing a strand of hair from her face.

"No problem at all," I replied, stopping the sewing machine and setting the fabric aside. "Let's get your measurements, then we can dive into the fun part."

She nodded and walked over to the fitting area. I gestured for her to step onto the small platform, grabbing my measuring tape and notebook.

As I worked, wrapping the tape around her and noting her dimensions, we chatted about the event.

"I'm so nervous," she admitted, glancing up at me through the mirror as I crouched to measure her hips. "It's my first show, and the press will be there. I really want to get everything right."

She paused, her fingers nervously fiddling with the hem of her blouse. "I want something classy but understated. The focus should be on the work itself, not the clothes. But I also want to make a statement… just not too loud."

"I get it," I said as I finished her measurements. "You want the dress to be elegant, but not steal the spotlight. Something that makes an impression without overshadowing the pieces in your exhibit."

She nodded eagerly. "Exactly. But I do want to look… special."

"I'll make sure we get it just right," I promised, already excited to design the perfect dress.

Before we could discuss the designs further, the door

jingled again, and I glanced up, curiosity flickering in my mind.

My heart skipped when I caught sight of the man in the doorway—tall and muscular, with dark hair falling messily to his shoulders, the breeze tousling it. He stood there like a force of nature, commanding the space around him. His gaze was sharp, intense, yet there was a calmness to him as well. I found myself holding my breath as our eyes met, unable to look away. His eyes were blue-grey—deep, stormy, flickering with a quiet intensity that I was inexplicably drawn to.

"Hey, Trigger," Melissa called out, breaking the spell.

"Mel," he said in a low voice, his eyes flicking briefly to me before returning his focus to her.

"Well, come on in, don't stand in the doorway staring like some creeper," Mel laughed, and he shot her an amused, yet annoyed look.

I cleared my throat, trying to shake the strange feeling that had settled in my chest.

"Trigger, this is Sara, the fantastic designer I was telling you about," Mel said. "Sara, this is my friend, Trigger."

"Nice to meet you, Trigger," I said, extending my hand, my voice a little unsteady despite myself, as he walked toward me.

His gaze flickered over me, his lips curling slightly at the corners. "The pleasure is mine," he said, taking my hand with a firmness that surprised me. His grip was warm, and there was something steady in it, like he was grounding me in that moment.

We shook hands, a tingle of pleasure shooting up my arm, and I couldn't help but notice the way his fingers held mine just a moment longer than necessary, his eyes studying me with unwavering attention. He was reading me, and for some reason, it both unsettled and intrigued me in equal measure.

I pulled my hand back slowly, trying to shake off the strange mix of emotions swirling inside me. His presence was magnetic—distracting in a way I wasn't prepared for. Shaking my head, I forced myself to focus on the task at hand. Taking out my sketchpad, I started working on an idea for Melissa, a long floaty-looking dress. While I was doing that, she wandered over to the black lace fabric I'd put aside earlier.

"This is gorgeous," she said, running her fingers over the intricate patterns. "Is this vintage?"

I nodded, smiling. "Yeah, I found it last week at an old factory sale. It's beautiful, and it has that old-world charm to it, don't you think?"

Her fingers lingered a moment longer on the lace. "It's stunning. I can see why you purchased it."

"Would you like me to design something with it in mind?" I asked.

"Absolutely," she cried.

Excited by the prospect, I set my pencil to the page again, sketching quickly. The soft scratch of lead against paper was soothing, and I allowed myself to get lost in it as I drew.

I looked up after a few minutes to find Melissa studying the design I was creating and the long dress I'd previously done, her brow furrowed as if deep in thought.

"Okay," she said, tapping a finger against her lips, "they are beautiful, but now I'm stuck between the two ideas. Do I go with something long and floaty, or…?"

Her voice trailed off as she bit her lip, studying the second design I'd sketched—this one a much simpler, form-fitting number that highlighted the body more clearly, the soft black lace wrapping around it like a second skin.

I gestured to the two designs. "Well, this is a long and floaty one that gives you that ethereal feel you mentioned when you called. And this,"—I pointed to the other one—"is sleek, more understated, but with enough detail to make it special. The lace and the shape of it should still make an impact."

"I love them both," she admitted, a little frustrated. "But I don't know which one is right for the show. The long one feels... elegant, but maybe too much like a statement itself. The short one is also beautiful..." She trailed off, her fingers moving over the edge of the fabric, her gaze searching the designs.

"What do you want your look to say?" I asked softly, catching her eyes. "Classy, but not over the top. Elegant, but with a bit of edge. What will make you feel the most confident?"

She tilted her head, her lips curving slightly. "That's exactly it," she said after a pause. "I want to make an impact and feel confident, but I also want to look effortless and not outshine my work." She bit her lip and sighed. "These are just so lovely, I can't choose which would be more suitable."

I nodded, glancing between the two designs. The short, fitted one—simple yet striking—would definitely be the perfect choice to let her confidence shine through. It would complement the art in her exhibit, not overpower it. I felt a sense of certainty that it was the right decision.

Just as I was about to speak, Melissa turned to Trigger, who had been leaning casually against the counter, observing our exchange in silence. I hadn't realised he was paying that much attention, but there was something in his posture that suggested he was taking everything in, even the smallest details.

"Trigger," Melissa said, catching his eye. "What do you think? Between the two... which one stands out more to you?"

His eyes flicked between the two sketches, narrowing slightly as he considered the options. Then, without hesitation, he spoke.

"The short one," he said, his voice calm and assured. "It's clean. Simple. Elegant. The long one's beautiful, but it could easily distract from everything else going on. The shorter one lets you stand out without stealing the spotlight from the exhibit."

I couldn't help but notice how sure he was in his response, how effortlessly his gaze moved from one design to the other, his eyes returning to the more fitted dress as if he'd already decided it was the right choice. The way he spoke made it sound like it wasn't just a suggestion—it was a conclusion he had drawn after thinking it through.

"That's what I was thinking," I said with a smile, feeling a little relieved that we were on the same page. "It's beautiful in its simplicity, and it'll let your art take centre stage, as it should."

Melissa's eyes lit up with excitement. "I love it," she said, turning to Trigger with a wide grin. "We've got a winner. Thank you."

Trigger gave her a nod, his lips twitching into something that might have been a smile. "No problem. Just keep it simple and let the dress do its job to build your confidence. Your work will speak for itself."

After a brief silence, Melissa spoke again. "I'll take the other one too. I don't know what I'll wear it to yet, but I love the design and I can't resist." She clapped her hands together. "Let's make that one red lace. With a silk underskirt?"

I nodded, already envisioning the design in my mind, it would look so good with her long, silky black hair. "Of course. I'll need to get my hands on some red lace, but I can make that work. I'll make sure it's a bit more dramatic, but still elegant. Like a statement piece, but with the same level of understated sophistication."

Melissa clapped her hands together. "Perfect! I knew I could count on you, Sara."

As we finalised the designs, I couldn't help but feel a small wave of pride. I had nailed exactly what Melissa wanted—and sold not just one, but two dresses. One that would perfectly complement her vision for her first show, and another she could use for her next special occasion. I felt the approval of Trigger's quiet, powerful gaze lingering on me, making my heart beat just a little faster.

As we wrapped up the details, Melissa stood there beaming, her excitement palpable. "This is going to be amazing, Sara. I can't wait to see it all come together."

I smiled, still feeling the buzz of satisfaction from getting the designs just right. "I'll make sure they are perfect for you."

She walked toward the door, her footsteps light, and paused with her hand on the handle. "I'll check in soon, but… thank you, really. This means so much."

"You're welcome," I said, my voice warm with the feeling of accomplishment. "I've got this."

"Oh, actually, before I go, can I use your loo?" she asked, hesitating and looking a little embarrassed.

"Of course, it's in the back beside the office," I told her.

With that, Melissa disappeared, and I was left alone in the small workspace with Trigger. The air between us seemed to hum with something unspoken, and I could feel my pulse quicken, even though he hadn't moved from his spot in the counter.

I turned back to my workbench, trying to focus on the sketches, but I could feel his eyes on me—lingering, as if he was watching every movement I made. The silence stretched out, and I wasn't sure if I should say something or just let it be.

Then, without warning, Trigger pushed off from the counter, his footsteps surprisingly soft for a man his size. He moved closer, the space between us shrinking, and I had to force myself not to take an instinctive step back. The heat of his presence pressed in on me, wrapping around me like a cloak.

"Thank you," he said. His voice, calm and assured, made the air between us crackle, an invisible thread pulling taut between us. "For helping Mel. She's been so excited to have one of your designs."

I glanced up, meeting his gaze, and for a moment, I couldn't look away. His eyes, still stormy and deep, held me in place, and the steady rhythm of his breathing seemed to sync with mine. I felt my heart beat faster, and the words I'd meant to say got lost somewhere in the space between us.

Gulping, I cleared my throat. "I'm happy to help," I said eventually when I found my voice again. "She's great to work with."

His lips twitched into something almost like a smile, but it didn't quite reach his eyes. Those eyes—so full of secrets, of things he wasn't saying—continued to study me with an intensity that made my skin prickle, but in a way that wasn't entirely unpleasant.

"I'm sure you make a lot of people happy," he murmured, his voice so quiet it almost felt like a confession.

I swallowed hard, my stomach doing a flip at the idea of him noticing me—really noticing me. I wasn't sure what to do with that thought. Or even if it was something I wanted.

"Maybe," I replied, trying to keep my voice steady. "I just try to do my job well."

He stepped a little closer, his gaze dropping for just a

moment to my mouth before coming back to mine. "I think you do more than that."

His words hung in the air like a challenge, like he was daring me to read between the lines. And I did, my mind racing, my pulse accelerating. Was he flirting with me? Was I imagining this? Was he going to kiss me? Did I want him to? Hell yeah! And his eyes... damn those eyes.

But after everything with Adam, I shouldn't let myself be drawn in so easily.

I quickly turned back to my worktop, feeling a flush rise to my cheeks. It was ridiculous to feel this way—this flustered, this off-kilter—especially after everything I'd been through. But somehow, in this small, quiet space, with his presence filling the room, everything felt... different.

"I'll see you out," I said, trying to regain my composure as I smiled shakily and gestured towards the door. The air was thick between us and breathing was becoming difficult. I licked my lips, my mouth suddenly dry.

Trigger's eyes flared as he tracked the movement. "No rush," he said, his voice so casual it made my heart skip a beat. "Melissa's still in the toilet."

He smirked as he openly ogled me. My face blazed. There was a long moment of silence between us, neither of us moving. Our eyes held, and it was as if a magnetic force was pulling me into his depths. And then, as though he couldn't help himself, he took another step closer. This time, I didn't try to move away. I couldn't.

He leaned in close. "It's been a pleasure meeting you, Sara," he said, his voice barely above a whisper. His breath fanned my ear, sending delicious shivers down my body and making my own breaths come out ragged. The pleasure was all mine. Oh god! What was happening?

Footsteps broke the spell, and he stepped back.

"Ready?" he said to Melissa without taking his eyes off me.

"Good to go," she replied cheerily.

Melissa's eyebrow raised, and she grinned as she looked between us, obviously catching onto the charged atmosphere.

"See you soon, Sara," she called as she walked past me and out of the door.

"I'll look forward to it," I replied, my voice croaky. I cleared my throat as I turned back to Trigger who hadn't yet moved.

"Me too," he said, with a slow smile, before turning and walking toward the door.

I stood frozen for a moment longer, watching him leave.

What the hell was that?

CHAPTER 6
TRIGGER
THE SAME DAY – DESIGNS ON SARA

"Sara's a beautiful woman," Melissa said, a hint of mischief in her eyes as we climbed into the car.

"I hadn't noticed," I replied with a small smirk.

"Yeah, right, you were practically salivating over her," she said, snorting.

I chuckled. "Okay, I admit, she is a beautiful woman."

"And talented," Melissa added, grinning.

"And talented," I agreed with a smile, masking the discomfort simmering beneath the surface. Flirting with Sara had been... unexpected. It wasn't something I did often. Usually, if I wanted a woman, I made it known—straightforward and to the point. Most times, it was clear from the looks I got whether she was interested, and if she was, things went from there. Simple.

But with Sara, it had been different. I'd taken the initiative, testing the waters with a playful remark, and her reaction had been worth it—shy but receptive. So receptive. There was something intoxicating about it, something I hadn't felt in a long time. Maybe ever.

Still, she was a single mum. Mel had mentioned that

already. I didn't play games, especially not with someone who had a kid or two to think about. And while the chemistry between us was undeniable, I could see Sara wasn't the type for a casual hook-up. Not that I'd even want it to be casual. That thought alone made me pause, a wave of uncertainty crashing over me. Could I give her more? Would she even want me if she knew the real me?

I pushed the thoughts aside, shoving them into the mental box where I kept things better left unanswered. Fishing around for something else to discuss, I asked, "Did you finish picking the last of your photographs for the exhibit?"

"Yes, all done. I decided on the last piece yesterday. Now I just need to pick the right frames and they will be ready for display," she said.

"Great stuff," I replied, and she smiled and sank back into her seat, her mind obviously back on the exhibit and away from the uncomfortable topic of Sara.

The rest of the drive to Glowacki's restaurant was thankfully quiet. Melissa sat beside me, staring out the window, her fingers tapping a rhythm against her thigh I couldn't quite catch. She looked relaxed, but I knew better. Melissa rarely sat still for long; she was always brimming with an energy most of us couldn't keep up with.

She caught me looking and raised an eyebrow. "What?"

I shrugged, focusing back on the road. "You're restless."

"Always," she replied with a grin.

As I drove into the small car park, Melissa's legs bounced, her eagerness to get moving again obvious. The second the car stopped, she was out, hurrying toward the entrance before I even cut the engine. I watched as she greeted the manager and staff, her energy filling the space effortlessly, her animated gestures drawing smiles all around. She'd been reserved when she first joined us, but it hadn't taken long for her to open up and show just how great a person she was. Melissa had a way of brightening up any room she entered, making people feel lighter simply by being around her. Maybe that was why Marko had paired me with her these last few weeks.

My role in the Bratva until now had always been flexible —me doing whatever was needed, whenever. But Marko knew me well. He must have realised how Mel's lightness could balance the shadows I carried. And how I'd guard her fiercely in return.

For a moment, I lingered in the driver's seat, hands resting on the wheel. My thoughts drifted back to Sara. She had a presence of her own—calm yet magnetic. I closed my eyes, her image coming easily: the curve of her lips as she smiled, the certainty with which her hands moved while sketching, the way her eyes met mine, causing my cock to thicken. I groaned and shifted uncomfortably. My reaction to her was unexpected, catching me off guard in a way that stuck.

A wave from the manager pulled me out of my thoughts of the sexy designer and back to my job. I stepped out of the car and made my way into the restaurant, nodding briefly to the staff as I scanned the room for Melissa.

She stood near the back of the room talking animatedly with Janusz Glowacki and his wife, Marta, aunt to the Rominovs, whose marriage to Glowacki had turned an alliance into family.

"Trigger," Glowacki greeted me as I approached. His Polish accent was thick but clear. "Good to see you," he said, shaking my hand with a firm grip.

"You too," I replied.

Marta leaned over and kissed me on the cheek. "Hi, Trigger, how are you doing?"

"Good, thanks," I told her with a smile, and for once, I meant it.

"What do you think of the new look?" Glowacki asked. "Marta has revamped the place and I think it looks amazing," he told me, pride gleaming in his eyes as he pulled Marta close and nuzzled her ear.

She swatted at him playfully. "You're biased. What do you think, Trigger?"

"It is beautiful. You've done a great job," I replied, genuinely impressed.

"She certainly has," Melissa chimed in, beaming.

The restaurant had been polished to perfection—real hardwood floors, glittering chandeliers, and an air of understated elegance. Staff buzzed around the dining room, arranging cutlery, and preparing for the evening service.

Glowacki and Marta escorted us through to the large banquet hall at the back, where decorators worked to renew the lighting to suit Melissa's needs.

"It's coming together beautifully," Melissa said, her eyes bright as she surveyed the space. "This will be perfect for the show."

"We're happy to host you," Glowacki grinned. "You are very talented and I'm sure many of my friends and family will want to buy your photographs. Just remember, I already own the ones of Marta and Magdalena," he added, smirking. "You can display them, but they're mine now."

Melissa laughed. "Don't worry, they'll have sold stickers on them, so no one else tries to buy them."

"Good. I'm looking forward to seeing them displayed at home," he said, his words meant for both women.

"Well, I'd really like Melissa to take some of you for our home too," Marta added, leaning in close and batting her lashes at him.

He laughed, and so did Melissa. The women had been happy to model for Melissa, while the men had been far more reluctant. Still, the women's determination was slowly wearing down their respective partners.

"All right, anything for you, my love," Glowacki said, smiling as he kissed the top of Marta's head.

She looked at Melissa and smirked. "We'll arrange a time for you to shoot him soon," Marta said excitedly.

"Oh, not again. Once was enough," Glowacki joked, placing a hand over his chest where he'd been shot in feigned protest.

"Not funny!" Marta pouted. "You'd better never get shot like that again, lover, or you'll have me to answer to," she chided.

Glowacki's lips twitched.

"Promise me," she said, elbowing him in the ribs.

"Oof, yes, my love. I promise not to get shot again if I can help it," he whispered, nuzzling her ear until she giggled.

Melissa chuckled at the sight, and I rolled my eyes. These two were another of the recently loved-up couples. Glowacki had originally arranged for his son Dariusz to marry Sonia Rominov to strengthen his allegiance with the Bratva. But when it was discovered that Sonia and Romi were secretly in love, Glowacki dissolved the arrangement, choosing instead to marry Marta—a decision sparked after she nursed him back to health when he was shot following an attack on the Rominovs drug Lab several months ago. Though it had started as a marriage of convenience, it was clear to everyone that it had become a genuine love match.

"All right, you two—get a room or let's get on with business," I said with a laugh, breaking into their little bubble.

Glowacki grinned. "I can't help that my beautiful wife is so distracting."

Marta blushed, but pulled away. "Let's finish up with Melissa so we can head home," she said, tossing a saucy wink over her shoulder as she walked toward a booth at the back.

"Mel," Glowacki said, catching her arm and tucking it into his own, "we've got business to finish." He smiled and tugged her along, clearly eager to wrap things up and spend more time being distracted by his wife.

Chuckling, I followed along behind, taking a seat next to Mel in the booth. The rest of the meeting was spent planning —lighting angles, table placements, guest lists, and security protocols. I listened more than I spoke, letting Melissa handle the arrangements while my thoughts drifted.

This restaurant had been one of the ones broken into and partially destroyed during the attacks by the Malia Boys and the Broxys. The very same enemies who later shot and almost killed Glowacki. Mathieson had been planning it all, through that weasel Simpson, but then we found out his brother was involved. After Mel and Marko broke into the MP's home and obtained evidence to send to the authorities, the MP was arrested.

I shifted slightly, my fingers tapping against the edge of the table, the thought of the bastard gnawing at me.

Out on bail, the arsehole was practically under house arrest at his country estate. Reporters had been camped outside since the day of his arrest, trailing him like a bad smell. It hadn't stopped him from pulling strings, though— he'd managed to get someone to stab Melissa just a few weeks ago. My fists clenched at the memory. The thought of her being hurt made my blood boil. That was the reason she needed a bodyguard. The sooner that fucker was behind bars and one of our allies took him out for good, the better.

Killing him ourselves wasn't an option. The risk of exposing the Bratva was too high. Instead, Miki had done what his father before him had mastered: using the authorities to do the dirty work. But now we were stuck waiting, tangled in a slow web of legal red tape, impatient for the day it was all over.

My phone vibrated. It was Boris.

"What's up?" I asked.

"Hey, just to let you know, that perverted little weasel, Simpson, has been lying low for the last couple of days, but now that his wife and kids are out of town, he's up to his usual tricks," he told me.

Bile rose in my throat, knowing what that meant. "Where is he?"

"That shabby flat where he takes his rent boys. He went inside with a couple after buying some coke. Looks like he intends making a night of it."

"Okay, I'm with Mel over at Glowacki's restaurant. I'll meet you there when I've dropped Mel back home," I told him.

It was my turn to watch Simpson tonight, and if he was at the flat he kept for his passionate liaisons, I didn't relish the task.

Nigel Simpson was another problem we needed to get rid of as soon as possible. Unfortunately, Eilidh, Miki's fiancé, had insisted on us keeping the pervert alive because she believed there was more to him than we knew, and also because she thought he might continue to be useful. I wasn't sure about that, but I did what I was told. One day, the guy would be dealt with, it didn't really matter to me if it were now or in the future, it was watching him enjoying his 'pleasures' that sickened me. However, it was all part of the job, so I'd suck it up and deal, like always.

By the time the meeting wrapped up, the sun had dipped below the horizon, and the city outside was cloaked in darkness. Melissa was still buzzing as we walked back to the car.

"That went well, didn't it?" she said, practically skipping beside me.

"It did," I replied, though my mind stayed locked on the bigger picture. "Glowacki will make sure everything's ready. He knows what he's doing."

Melissa grinned up at me. "And so do you. Thanks for coming with me tonight. And I liked your suggestion to have individual lights placed over each photograph. It will really showcase them well."

I opened the passenger door for her, pausing as she climbed in. For a second, Sara's face flashed in my mind—her bright smile, the way she'd looked at me like I wasn't broken. I swallowed hard and slid into the driver's seat.

The drive back to the Rominov estate started in silence, the hum of the engine filling the space between us. Melissa's fingers tapped on her thigh again, but this time she spoke.

"You seem distracted tonight."

"Just thinking." My voice came out flat as I kept my eyes fixed on the road.

"About what?"

The corner of my mouth twitched. I was not about to tell her I'd been thinking about a gorgeous blond dress designer. "About how you're making me soft. I'm supposed to be scary, you know. Yet here I am discussing dress designs and lighting arrangements and all sorts of girly stuff with you," I joked.

Melissa's laughter broke the quiet, light and free. "You? Scary? Please. You're intense, sure, but you're one of the good guys."

I didn't reply, but something inside me sparked. Was I? I'd once believed I was when I fought for my country, but after I left and since joining the Bratva well, let's just say, the lines between good and bad had blurred. But the more I thought about it, the more I wanted to believe that she was right. That, deep down, I was a good guy, despite the things I'd done in life.

The estate appeared up ahead, its sprawling grounds glowing under the moonlight. Melissa sighed softly, the contentment in the sound hitting me in a way I hadn't expected.

"You are a good guy, Trigger," she said, turning to me as I pulled up to the front steps. "Don't doubt that."

Her words settled in my chest, heavy and warm.

"And I happen to think that Sara didn't find you at all scary. Quite the opposite, really. I believe that beautiful lady was just as enamoured with you as you seemed to be with her." She grinned. "You should ask her out."

I gulped and cleared my throat. Shit. It was all very well imagining something with Sara, but I wasn't sure I was up to pursuing her.

"I'm not sure I can do it. I don't know if I can have a relationship," I admitted to Mel, my voice steady but laced with uncertainty.

Over the past few weeks, I'd come to know her well. I liked to think she saw me as more than just her bodyguard or friend, but as a sort of big brother. I certainly thought of her as the little sister I never had. So, if I could confide in anyone about my fears, it was her.

She smiled gently at me. "Trigger, I know you suffer from PTSD. I can't pretend to understand what it's like or the horrors you've been through, but I can tell you this: you're a good man, a great friend, and any woman would be lucky to have someone as honourable and caring as you. Besides, a relationship with a lovely woman like Sara might be another step toward healing. Don't let your past define your future. You deserve happiness, and if there's even the slightest chance, you could find that with Sara, you should go for it. Give it a shot. Life's never easy, but if it's meant to be, the challenges will be worth it."

I nodded, unable to trust my voice. Melissa was one wise woman, and her words hit home. She climbed out, and I said, "Thanks, Melissa. Goodnight."

"You're welcome. Night, Trigger," she replied, throwing me a grin before disappearing inside.

I stayed in the car a little longer, staring out into the darkness. I'd found a family here—men, and now women, I'd fight for, people who'd pulled me out of the wreckage I'd been drowning in. Yet, the more family I let into my heart, the more empty it felt.

The realisation hit me like a kick to the stomach. I was lonely. It had always been there—growing up with just my grandad, throughout my army days, when my team had died, in the desolation of the streets—I'd just never recognised the fact until now.

Sara's face came to me again, unbidden and unrelenting. Maybe it wasn't just loneliness haunting me. Maybe it was the hope of something more—a flicker of something I'd buried so deep, I'd forgotten it existed until she brought it back to life. Love. Or at least the first sparks of what could be love. Something I hadn't felt since I was a child.

And that scared me more than anything else ever could. I was due to see her again soon, when I took Mel to her next dress fitting.

What if I wasn't ready for this? What if I didn't know how to let someone in again without it all falling apart?

CHAPTER 7
SARA
A FEW DAYS LATER - COULD I RISK IT?

I moved around the shop, tidying the counter by the fitting room, trying to keep my hands busy and my mind occupied. Melissa was due for her final dress fitting soon, and I couldn't help but wonder if Trigger would be with her. From what Marcie had told me, he worked as a driver and bodyguard for the Rominovs, and was assigned to Melissa now that she'd moved in with Marko. It made sense —the Rominovs were rich and influential—but it still felt strange to think anyone I knew might need personal security.

Since our first meeting, the intriguing man's presence had remained at the edge of my thoughts. I told myself it was nothing, just a fleeting connection. But the memory of those stormy orbs, his subtle smile, the way he carried himself—it stirred something in me. Our brief encounter had left a stronger impression than I cared to admit, and the thought of seeing him again brought a mix of nerves and anticipation I wasn't sure how to handle.

The bell above the door announced the arrival of a customer, and my breath hitched. I glanced up to see Trigger standing in the doorway with Mel. Just like the first time, my heart skipped a beat. It was ridiculous—how could he have this effect on me? I tried not to stare, but my eyes betrayed me, lingering on his broad shoulders and the way his worn leather jacket stretched across his frame in such a sexy way, before flicking up to his face. He was just as striking as before, maybe even more so now that I had a second chance to take him in. A small smile spread across his lips, and my cheeks flushed.

My pulse quickened as we stared at each other, and then, without warning, a traitorous throb between my legs made me freeze. Bloody hell. That had never happened before. Even in the early days with Adam, it took more than his mere presence to make my body react like this. Mortification flooded me. It was absurd to feel this way over someone I barely knew, but no matter how I tried to fight it, it was impossible to ignore—and threw me completely off balance.

"Morning, Sara," Mel greeted me cheerfully as Trigger held the door open for her to enter. "I can't wait to see the dresses. You said you've already finished both of them?"

Her question snapped me out of my trance and I blinked, finally managing to shift my focus from the intoxicating presence beside her.

I took a deep breath to steady myself. "Absolutely," I said. "Come on, I'll show you."

"Oh, I'm so excited!" Melissa rounded the counter, her enthusiasm radiating from every pore. I just hoped my designs would meet her expectations.

Lifting a garment bag, I unzipped it and pulled out the black dress first.

"Oh my, that is gorgeous," Mel said, her eyes roaming over it. She reached out to touch the fabric. "God, this lace is as beautiful as I thought it would be."

"Wait until you see the red one. Honestly, when I found

that lace, I almost wanted to keep it for myself," I admitted with a chuckle. "If I hadn't already promised you a red lace dress, I probably would have."

I gently removed the dress from its bag and held it up.

"Wow, it is stunning. I can see why you wanted it for yourself. The pattern is exquisite. I'm so glad you let me have it. Both dresses are beyond my expectations, Sara. You are amazing." Melissa clapped her hands together and, with a little squeal, pulled me in for a quick hug. "Everyone is going to be so jealous when I wear them. Especially Marcie," she added with a wicked giggle.

I laughed. "I'm glad you like them."

"Like them? I love them!" she cried, and my insides leapt with pride. It was still such a new feeling to have someone love my designs as much as she did.

"Let's try the black one on first," she said, beaming at me.

"Good idea," I agreed. "It's the one you need sooner, anyway."

I handed her the dress and ushered her inside the tiny cubicle to change.

"Come out when you're ready, and we'll check what adjustments it needs," I said. She nodded and grinned before disappearing inside.

The moment Mel disappeared into the fitting room, I felt exposed, as though the room had shrunk, leaving me nowhere to hide from Trigger's attention.

When I turned to face him, I swallowed hard at the unfiltered lust in his expression as he looked me over. Clearing my throat, I caught a flicker of sheepishness crossing his face, as though he'd only just realised how blatant he'd been. It made me want to laugh, but instead, I bit the inside of my cheek and walked past him.

"It's good to see you both again. Have you had a good

week?" I said, unsure what else to do but make small talk while we waited for Mel to be ready. But I couldn't look at him, so I busied myself with collecting the items I would need to pin Mel's dresses.

"I did, thanks. Although I was a bit distracted," he said.

"Distracted?" I asked, wondering what he was getting at.

"Yes," he replied, his voice low and sultry, "by a certain dress designer I couldn't stop thinking about."

My eyes flew to his, my jaw dropping open at the blatant flirtation. Before I could gather a response, he leaned in just slightly, a teasing grin on his face.

"I guess you could say you're a cut above the rest."

"Cheesy," I muttered, unable to hold back the smile that broke free despite myself.

He chuckled, his eyes twinkling with mischief. "Maybe, but it made you smile. That's a win in my book."

For a moment, his presence wrapped around me, warm and intoxicating. The faint scent of leather and sandalwood teased my senses, making my pulse flutter with the thrill of his attention. Once again, I found myself caught in his pull, unable to look away.

"So, did you think of me?" he whispered.

Before I could respond—or even process how much I liked that strange, heady feeling—Mel emerged from the fitting room, a smile of satisfaction on her face.

"Perfect," she announced, spinning to show off the dress. "At least I'll look confident when I give my opening speech, even if I don't quite feel it."

I smiled, trying to ease her nerves. "You look amazing, Mel."

Trigger's voice was low but sincere when he spoke. "You've got this. You look incredible."

Mel hesitated, her fingers smoothing over the fabric. "I'm

just worried about everything. What if my photos don't measure up?"

I nodded, giving her a reassuring smile. "I've heard nothing but great things about them, Melissa. Marcie told me how amazing your work is."

Trigger agreed with a confident smile. "Your photos are going to impress, Mel. You just have to believe in yourself."

Mel's smile returned, the uncertainty easing from her expression. "Thanks, guys. That really helps."

"Okay, just let me double-check everything," I said, stepping back to take a closer look. After a quick inspection, a grin spread across my face. "You're right. It fits perfectly. No adjustments required to the body, but how about altering the length slightly so it cuts off just above the knee?"

Her eyes lit up. "Sounds great."

I knelt down, securing several pins in the length. It took longer than it should have, my fingers fumbling slightly, aware that Trigger's attention was fixed on me once again.

Was he still waiting for a response? Did he expect me to admit I'd been thinking about him, too? I bit my lip, chewing it absently as I pretended to concentrate on pinning the hem. Shit, should I say something? Or keep quiet?

I had no idea. I was so out of practice with this stuff, but one thing was clear—I couldn't delay any longer. "Okay, you can take that one off now and try on the red," I said, my voice managing to sound a little steadier than I felt.

Mel disappeared back into the cubicle, and I busied myself with rearranging fabric and adjusting the mirrors, anything to avoid looking directly at him. What was I supposed to do now?

Eventually, he cleared his throat, and I turned to find him leaning against the counter, right next to me. His expression was unreadable, but the tick in his jaw told a different story. He wasn't as casual as he seemed.

"You alright?" he asked, his voice low. "I didn't mean to make you feel uncomfortable."

"You didn't," I said, but his raised eyebrows told me he knew I was lying. "Alright, you did. But only because I wasn't expecting that. I'm a little out of practice with flirting," I admitted.

"Me too," he said, surprising me.

"Really?" I asked, unable to believe that such a confident and handsome man would not be well versed in flirting.

"I'll let you into a little secret, Sara. I haven't had a relationship in years. A few one-night stands but not much more than that," he told me, his voice hushed and a look of vulnerability crossing his face.

I gaped at him, then swallowed, suddenly self-conscious, a flutter of nerves making my stomach twist. "Me neither. In fact, it's been years since I've been with anyone at all," I confessed, my voice barely above a whisper.

He smiled widely and took a step closer, his eyes flickering between mine and my lips. The air between us was thick, charged with mutual desire. Was he going to kiss me? My breath hitched in anticipation.

"Wow, Sara, this dress is even more amazing on. Isn't it, Trigger?" Mel grinned, interrupting the moment.

We pulled away from each other quickly, neither of us meeting the other's gaze, the moment entirely shattered.

"It certainly is," he said, his voice sounding a little strained.

I shot him a look, and he glanced at me out of the corner of his eye while subtly adjusting his pants. Oh fuck!

Mel caught the looks, glancing between us with a raised

eyebrow. "You two should go for coffee or something when this is over. You look like you could both use it."

I felt the heat rise in my cheeks again, but before I could say anything, Trigger's low voice cut in, his words seemingly directed at Mel but clearly aimed at me. "I need to get you back to the estate. Besides, I'm sure Sara is busy. Don't want to keep her from her work."

Mel frowned at him but didn't comment further.

I took a steadying breath, trying to regain control over my racing heart. It was hard to concentrate when the charged energy of what had just passed between Trigger and me still lingered in the air. Shaking off the moment, I forced my attention back to Mel. "Just some minor adjustments to the neckline and the length here too," I told her quickly, changing the subject and aiming to sound businesslike, even as my insides ached with desire.

She smiled but said nothing as I worked, my hands trembling with the effort to keep them steady.

The flirty banter had knocked me for six, but his words after Mel's coffee suggestion were confusing. Did he want to, but couldn't? Or was he telling me this was just a flirtation for fun, nothing more? I had no idea. God, I really was rusty at this stuff.

"All done, you can get changed," I said after a beat, clearing my throat.

"Okay, won't be long," she replied, her eyes darting between us before slipping behind the fitting room curtain again.

Trigger and I stood in the silence, staring at the closed curtain of the cubicle. He stepped in a little closer, his breath warm on my skin as he spoke again, "That's another beautiful dress, Sara. You're very talented." His words sent a flutter of warmth rushing through me, my pulse quickening as I struggled to maintain my composure.

Just then, the door to the storeroom opened with a soft creak, and Lolita stepped out. She stopped mid-step, her eyes flicking between me and Trigger. A sly smile curled at the corners of her mouth as she took in the charged atmosphere. "Am I interrupting something?" she asked, her tone teasing.

I felt my cheeks warm and quickly shook my head. "Not at all," I said, my voice betraying me by rising a little higher than usual.

Thankfully, I didn't have to say anything else because Mel appeared.

"Oh, hi," she said, noticing Lolita standing beside me.

"Lolita, this is Melissa Martin and Trigger," I said, trying to regain some composure.

Lola stepped forward and shook Mel's hand. "Hi, I'm Lolita, Sara's best friend and assistant," she said with her usual brightness.

"It's nice to meet you both, I've heard so much about you," she said, the emphasis on *you* a little too obvious as she looked directly at Trigger.

"You were right, Sara, he is drop-dead gorgeous," she said to him before leaning in conspiratorially and stage whispering, "Her words, not mine." She winked at him and then threw me a mischievous look. Trigger's eyes flicked to me and quickly away again, but not before I noticed the slightly uncomfortable look he tried to mask behind his smile. Mel smirked at me, and I wanted the ground to swallow me up.

"Well, we need to leave. It's been lovely seeing you again, Sara," Trigger said, his voice a little tight as he cleared his throat, clearly trying to avoid the awkwardness creeping in.

I nodded, unable to trust my voice. I was going to kill Lolita.

"Thanks for making me such wonderful dresses," Mel gushed, giving me another quick hug.

"You are welcome. I am just so happy you love them. I will have the final adjustments done the day after tomorrow," I said, refusing to look at Trigger.

"Wonderful. Trigger will come and collect them for me when they are ready then," she grinned at us both, and the mischievous glint in her eye made me wonder if she was trying to matchmake. Especially when I noted the look of annoyance Trigger threw her way.

"Great, I'll look forward to it," I said, not sure my voice quite conveyed that sentiment. My mind churned with mixed feelings about the prospect of seeing the man alone again. And so soon.

"Well, bye for now and thanks again," Mel called as she left. Trigger nodded, his expression slightly strained as he followed her out.

I huffed a breath of relief as I watched them go.

Rounding on Lolita, I glared. "I cannot believe what you said to him," I snapped.

She laughed, brushing it off with a wave of her hand. "Oh, I'm sure he's been told how hot he is before. Anyway, it's true."

"I'm not so sure about that. He looked uncomfortable to me," I retorted, crossing my arms.

"Nah, he was just a bit thrown by my comment, but I'm sure he was secretly pleased to learn how much you like him," she teased with a grin. "So, what's going on with you two, anyway?"

I rolled my eyes, half-exasperated and half-amused. "Nothing."

"Nothing?" Lolita shot me a look, arching a brow. "Sara, I've known you for years. Don't try to tell me there's nothing going on. Besides, you've got that look."

"What look?" I asked, feigning innocence.

"That whole 'I don't want to be interested but I am' look," she quipped, smirking knowingly.

Running a hand through my hair in exasperation, I sat down on the stool beside my workbench. "Alright, yes, I'm interested. I've never been more interested in a guy in my life. I mean, whenever he looks at me, my whole body feels like it's on fire. His mere presence sends me into a dizzying mix of nerves and excitement. I'm not sure how to deal with it."

"Wow, that sounds like some chemistry to me," she said, taking the stool next to me.

I nodded. "Yeah, but I haven't even thought about dating anyone since Adam, and I don't know if I'm ready for that again," I muttered, rubbing my temple.

Lolita leaned in, her tone serious. "He's a handsome guy, Sara. You're getting divorced. It's time you thought about relationships again. Not all men are abusive bastards. You know that, right?"

My fingers pressed against the edge of the workbench, the cool surface grounding me as doubt swirled inside. I knew that I really did. But the thought of trusting someone again felt like a betrayal of the walls I had so carefully built up around my heart. "I do. But… I've been hurt before. I don't think I can risk opening myself up to someone again."

"But if you don't take a risk, you'll never know what could be," she said gently.

"I'm not sure," I said softly, looking down at my hands. "I don't know if I can do it. And I have the girls to think about."

Lolita took my hand and squeezed it gently. "I get it, I do.

But if there's chemistry there, you shouldn't ignore it. You deserve to be happy, to have someone who wants you. And from what I can tell, Trigger's definitely interested. Besides, you can start small. Go for lunch or a coffee and take it from there," she urged.

"Mel suggested he take me for coffee, but he said he had to take her back and that I must have other things to do. So, I'm not sure if the whole chemistry thing was something he really wanted to explore, anyway. We flirted, that's all. I doubt it was more than that," I said, pursing my lips as I dismissed the topic. The whole idea of dating anyone made me feel exposed. Yet, there was a part of me that longed for connection, even if I was too scared to admit it.

Lolita gave me a soft, understanding smile. "Just think about it, alright? You deserve happiness. It's time to open your heart again, Sara. If the guy asks you out, go. Give him a chance, and see what happens. You can always walk away if it doesn't feel right."

I sighed heavily, biting the edge of my thumbnail in that nervous habit of mine. Maybe it was time to consider letting someone in. But the real question was: could I take the risk?

CHAPTER 8
TRIGGER

THAT NIGHT – SHADOWS ON MY SOUL

After taking Mel back to the estate, I spent the early part of the evening watching Simpson. Boris took over later, giving me the chance to head home and get some rest—not that my mind would let me.

As I drove back to my flat, thoughts of Sara still consumed me. The way she looked, her scent—a subtle, sweet fragrance that clung to me like a damn drug. Intoxicating didn't even begin to describe it. Those bright blue eyes, so expressive, had a way of making me feel like she could see straight through my walls, right down to the mess beneath.

I'd found myself watching her closely earlier, everything about her drawing me in. That sultry voice of hers sent a shiver down my spine. It was soft yet commanding, and I'd leaned in, just to hear it again. The cascade of her blonde hair had tempted me to reach out, to wrap a strand around my finger and see if it was as soft as it looked. And her body... Christ. A man could lose himself in those curves. Just thinking about the sway of her hips made me hard.

I clenched my eyes shut, biting off a groan, but it was no

use. Every detail of Sara replayed in my head on an endless loop. The way she'd blushed so prettily when I teased her, pretending to be annoyed but unable to hide the faint smile tugging at her lips. That smile—it was rare, I'd bet, but worth every bit of effort to coax out. And when she'd mentioned she hadn't been in a relationship in years? Relief and excitement had surged through me like a shot of adrenaline.

Then she'd laughed at my cheesy line, her eyes lighting with humour. She hadn't dismissed me or looked at me like I was damaged goods. That had felt good. Better than good. It had been so long since I'd let myself truly connect with a woman—even in something as simple as harmless banter.

It made me want to see where we could go. But what if I screwed it up? Survivor's guilt had a way of sinking its claws in deep, making a man second-guess every good thing in his life. She deserved better than a broken soldier barely holding himself together most days. The thought of dragging her into my darkness made my chest tighten.

And yet, I had a feeling she'd understand me better than most. We had something in common. She was a survivor too, and I wasn't the only one struggling to move on from the past. She'd hinted at it without saying much, but I could see the pain Sara carried in the way she avoided meeting my gaze for too long, the way her fingers fidgeted when I pushed her boundaries. It made me want to protect her—to be the one to put her at ease. At the same time, it scared the hell out of me.

By the time I got home, my pulse pounded in my ears, refusing to settle. The night air had done little to cool the fire coursing through me. Shutting the door behind me, I flicked the lock, the sharp click echoing in the quiet flat. The stillness felt oppressive, every inch of the place too empty, too cold, compared to the warmth Sara had stirred in me.

Kicking off my boots, I shrugged my jacket, tossing it

over the back of a chair. My fingers fumbled with the buttons of my shirt, my chest heaving as I tried to catch my breath, but the effort was futile. Thoughts of her swirled in my mind, relentless and consuming. Stripping out of my jeans and shirt, I sank onto the edge of the bed, running a hand through my hair. My body felt hot, Sara was like a fever raging through me, burning down my defences. I wanted her more than I'd ever wanted anyone in my life.

Every nerve in my body was alive with the memory of her. The curve of her lips, soft and inviting, and the way her laugh had cut through the icy barriers I'd spent years building. Her voice lingered in my mind, teasing me like the faint echo of a melody I couldn't stop humming. My cock throbbed insistently, the ache impossible to ignore—a stark, physical reminder of just how deeply she'd got under my skin.

I leaned forward, my elbows resting on my knees, head bowed as I let out a slow, unsteady breath. The room was dim, the glow from a nearby streetlamp casting long shadows across the walls. I scrubbed a hand over my face, trying to will away the tension coiling low in my gut. It was useless. Every time I closed my eyes, Sara was there, vivid and untouchable, her image burned into my mind.

Her wary gaze when she'd looked up at me was a mix of curiosity and caution that made me want to earn her trust. The way her tongue had darted out to wet her lips, leaving them glistening like a silent invitation she didn't even realise she'd issued. I groaned, the sound low and rough, as frustration warred with desire. My chest tightened with the pressure of wanting something I wasn't sure I had the right to claim.

For a moment, I thought about ignoring it, shoving the thoughts into the same locked box where I kept all the things I couldn't afford to feel. But she'd already shattered my defences with a single glance, and now there was no escape. Giving up the fight, I leaned back against the pillows, the cool fabric brushing against my overheated skin. My hand drifted lower, tentative at first, before I let go of restraint and gave in to the fantasies clamouring for release.

I pictured her hands, small and delicate, splayed across my chest. Her lips, soft and warm, trailing a path down my neck, leaving a searing heat in their wake. The thought of her body pressed against mine, her curves fitting against me perfectly, made my pulse race. In my mind, her breath hitched as I touched her, her eyes fluttering shut as she surrendered to the moment. I imagined the way she'd arch beneath me, her name a whispered plea on my lips as I lost myself in her entirely.

My movements increased and the tension built rapidly, every sensation amplified by the vivid images in my mind. My breaths came quicker, sharper, until the release hit me like a wave crashing against the shore. A guttural groan tore from my throat, her name slipping past my lips like a prayer. My body shuddered, the fever finally breaking, leaving me momentarily weightless. For a brief, fleeting moment, there was peace, soft and welcome.

But it didn't last.

Reality returned, creeping in like a cold draught under the door. I reached for a tissue, cleaning up mechanically, my movements slower now as my old doubts returned. Tossing the tissue into the bin, I swung my legs over the side of the bed and sat there, staring at the floor. My chest rose and fell as I tried to even out my breathing, but the hollow ache in my ribs refused to go away.

Could I really offer her anything more than this? Could I be the man she needed? The scars I carried weren't just physical—though there were plenty of those to go around. It was the unseen ones that truly scared me, the ones that twisted my thoughts and made me wonder if I'd ever feel whole again. Would she see those scars and run? Or worse, would she stay and end up broken because of me?

I dragged a hand over my face, weariness seeping into my bones.

Melissa said a relationship with Sara be another step in my healing, could she be right? That thought sparked another. If she was battle-scarred too, could we help each other mend? Heal together?

Turning onto my side, my gaze fell to the empty space beside me on the bed. It felt colder than usual tonight—a stark reminder of the loneliness I'd grown used to but never quite made peace with.

My life was built on carefully controlled routines—structures designed to weather the bad days. My workouts, my guitar, my therapy. Adding someone like Sara to the mix felt like inviting a storm to tear through it all. Yet as I shifted beneath the covers and closed my eyes, her image lingered in the darkness. Her rare, fleeting smile stayed with me like a beacon, guiding me toward something I couldn't seem to resist chasing. That flicker of possibility Sara had stirred inside me couldn't be ignored.

I woke in the dead of night, my skin slick with sweat, the sheet tangled around my legs like a snare. My heart thundered in my chest, its rapid beat echoing in my ears as I blinked against the darkness. Another nightmare. Another losing battle fought in the treacherous landscape of my mind. The echoes of distant screams and the sharp, metallic scent of blood clung to me, dragging the nightmare into wakefulness.

My ragged breaths filled the room, the only sound in my otherwise silent flat. My gaze landed on the guitar propped in the corner, its silhouette both familiar and grounding. Shaking and restless, I slipped out of bed and reached for it. The smooth wood of the neck felt cool under my fingertips as I cradled it in my lap. Brushing the strings gently, I let the notes emerge, soft and hesitant, like a whispered conversation in the night. Each chord unravelled the tangled knot of emotion lodged in my chest, the melody flowing from somewhere deep inside me.

I played quietly, mindful of the neighbour upstairs who worked nights at the hospital. The music filled the flat, weaving through the air like a fragile thread of solace. It worked, as it often did, easing the remnants of the nightmare. But as the music faded, it left behind a different kind of haunting—this one far more pleasant.

Sara.

Her name echoed in my mind, vivid and insistent. When I closed my eyes, her face appeared—a teasing smile that danced just out of reach, her lilting voice a melody all its own. Everything about her was unforgettable.

My fingers faltered on the strings, the sound dying abruptly as frustration surged. I wasn't good enough for her, not with the shadows that dulled my world.

I set the guitar aside, its gentle thud against the wall breaking the stillness. Stretching, I rose to my feet, the early light of dawn creeping through the window to paint the room in soft amber hues. As I moved through the motions—dressing, brushing my teeth, pulling on my boots—her image stayed with me. What if she was the missing piece I'd been searching for all this time?

Maybe I wasn't the man for her… but wasn't that for her to decide? The thought struck like a sharp note ringing through silence. I'd been so focused on what I lacked, so sure of my shortcomings, that I hadn't stopped to consider the possibility that she might see something more in me. And with her, I might actually *be* something more.

The thought gripped me, equal parts comfort and torment. I couldn't let her go—not yet. For the first time in years, hope sparked inside me and whether things worked out between us or not, I wanted to give it a try.

CHAPTER 9
SARA
THE NEXT DAY – EMILY'S PARTY

The door buzzer rang, and Emily rushed to open it, eager to greet the last of her party guests for her tenth birthday. It warmed my heart to see her beaming with joy as she welcomed the little girl from her school and accepted the gift she brought. The pile of presents in the corner was steadily growing, and Emily giggled every time she added another to the stack.

My youngest, Lily, was the more outgoing of my two daughters. Emily tended to be the quiet thinker, more reserved than her sister, but today was Emily's day, and she was making the most of it.

Our small flat was abuzz with the laughter of children and enough noise to rival a Taylor Swift concert. It wasn't a big space, but we'd made it work. Balloons in bright colours bobbed around the room, scattered in every corner. Streamers hung from the ceiling, crisscrossing above the partygoers and adding a playful touch. The dining table was prepped for the buffet, covered with a Barbie tablecloth, complete with matching paper cups and plates.

Lily had taken charge of the decorations. She had no

shortage of energy and no fear of making the place look like a funfair. She'd even convinced me to let her hang a piñata from the ceiling. My eyes flicked to the lampshade where I'd hung it, praying it would hold up against the onslaught it would face from ten children armed with wooden sticks, all desperate to break it open for the sweets inside. The image of the ceiling crashing down made me bite my lip, but I quickly shook off the thought. There was no way that was going to happen. The building we lived in might be old, but it was sturdy enough.

Tears pricked at my eyes as I looked around. The place felt alive, full of joy. When I left Adam, I'd worried about how I was going to look after us, but now, as I took in the scene, I felt proud of how far I'd come. My eyes flicked back to Emily. For once, she was basking in being the centre of attention, and it made my heart sing.

After several rounds of *Musical Chairs, Musical Statues*, and *What's the Time, Mr Wolf,* along with the destruction of the unicorn piñata—the ceiling and lampshade both thankfully surviving—I snuck into the kitchen to check on the mini sausage rolls and pizza for the kids' buffet.

As usual, Lily was in full party mode. She bounced around, trying to get everyone to play some sort of game that involved running in circles and yelling at the top of their lungs. I loved her boundless energy, though it often had me wishing for a moment of peace. By the end of the party, I was going to have one hell of a headache if things continued like this. I smiled. Headache or not, it would be worth it. It was always worth it to see how well my girls had flourished in the years since we'd left their dad.

"Christ, the party's only halfway through and already my head is bursting. Yours?" Lolita's voice broke through my thoughts as she rubbed between her eyes. She was leaning against the kitchen doorframe, watching me. I hadn't heard her come in, but I wasn't surprised. She had a way of sneaking up on me.

I nodded. "Yeah, pounding. It's hard keeping up with them all." I gestured toward the living room, where the kids were now in the middle of a game of *Pass The Parcel*, the music playing from the stereo and the girls squealing every time it stopped. Lily had opted to play the music for this game. She loved taking charge of things and was in her element stopping and starting the music and pronouncing whoever had the parcel when the music stopped 'out.'

"They're having a great time. Even Emily is louder than usual. It's good to see. Sometimes, she seems far too quiet for her own good. Lily runs rings around her, but not today," Lolita said, glancing toward Emily, who was laughing loudly with her friends.

"I know," I said quietly. "She saw too much when I was with Adam. I sometimes worry that it's affected her more than I know."

Lolita smiled, but there was a trace of concern in her eyes. "She's been through a lot for her age, but she is strong and resilient, just like her mum," she said, patting my hand. "And she has a good head on her shoulders. She knows what happened was wrong, and that you got out when you could. You've given her a good life since, and each year has only got better. Quiet is just her nature. I don't think you have to worry about her. She comes out of her shell when she wants to."

"She does, but it's not as natural for her to be outgoing, not like it is for Lily," I sighed.

"They are each their own person. They might be different, but both are amazing little girls and you should be proud of them and how well you're raising them," she said, giving me a reassuring smile.

"I just… want to make things easier for her. You know?" I paused, my voice softening with the weight of it.

Lolita's voice softened, but there was an underlying, teasing tone to it. "I think you could use something a little easier in your life too, Sara."

I glanced at her, raising an eyebrow. "What do you mean?"

She didn't hesitate. "Trigger, of course." Lolita leaned in slightly, her eyes glinting with mischief. "He's certainly easy on the eye."

I chuckled. "He certainly is."

"And the way the two of you looked at each other was hot," she added with a wink. "Phew, I almost passed out from the heat coming off the pair of you at the shop yesterday." She fanned herself with a paper plate, and I laughed. "So, have you decided to give the guy a chance if he asks you out?"

"I… I'm still thinking about it," I admitted.

"Well, you don't get all flustered or blush like crazy when we talk about anyone else. You really like the guy, so take a risk. I would," she said, her voice light, but I could hear the encouragement there.

I groaned. There was a part of me that screamed to do just that, but the other part, the more cautious side, was still unsure.

"Look, I don't know," I said, my voice quiet. "It's not that simple. There's so much… so much to think about. Emily, Lily… everything. I'm not sure I'm ready for something like this."

Lolita's tone softened, though her eyes still held that teasing gleam. "You don't have to jump in headfirst, you know. Just take it slow. See how it goes. If you like him, and if the girls like him too, then maybe… Maybe he's worth taking a chance on."

I was about to respond when Emily asked, "Who's Trigger?" She frowned. It was obvious she had overheard.

Lolita shot me a quick look, and I felt my heart race. It wasn't supposed to come up like this—not now, not at Emily's party.

I swallowed, trying to push down the nervousness twisting in my stomach.

"Trigger is… a customer's friend," I said, trying to sound casual.

Emily didn't seem entirely convinced. She bit her lip, her brow furrowing. She didn't ask anything more, but I could tell the question was still there, hanging between us.

"Mum, when's the food going to be ready?" Lily demanded, running into the kitchen and interrupting the awkward moment. "I think I'm going to die if I don't have something to eat soon."

I chuckled and handed her a bowl of crisps. "Patience, sweetheart. We're going to eat in a minute. Go and put these on the table and I'll bring the rest out." She beamed, grabbing a handful of the crisps and hurrying back to the living room.

"Here, you take these in and put them on the table, love," I said to Emily, kissing her forehead and handing her several other bowls. She smiled, and it seemed any worry she had was forgotten as she turned and rushed off.

"We'd better get these out before we have any more hungry kids to deal with," I said, shoving a platter of mini pizzas at Lolita.

The rest of the party continued, but the energy shifted slightly. Emily was quieter now, her smile more fleeting. She still participated in the games, but something had changed.

Lolita stepped closer and nudged me gently. "She'll be okay. Give the guy a chance and if you find you like him, then you can introduce them and take it from there. In the meantime, just act normal and keep reassuring her there is nothing she needs to worry about," she murmured softly.

I chewed at my lip as I watched my daughter playing a game of *Duck Duck Goose*, squealing as she ran around the circle being chased by Cammy.

"Emily is a good kid. If you really like him and he makes you happy, she'll like him. You deserve love and happiness, Sara. And just maybe he's the guy to give it to you. If he is, everything will work out. Trust in yourself, and trust in her," Lolita said. I nodded, her words settling heavily in my chest.

My Emily knew what abuse was. It was understandable that she would be cautious about any man I might get involved with, but I didn't want her to think all men were abusive. My instincts told me that Trigger was not a man who'd hurt me; I'd been wrong before, but this time I believed them.

Perhaps Lolita was right, and it was time to take a chance, not only for myself, but for Emily. To show her that good men did exist and loving relationships were possible. Not that this was love, at least not yet, but deep inside me, I thought that given the chance, something special might develop.

A thrill of anticipation ran through me. When Trigger came for Melissa's dresses, if he even hinted at going on a date, I'd jump at the chance and see what happened.

CHAPTER 10
TRIGGER
THE FOLLOWING DAY – TWO FOR THE PRICE OF ONE

As I stepped into Sara's boutique, the familiar scent of vanilla and freshly pressed fabrics enveloped me, instantly transporting me to a place of comfort and serenity. The soft chime of the doorbell announced my arrival, and I took a moment to appreciate the shop's ambiance. Sunlight filtered through the large front windows, casting a golden glow over the neatly arranged bolts of fabric that lined the walls. The gentle hum of a sewing machine in the background added a rhythmic cadence to the tranquil atmosphere.

Sara looked up from her work, her eyes sparkling with recognition as a warm smile spread across her face. She was dressed in jeans and a simple yet elegant blouse, her hair pulled back in a loose bun, with a few stray strands framing her face. God, she was a vision.

"Trigger, it's good to see you," she greeted, her voice soft and welcoming, carrying that sexy lilt that always made my cock thicken. "I'll go get Mel's dresses. Be right back," she said, disappearing into the back of the shop, leaving me alone with my thoughts.

As I waited, I let my gaze wander around the shop, noticing a few changes she'd made since the last time I was here. The walls were adorned with framed sketches of dress designs, each showcasing Sara's impeccable talent and attention to detail. I recognised those of the dresses she'd designed for Mel. I knew she hadn't been designing for long, so these must be the first of her commissioned designs.

A vintage mannequin stood in the corner, draped in a half-finished gown, the delicate lace cascading down like a waterfall.

From the back room, I heard a muffled conversation, punctuated by a playful exclamation of, "You go, girl!" followed by a chorus of giggles. The sound brought a smile to my face, a reminder of the close-knit camaraderie that thrived within these walls.

Moments later, Sara re-emerged, carrying two garment bags draped over her arm. "Here they are!" she announced brightly, a faint blush colouring her cheeks as she handed the dresses over to me.

As our hands brushed, a tingling sensation shot up my arm, sending a jolt of awareness racing through my body. The intensity of the reaction left me momentarily stunned, my mouth going dry as I locked eyes with her. In hers, I saw a reflection of my own surprise, a silent acknowledgment that she had felt it too.

I knew I had to seize the moment. My heart pounded in my chest, and I licked my lips, trying to summon the courage to speak. "I… I know it's late notice, but I was wondering if you would come to Melissa's exhibit on Saturday night as my guest? She's given me the night off," I said, my voice wavering slightly.

Before Sara could respond, Lolita, her assistant, poked

her head out from the back room with a mischievous grin on her face. "She certainly will."

Sara turned to Lolita, concern etching her features. "But what about the girls?"

Lolita waved off her worries with a wink. "I'll have them for a sleepover."

Sara hesitated, biting her lower lip, clearly unsure. I was about to backtrack, to tell her it was fine, and that she could forget about it, when she smiled and nodded. "I'd love to."

A surge of elation washed over me, and I grinned, feeling as though I'd just won the lottery. Not wanting to give her a chance to change her mind, I pulled out my phone. "What's your number? I'll text you, and you can send me your address," I suggested, trying to keep my hand steady as I entered her contact information.

Once I'd saved her number, I sent a quick message. Her phone vibrated, and she smiled shyly as she read my simple text, and replied:

Me: Hi.

Sara: Hi back.

Her cheeks dimpled with a smile as she provided her address.

Me: I'll pick you up at 7 pm.

I smirked at my phone as I typed.

Sara: Fantastic. *smiley face emoji*

As I slipped my phone back into my pocket, a fleeting thought of engaging in playful banter with her crossed my mind, but I quickly dismissed it, reminding myself to take things one step at a time. I'd been privy to Marko and Mel's flirtatious exchanges recently, and while they often over-shared, the idea of having someone to share such moments with was becoming increasingly appealing.

Excitement bubbled within me at the prospect of our

upcoming date. Yet, as I observed the mirrored excitement in her eyes, I realised that waiting two days felt like an eternity. Taking a deep breath to steady my nerves, I decided to take a bold step. "And… I was wondering if you'd like to come to lunch with me today?" I blurted out, the words tumbling over each other in my haste.

Sara's eyes widened in surprise. "That… well, um…" she stammered, her uncertainty evident.

Lolita, ever the matchmaker, interjected once more. "She absolutely will. I'm happy to hold down the fort here, as long as you bring me a to-go box," she added with a playful wink.

I chuckled. "It's a deal." Then, turning to Sara, I added, "Well, as long as it's okay with you, of course."

Sara's hesitation melted away, replaced by a radiant smile that sent a jolt straight to my core. "Yes, that's okay with me."

Her response ignited a whirlwind of emotions within me. It was clear that this woman had the potential to be either my salvation or my downfall, and I was eager to discover which.

"I'll drop the dresses off to Mel and then come back around midday, if that suits you?" I proposed, anticipation lacing my words.

"That's perfect," she replied, her eyes sparkling.

As I left Sara's shop, the anticipation of our upcoming lunch date filled me with a sense of excitement I hadn't felt in years. The prospect of spending time with her outside the confines of her shop was both exhilarating and nerve-wracking. I couldn't help but replay our conversation in my mind, analysing every word and gesture.

Driving to the Rominov estate to deliver Melissa's dresses, I found it difficult to focus on the road. My thoughts kept drifting back to Sara—the way her eyes sparkled when she agreed to join me, the subtle blush that coloured her cheeks, and the warmth of her smile. I wondered what she was thinking now. Was she as eager for our lunch as I was?

When I arrived, Melissa met me at the door, her eyes lighting up as she saw the dresses. "Trigger, go grab a coffee or something while I take these upstairs. Then come help me, please. Marko's made me a simulation of the exhibit space, and I need to check that each of the photographs is in the best spot to show them off properly."

"Sure," I said, heading to the kitchen to grab myself a cup before making my way upstairs to Melissa's new office. Marko had set up a small darkroom for her old-style development, but he'd also recently transformed an unused bedroom into a combined studio and office for her.

She was already there. Melissa had the 3D simulation open, showing her photographs in situ.

"What do you think?" she asked, tilting her head as she surveyed the display.

My eyes swept over the familiar works. Having spent the last few weeks as her bodyguard, I'd spent a lot of time with her and found myself enjoying the process of learning how she worked. Turns out, I had an eye for precision and detail, and I was good at discerning the best lighting effects—probably thanks to my years of training as a sniper.

"They all look perfectly positioned to me," I said with a nod.

"These will be the highlight of the exhibit," Melissa said, her voice filled with excitement as she showed me what she called her pièce de resistance, being vibrant photographs of Glowacki's daughter, Magdalena, dressed life a woodland fairy, taken in the small walled garden here on the Rominov estate which Miki's mother had made. Marissa had loved gardening and enjoyed tending to her wild flowers. It was the perfect location for the fairytale-like scenes and Mel had only let me and Marko see the results, keeping these a secret for full impact on the night.

"I can't wait to see everyone's reactions. Especially Magdalena's," she said, barely able to contain her excitement.

"I'm sure they'll not only be impressed, but everyone will be fighting over them," I replied, "I have a feeling once Magdalena and Glowacki see these, Glowacki's wallet will be even lighter than it already is."

Mel chuckled. "Yes, he's turning out to be one of my biggest customers and supporters. I'm glad Marta has convinced 'daddy Glowacki' to do a few poses himself," she said with a wicked wink. I burst out laughing. The ladies all thought Glowacki gave off daddy dom vibes. They were likely right.

My mind kept drifting back to Sara, a habit I was quickly forming. I couldn't help but wonder if she shared a thing for daddy doms, too. I hoped not—I didn't mind taking control, but I didn't consider myself one. Still, once she was in my head, I couldn't shake the thought of her. What was she doing right now? Was she thinking about our lunch, or was she just as nervous as I was?

After assuring Melissa that her plans were spot-on, I made my way back to my car. The drive to Sara's boutique felt like it took forever, every minute stretching the anticipation tighter. I couldn't wait to see her again, to spend time with her outside the shop, and to figure out where this connection was heading.

CHAPTER 11
SARA
THAT AFTERNOON – THE LUNCH DATE

As noon arrived, I closed up the shop for lunch, my heart fluttering with a mix of eagerness and nervousness. It had been a long time since I'd agreed to go on a date—and even longer since I'd felt this kind of anticipation.

Meeting Trigger outside the shop, I couldn't help but smile as I caught sight of him. He'd changed his clothes from earlier and the effort to do so pleased me, like he wanted to make a good impression.

He was still dressed casually, but had tied his long brown hair back neatly and the blue shirt he wore under his trusty black leather jacket, highlighted the colour of his blue-grey eyes beautifully. Between the effort, and his quick grin when he greeted me, I felt my nerves ease slightly.

"Ready?" he asked, his deep voice sending tingles through my body.

"I think so," I replied, stepping into pace beside him as we set off for the new sushi restaurant down the road. The crisp spring air nipped at my cheeks, but his steady presence beside me had me glowing so much I barely noticed.

The restaurant, "Sakura Sushi," was a bright and lively spot, buzzing with the hum of lunchtime chatter and the soft whir of the sushi carousel. A waitress guided us to a table bordering the conveyor belt, where colourful dishes passed by in a mesmerising display. Trigger pulled out a chair for me—a small gesture, one that sent a flutter through my chest. For a moment, I hesitated, the action so simple yet unfamiliar. My ex had never been the type to do something like that. He'd always dismissed such gestures, calling them pointless. But Trigger's quiet thoughtfulness felt meaningful, almost disarming.

"This was a good call," he said, glancing around. "I wasn't sure where to go, but this place looks great."

"I've been wanting to try it for a while," I admitted. "It's new, and I've heard good things."

"Well, here's hoping it lives up to the hype," he said with a grin.

We each picked a dish from the conveyor belt to start, tentative bites filling the first few minutes. The silence wasn't awkward, but it stretched on until Trigger broke it.

"What do you think of that one?" he asked, nodding toward the plate I'd just finished.

"Not bad," I said, my tone light. "But I think I'll avoid anything with sea urchin in the future."

He laughed, the sound rich and warm. "Fair enough. I'll admit, I'm playing it safe so far."

"Trying new things is the whole point, though," I teased. "Come on, let's both pick something we'd normally avoid."

He raised an eyebrow, but reached for a plate with a daring flourish. "Alright, you're on."

The small challenge broke the initial unease, and soon we were laughing over our adventurous (and sometimes regrettable) choices. As we settled more in each other's company, the teasing took on a playful edge.

"Alright, try this," Trigger offered, holding up a piece of eel nigiri with his chopsticks.

I eyed it suspiciously but leaned forward, taking the bite he offered. The buttery texture and smoky flavour surprised me, and I couldn't help the soft moan that escaped. For a moment, the air between us felt charged, and I noticed the way his expression shifted, as though the sound had caught him off guard. Something unspoken passed between us—a flicker of awareness that sent a shiver racing through me. My cheeks burned, and I looked down at the table, suddenly hyperaware of the closeness between us. I needed to break the moment before it overwhelmed me.

Your turn," I said quickly, picking up a piece of tuna tartare. When he leaned forward to take it, his lips brushed my fingers lightly, sending a shiver through me. I drew back, my breath catching as his stare locked onto mine, intense and unwavering.

"I like that flavour," he said softly, his voice rough.

"You like the tuna tartare?" I asked, though my pulse already knew the answer.

"That's not what I meant," he said simply with a slow, sexy smile.

Electricity crackled between us, but before it could become too much, I reached for another plate to break the moment. "Alright, what's next? How about this?" I held up a piece of tuna maki, and he chuckled, the tension easing just enough to bring us back to laughter.

Between bites of tempura prawn rolls, spicy tuna maki, and avocado nigiri, and casual conversation, the playful flirting lingered, each shared bite a small spark that kept the connection alive.

"So, how did you get the nickname Trigger?" I asked, unsure what to make of it.

There was a quiet reflection in his reply.

"Army. I was a sniper and one of the best. Won a competition and earned the nickname as a result. Since then, it's just sort of stuck," he replied, his smile slipping for a moment, as if the memory still had a hold on him. "Guess I just never really shook off the name. Didn't really think about it." It was brief, but something about it caught my attention—the way his tone shifted just slightly, like a man who'd learned to bury a lot of things, but still couldn't quite erase them.

A flash of sympathy and understanding hit me. Everyone carried their past with them, whether they realised it or not. I certainly still carried mine. We had that in common, it seemed. The thought tugged at me, threatening to shift the mood.

He must have felt it too because he took a slow sip of his drink before clearing his throat. "So, tell me about your girls," he finally asked.

I smiled, grateful for the change to a lighter topic. "Lily is seven, almost eight, and Emily just turned ten. They're growing up so fast it's hard to keep up. Lily's in primary four now and obsessed with art. She's always drawing something. And Emily…" I paused, my smile softening. "Emily's the serious one. She loves science and animals. We've been to the zoo more times than I can count."

Trigger's lips curved into a genuine smile. "They sound brilliant. A bit of a handful, maybe, but in a good way."

"They keep me busy, that's for sure." I reached for another dish from the carousel, my movements more relaxed now. "I know this is a first date, but I feel I need to mention right away that they're the most important part of my life. If things ever got serious with someone, they'd have to understand that I come as a package, which includes my girls."

Trigger appraised me with a soft smile, nodding. "I respect that they are your priority."

"What about you? Any kids?" I ventured. He shook his head.

"No kids, but any nieces or nephews you're close to?" I pressed.

"None of those, either," he said with a wry grin. "I was an only child. Grew up with my grandad. His name was Hugh too."

"Your real name is Hugh?" I asked, surprised by the old-school name. Trigger fit him, but for some reason, I liked Hugh even more.

"Hugh Scott," he smiled wryly. "Not that anyone ever calls me that nowadays."

"Can I?" I asked before I could stop myself.

"What?" he replied, brows raised.

"Can I call you Hugh?" I asked again, my voice more tentative and my cheeks flaming as I realised how intimate that was—asking to be able to call him something nobody else did. Even if it was his real name, it seemed a bit forward.

He beamed.

"I've never really liked the name, to be honest," he replied. God, I wanted the ground to swallow me up. "However, nobody has ever said it quite like you do, and I think I enjoy hearing it from your lips." His smouldering look made my core throb. It suddenly felt unbearably hot in the restaurant, and I had to fight the urge to fan myself.

"So, please feel free to call me Hugh, Sara. I'd like that. I'd like that very much," he said, his voice was low and intimate. "As long as I can call you darling?" he smirked.

I cleared my throat. Butterflies erupted in my stomach like they were trying to break out of a jar, my pulse quickening with every beat. Dear Lord, the man prompted such intense, uncontrollable responses from me. My eyes flicked down, and I shifted, trying to disguise how the throbbing sensation between my legs was making me ache with need.

Trigger…Hugh, I mentally corrected myself, noticed, his eyes sparking with fire at my reaction, but thankfully toned his flirtation down, quickly changing the subject again.

"Closest thing I've got to family these days are my mates—the ones I work with. It's a different kind of bond, but it's solid."

His mention of work stirred my curiosity, and I was glad to have something else to latch onto other than how his lips looked when he smiled, or when he said my name, or when he laughed… "You've mentioned your job before, but I don't think I know much about what you do," I said, trying hard to keep my voice steady and controlled, despite the turmoil of the emotions within me.

Trigger hesitated, his fingers brushing over the rim of his glass. "It's… complicated," he admitted. "Like I said before, I was a sniper in the army and did a lot of tours, saw a lot of things I'd rather not remember. When I got out, adjusting wasn't easy. Spent some time homeless, dealing with… well, everything that came with that. PTSD, mostly."

My heart ached at the raw honesty in his voice, and I reached across the table, my fingers brushing his hand. "That sounds like a lot to carry. I'm sorry you went through that."

He glanced at our hands but didn't pull away. Instead, he turned his hand to clasp mine lightly. "I've come a long way since then," he said, his tone steady. "But it's still part of who I am. Anyway, Marko befriended me when I was at my lowest and then Miki offered me a job, a purpose, and things have been better ever since."

"Thank you for sharing that with me," I said softly. "It means a lot. And I'm glad the Rominovs were there to help you."

The vulnerability in our conversation seemed to break down the last of the barriers between us. The words flowed effortlessly as we swapped stories about our childhoods, shared laughs over some of the more adventurous dishes on the menu, and found more common ground in our mutual love of heavy metal and rock music, and the greatest bands of all time—Metallica, AC/DC, Led Zeppelin, Iron Maiden, basically all the oldies.

"You'll have to come see me play in my friend's band sometime," he murmured.

"You're in a band?" I asked, trying to mask the awe in my voice. It was surprising—Trigger had turned out to be far more complex than I'd imagined.

"Well, not really, but their guitarist works on the rigs and when he is away and they have any gigs on, I fill in for him. Boris and Vlad both love the same music, so they tend to get cover for me when I need to take the time off to play," he told me.

"Music is great for the soul," I said. "Whenever I've been going through a rough time, I've always used music to help me through," I told him.

He blinked at me, silent for a moment, and I wondered if I'd said something wrong.

"I understand that completely," he eventually said.

He took a deep breath and continued, "I already mentioned that I suffer from PTSD and I go to counselling to help, one of the things I learned there was how much music can be a therapy. I'd always played guitar when I was young, but I hadn't realised how helpful it could be."

I nodded. It had certainly helped me during my years with Adam and since then, so I could understand exactly where he was coming from.

As the conversation deepened, Trigger opened up more about his time in the army. He spoke about the camaraderie he'd shared with his unit, his eyes lighting up with fond memories, only to dim when he mentioned how they hadn't made it home. I listened intently, touched by his willingness to share such personal parts of his life.

"It's why I'm so close to the guys I work with now," he said. "They've got their own scars, their own stories. We've all been through hard times in one way or another."

"It's good to have people you can rely on," I said, understanding the value of a strong support system. "Everyone needs people they can count on.

"Yeah," he agreed, looking intently at me. "And sometimes, you find it in the most unexpected places."

By the time we finished our meal and stepped back out into the crisp afternoon air, I felt lighter than I had in years. Trigger walked me back to the shop, his hand brushing mine occasionally as we strolled. At the door, he paused.

"I'll see you Saturday night," he said. "Seven o'clock, right?" His expression was hopeful yet hesitant, and I wondered if he was expecting for me to change my mind. Maybe he thought sharing all he had would put me off. It hadn't, not in the least. Quite the opposite in fact. By him telling me about all of his issues, I'd found a kindred spirit. Someone who'd not only survived unspeakable things but could understand the trauma I'd faced in fighting my own battle.

"Right," I replied, smiling. "And thank you for today. It

was wonderful. And I can't wait for Saturday," I said, determined to reassure him.

"Likewise," he said, his smile softening. "I'm also really looking forward to Saturday."

As he turned to leave, I watched him go, a quiet warmth settling in my chest. It had been just lunch, just a conversation. But it felt like the beginning of something that could be so much more, something worth waiting all these years for.

Back inside the shop, I leaned against the counter, replaying the day's events in my mind. Lolita emerged from the storeroom, a knowing smirk on her face. "So... how was it?"

I laughed, the sound light and genuine. "It was slightly awkward at first since neither of us have dated in so long, but it didn't take us long to relax and then it was good. Really good."

"Really good, huh? I bet you're looking forward to Saturday then?" she pressed.

"Absolutely," I admitted, a small smile tugging at my lips.

"And was that a kiss on the cheek I saw?" Lolita asked with a knowing grin.

"Yes, he was very gentlemanly, insisted on paying. I wasn't so sure because I didn't want him to think that entitled him to anything. After Adam, I want to make sure no man ever thinks they can take what they want or are entitled to my body just because I've been nice. He seemed to understand there was more behind my reticence than merely me asserting my independence. So we made a deal. He paid this time and I can treat him another time." I said with a sly smile. The fact he'd said such a thing showed me how interested he was in seeing me again, even beyond Saturday night.

Lolita wiggled her eyebrows. "A man who knows how to treat a lady. I like him already. So, are we talking sparks flying? Or is it more of a slow burn?"

I rolled my eyes, my smile widening. "Definitely sparks. Big sparks—fireworks, even."

"So, you'll be taking full advantage of a kid free evening on Saturday to jump on him then? I'm going to live vicariously through you now. It's been forever since I've found anyone worth dating. My 'doo dah' is probably closed up by now."

I choked at her words and laughed. "I know the feeling. But I think it's a bit too soon for that. I'm still working up the confidence to date, let alone take it further. But… I'm definitely looking forward to getting to know him more."

My fingers drummed lightly on the counter as I recalled my time with Hugh. He had opened up, sharing parts of himself with me that I was sure few had ever seen, yet there was also an underlying uncertainty in him as he did so. As if, by laying bare his past, he was testing whether I would still want to be a part of his future. That vulnerability, wrapped in his strength, had drawn me to him like a moth to a flame. I wanted to dive right into whatever this was and bask in it, but I reminded myself we needed to take it slow. Not just for me and the girls, but for him too.

I told Lolita as much. "I think he wants to take it slow himself. At least that's the vibe I got from him. He seems open to the idea of pursuing something with me yet cautious. Like me. I think that's one of the things that make him so appealing. We have so much in common. He's been through a lot in the past, and there's a rawness to him, something he tries to keep hidden." I ran my thumb over the edge of the counter, the cool surface a contrast to the warmth of my thoughts. "I'm looking forward to exploring things together and seeing where it leads."

"Well, if you don't get some action soon, I'm filing a complaint on your behalf," Lolita teased with a wink.

Shaking my head, I couldn't help but laugh. For the first time in years, I felt attractive and ready for something new. Hugh didn't just spark fireworks inside me—he made me feel seen, understood, and listened to. Something I'd never had before. In just one short date, he had made me happier than Adam ever had. The thought of seeing him again on Saturday—spending a whole evening with him, getting to know him more—was the most exciting thing I'd looked forward to in ages.

The rest of the day, I replayed every minute detail of our lunch date, a slow smile curling on my lips, before finally turning my attention to our next date. And in particular, what to wear? I'd recently designed a black sequined dress that came to just above the knee, showing just the right amount of leg without seeming to try too hard, and a crossover neckline that allowed a hint of cleavage without being overpowering. That would work. I had been planning on showing it to a client due to come in next week, but I could easily draw up something else for her. With a rush of giddiness, I sketched out my dress. It was rare I ever indulged myself in anything like this because I never really had anywhere to wear something so dressy, but this was the perfect occasion for it. After cutting out the pattern, I stitched it up, all the while wondering how Hugh would react when he saw me in it.

As I finished stitching the last seam, my mind drifted to what I could do to repay Hugh for lunch. If the date to the exhibit went well, I could plan another one—a quiet drive out to a country pub for some food. I frowned, pursing my lips as

I thought it over. Or perhaps the cinema. No, it would be too hard to talk there.

I blew out a breath, feeling the uncertainty rise. I bit my lip, frowning. Should I invite him over for dinner? But no, that was probably too soon. Either of us going to the other's place at this stage might push things further than we were ready for. I sighed, my shoulders slumping slightly. This whole dating thing was a minefield.

A laid-back pub lunch in the countryside it was then. The idea of dating was thrilling, but navigating the complexities of it was going to be a nightmare. Still, if it meant time with Hugh, it was something I'd gladly endure.

CHAPTER 12
TRIGGER
SATURDAY NIGHT – THE PHOTOGRAPHY SHOW DATE

Ever since our lunch date, I hadn't stopped thinking about a certain sexy little designer who I couldn't wait to see again. As I pulled up outside the block where she lived, my gut churned with apprehension. Why did dating feel so much harder than walking into battle?

As I sat in my car outside Sara's flat, waiting to take her to Melissa's photography exhibit, my leg bounced with restless energy. I glanced at my watch. I was too early and I didn't want to make her feel rushed, so I forced myself to wait, taking long, deep breaths to calm my racing heart.

It had been a long time since I felt this way and my mind swirled with memories. Particularly, double dating with Alan, or acting as his wingman before he met and married the love of his life. Unusually, thinking of him didn't pull me into despair. Instead, I felt uplifted as I looked up at the window I suspected was hers.

This morning, I'd sent Sara a gift that I'd purchased on a whim yesterday while Melissa was shoe shopping. A pair of black patent Louboutin's, the ones with the famous red soles. I didn't know much about women's shoes, but Sonia

Rominov was a big fan of this particular style, and Mel had said that since Sara was a dress designer, she would likely love them.

I hoped so, but my mind went back to how she'd wanted to pay for lunch the other day and the way she'd looked. It hadn't taken much to understand that she didn't want me to expect anything in return. I'd been quick to reassure her, telling her she could take me somewhere sometime to make up for it—something I'd been glad to do, anything to get to spend more time with her. But now, I was second-guessing my gift. Would she think this was some sort of bribe? Would she feel insulted or flattered? God, I was so out of practice with this sort of thing. Not that I had ever sent any woman a gift like that before. Sara just made me want to do things. Things I'd never done before, and that wasn't just in the bedroom, though I smirked at the thought.

The minutes dragged, but eventually, it was seven, and I made my way over to her building.

Pressing the buzzer to her flat, my heart leapt when she answered, "Hello?"

"It's me," I said. The door buzzed and I pushed it open, noticing how my hands shook a little.

Taking the steps two at a time, I reached her flat door in less than a minute. Just as I arrived, the door opened and there she was. My stomach dropped, and my heart battered against my chest at the sight of her.

She wore a sleek black dress that sparkled and hugged her curves in all the right places, her hair cascading down her shoulders in loose waves.

"Hey, Hugh," she greeted me in that soft, sultry voice that made my cock jerk in response.

"Hey yourself," I replied, leaning forward to brush a light kiss on her cheek. "You look stunning," I told her, stepping back to admire her. "No, stunning doesn't adequately describe you. Vision, Goddess... or maybe Exquisite Angel still might not be enough," I murmured.

My heart hammered hard, and I forced myself to take in a long, slow breath as I fought to steady myself, my eyes still roaming over her.

Sara blushed, a delicate pink tinting her cheeks. "Thank you. You don't look too bad yourself," she teased, giving me a playful once-over.

"You're wearing the shoes," I said, my grin splitting my face.

"Yes, how could I not? They are beautiful. Thank you, Trigger," she said, and my worry fled. The look in her eyes told me she was pleased with the gift, and there was no sign of discomfort. She didn't seem concerned by the gesture, so I took it that she wasn't feeling pressured.

"Trigger? I thought you were going to call me Hugh?" I teased.

"Can I call you both?" she asked with a playful glint in her eyes.

"Darling, you can call me anything you want," I replied, grinning. "I love the sound of your voice, and frankly, you could recite the alphabet or the whole of the telephone directory to me, and I'd still find it the sexiest thing ever."

She blushed again and I chuckled, offering her my arm. "Shall we?"

―――

It was only a short drive to Janusz Glowacki's restaurant, Marta's, named in honour of his new wife after its recent refurbishment.

"What's that?" Sara asked, pointing to a CD lying in the shelf under the glove compartment.

"Oh, it's my mate's band's CD," I replied.

"Are you on it?"

"Actually, I'm playing on the first track. Paul—the usual guitarist—did the others, but I recorded that one." I couldn't help the pride that crept into my voice. Not that it was anything to brag about. Playing guitar occasionally for a rock band that mostly did weddings and the odd pub gig wasn't exactly headline news, but it was another step in my healing. Being able to perform at all was progress.

"Can I hear it?" Sara's curiosity brought a smile to my face, snapping me out of my thoughts.

"Sure, but don't get too excited—they're not that great," I warned, sliding the CD into the player.

This was what drew me to my new car—an older model black Mercedes-Benz S-Class with the CD player I'd wanted, a rare touch of nostalgia in a world that had moved on to Bluetooth everything. It had an understated elegance, the kind that spoke quietly of quality rather than shouting for attention. It wasn't flashy or over-the-top like the Rominovs' fleet of luxury vehicles, which suited me perfectly.

I'd only bought it yesterday, after much internal debate about what would work best for tonight. The bike was out of the question; a woman in a sleek dress and Louboutin's didn't belong on the back of a motorcycle. The Rominovs' SUVs were too businesslike, too impersonal. This car struck the perfect balance. It was classy enough to complement Sara's elegance and still practical enough to feel like a natural fit for me.

The fact that it was an older model meant I snagged a great deal, but what sealed the decision was a casual comment from the salesperson. "A great family car," they'd said. I hadn't been expecting the mental image that followed —Sara in the passenger seat, two little girls chattering away in the back. The words "I'll take it" left my mouth before I could even think twice.

I shook my head, realising how much I'd changed lately. I was doing things impulsively and with Sara in mind, something unusual for me. Yet, it felt… right.

"It's good," Sara said, her voice snapping me back to the present. She hummed softly along to the melody, her appreciation tugging at something deep inside me.

I chuckled. "Yeah, it's probably their best track, to be honest. The crowd always loves it, but they're more of a cover band than anything else. Songwriting isn't their strongest suit. Still, they're a good group of guys, and I enjoy playing with them when I can."

"Don't want to do it full time?" she asked, glancing at me with curiosity.

"Definitely not," I replied, shaking my head. "I'll stick to dipping in and out. It's more fun that way."

I pulled into a parking space a few blocks away. There was a small lot behind the restaurant, but all the spaces had been reserved for Glowacki's family and the Rominovs, leaving everyone else to fend for themselves. Jumping out of the car, I strode around to the passenger side and opened the door for Sara.

This kind of thing came naturally in my line of work, but tonight it felt more personal. I wanted to make her feel special, show her how good things could be between us. From what Marcie told me when I rang her yesterday to glean some more information from her, Sara had been in an abusive relationship. I didn't know all the details, but it didn't take a genius to understand that she deserved better. I wanted her to know I'd treat her well, that she'd never have to be afraid of me.

Sara took my arm with a graceful ease that made my chest tighten. We walked towards the restaurant at a leisurely pace. The chill in the spring night air made me glad she was wrapped in that black faux-fur jacket, even if it covered her luscious curves. Although despite that, she still looked good enough to stop traffic.

As we strolled along, I couldn't help but steal glances at her, the way her hips swayed with each step, making my pulse quicken. The soft curve of her neck, the way the streetlights caught in her hair, it was enough to make my mouth dry. Whatever she'd been through, it hadn't dulled her beauty, and I found myself wanting more—needing more. I wanted to touch her, to feel the smoothness of her skin beneath my fingertips.

"So," I said, breaking the comfortable silence and forcing my thoughts away from the way she made my body hum, "tell me something about yourself."

She glanced up, her lips curving into the hint of a smile. "What do you want to know?"

"Anything," I replied honestly. "Everything. I want to know what makes you tick."

Her smile softened, tinged with a wistfulness that pulled at something deep inside me. "Well, where do I start? As you know, I'm a mother of two beautiful girls, all of us survivors of a past I'd rather forget. I'm a designer by day, a dreamer by night. And I suppose, in this moment, I'm just a woman trying to find her place in the world."

I listened intently, my heart swelling with admiration for the strength and resilience she exuded, even as a part of me couldn't stop thinking about how badly I wanted her. "You're more than just a survivor, Sara. Anyone can tell you're a fighter. You're bringing up two kids by yourself, running a home and a business, and now branching into the world of fashion design. And from what I've seen, you're doing a bloody good job of it. According to Marcie, and now Melissa, you're a talented designer who's about to take London by storm. I think you're well on your way to finding your place in the world."

Sara's smile widened, and a glimmer of something unspoken passed between us. "Thank you, Trigger. That means a lot, although I still feel like I have a long way to go before I can feel properly settled in life."

A shadow flitted across her face, but she quickly composed herself. "And what about you? Have you found your place in the world, Hugh?" she asked, her voice soft and curious.

I tilted my head slightly, considering her question as my hand brushed hers. "I've made a start, but I've a long way to go before I can truly say that. Although being here with you... certainly feels like I'm on the right track," I said with a wink, trying to keep the mood light. The last thing I wanted was to come across as too intense, so I decided to change the topic.

"So, tell me what rock bands you like?" I asked, shifting the conversation to something lighter.

As we neared the restaurant, the sound of laughter and music spilled out onto the street, creating a lively backdrop to our easy conversation. I held open the door for Sara, watching her smile up at me as though she was pleased by the small gesture. Yes, my sexy designer enjoyed being treated like a lady. That made me want to do it more.

Inside, the restaurant buzzed with activity, the air thick

with the scent of Polish cuisine and animated chatter. I guided Sara through the crowd, my hand resting on the small of her back, a quiet promise of protection, support—and a little more. I wanted everyone to know she was with me. And in that moment, I couldn't help but feel like she already belonged to me.

We entered the main hall, the buzz of conversation and laughter filling the space. I took in the vibrant displays of Melissa's photography and the eclectic mix of guests mingling among them. Pride swelled inside me as I introduced Sara to everyone I knew.

"Sara," Marcie called, rushing over with her friend Claire in tow.

"Hey, it's lovely to see you," Sara said as Marcie grabbed her and kissed her on the cheek.

"Hi, Sara, I'm looking forward to my design consultation with you next week," Claire said, leaning in to give Sara another quick kiss.

I moved closer to my sexy designer, a flicker of jealousy sparking inside me at how easily they could kiss her when I longed to do the same.

"Hi, Claire, it's good to see you again, and I can't wait to explore some new ideas with you," Sara replied, and Claire grinned.

"Hey Trigger," both women said in unison as they seemed to notice me for the first time.

"Ladies," I replied with a nod.

The crowd quietened as Glowacki took to the small makeshift stage to make a speech. Melissa stood behind him, looking a little nervous. My attention shifted to Marko, positioned in her line of sight. His soft smile sent her the support she needed.

Glowacki thanked everyone, and Melissa introduced her

photography exhibit, declaring it open, and I felt like this was the right time to take a chance. My hand moved from around Sara's waist, slipping up to her shoulder, and I gently pulled her into my side. Her breath caught for a moment, and she tensed before relaxing against me. My heart hammered in my chest, but I was glad she'd allowed the action and seemed comfortable enough to stay in my embrace. It felt like another step forward for us, and I couldn't help but feel proud for listening to Melissa's advice and finally giving this a shot.

Sara clapped at the end of Melissa's speech. Reluctantly, I moved my hand off her shoulder just long enough to join in, before quickly placing it back around her. She gave me a sly smile, a playful spark flickering in her expression before she turned into my arms.

"Well, are you going to kiss me or what?" she asked.

I was caught off guard. I'd imagined our first kiss happening later, somewhere more private, but here she was, asking for it in the middle of a crowded event. Without hesitation, I seized the moment. I leaned down, my hand going around her waist, the other slipping into her hair, pulling her closer. Our lips met, and everything else in the room fell away. The noise, the people—it all disappeared. There was only the press of her body against mine, the softness of her lips, and the rush of heat that spread through me. Her taste was intoxicating, and I deepened the kiss, hungry for more.

The thickening of my cock grew uncomfortable, and I reluctantly pulled back, still holding her close. Sara's breath was shallow, her body warm and pliant in my arms. She looked... exquisite.

"Wow, that was..." she murmured, her voice a breathless whisper.

My smile was slow and satisfied as I leaned down again,

murmuring in her ear, "It was fucking incredible, darling. And something I can't wait to repeat."

Unable to relinquish hold of her, I held her hand as we made our way through the exhibit, stopping to admire each of Mel's works thoroughly before moving on. I couldn't help but notice Sara's looks of wonder and admiration as she studied each photograph. I guessed being a creative person in her own right, she appreciated the nuances and details others might miss, seeing the world through the lens of an artist herself.

"These are incredible," Sara breathed, her voice filled with awe as she paused in front of a particularly striking black-and-white portrait. "Melissa has such a gift."

I nodded in agreement, my eyes never leaving her face. "She does. Each photo tells a story, doesn't it?"

Sara turned to me, a soft smile playing on her lips. "Just like you, Trigger. I get the feeling there's more to your story I've yet to discover."

My heart hammered rapidly at her words, a rush of emotions flooding my chest. "Maybe someday, I'll let you in on all my secrets," I replied, my voice laced with a hint of playfulness.

Sara's laughter rang out like music in the crowded room, a melodic sound that warmed me to my core. "I'll hold you to that," she teased.

As we continued to explore the exhibit, we chatted with some of the other guests and the more I learned about Sara, the more I fell under her spell.

Eventually, hunger beckoned, and I led Sara to a table near the back of the restaurant, where a buffet feast awaited us. We dug into the delicious spread with gusto, exchanging playful banter and stolen touches that spoke volumes about the growing attraction between us.

"You know," Sara began between bites of pierogi, a dish she seemed to like, "I never imagined I'd be dating a man like you."

I raised an eyebrow, a smirk tugging at the corners of my lips. "And what kind of man is that?"

She chuckled, her eyes sparkling with mischief. "A man with a scarred past, a dangerous present, and an uncertain future."

I leaned in closer, my voice low and husky. "Sounds like someone you'd want to steer clear of."

Sara shook her head, her expression flirtatious. "On the contrary, I find myself drawn to you like a moth to a flame."

After I walked her up to her front door, I leaned over and pecked her on the lips. "I had another great time, Sara. Thank you for accompanying me tonight."

"Thank you for asking me. I had a wonderful time, too. Would you like to come in for a coffee?" Sara asked when we arrived back at her flat. Her voice soft and inviting, but I could detect the tiniest hint of reticence.

I hesitated for a beat, then gave her a small, almost apologetic smile. "I'd love to, you have no idea how much, but I think we should take things slow. You're special, Sara. You deserve to feel that way, and I'm going to make sure you do before I let myself give in to… well, everything else."

The smile she gave me told me I'd made the right move. While I really wanted to take her inside and throw her down on the nearest soft surface to ravage, I knew that we needed to build more trust between us before I could allow myself that pleasure.

So, instead, I leaned in for one last kiss, this one a little longer, slower, like I was soaking in everything about her. But as much as I wanted to stay, I knew it was time to go.

"I'll call you tomorrow," I told her before forcing myself to turn and walk away. At the top of the stairs, I turned to find her still standing in the doorway, watching me leave. A slow smile lit my face, and I winked at her, glad that she was still standing there, waiting. Whistling, I ran down the steps and out the front door before I could do something stupid and push her inside, kiss her the way I desperately wanted to. The only thing stopping me was my promise to myself that I would build things slowly between us and ensure she trusted me completely before taking things further.

As I climbed back into my car and headed home, happiness settled over me. I cranked up the volume on the radio and sang along to "Enter Sandman" by Metallica as my mind filled with images of the woman who was fast becoming everything to me. I checked my watch, it was almost one o'clock in the morning. Already tomorrow. Was it too early to call? Yeah, but a little text should be fine.

When I got home, I pulled out my phone, ready to send a message, and my breath caught when I saw one from Sara.

Sara: Thanks for a wonderful evening. I'll look forward to talking to you tomorrow, Night Hugh x.

I stared at the words and my insides warmed. Quickly, I fired off a reply.

Me: The pleasure was all mine darling. Speak soon. x

I hummed and hawed for a good few minutes about how to end the text, at last settling on copying Sara, and added a kiss.

Climbing into bed, I couldn't keep the smile off my face. For the first time in years, I was excited not only about my life, but about the future. It was a feeling I wasn't used to, but one I hoped would become familiar—and it was down to one person. Sara. This had been one of the best evenings of my life, and I knew that it was the beginning of something truly extraordinary.

CHAPTER 13
SARA

THE FOLLOWING DAY – PLAY DATES
AND PLAYFULNESS

When I woke the following morning, all I could think about was how amazing the evening had been, and how I'd practically melted into a pile of goo over Trigger's kisses. Each one made my toes curl more than the one before. Lord, that man could kiss, and just the thought of his soft lips on mine made my insides mushy.

As I went to collect the girls from Lolita's, I couldn't contain my grin. It felt like I was literally walking on air as I crossed the hall to her flat. I'd always scoffed at these kinds of thoughts, but now here I was, not only thinking them but fully understanding their meaning.

I rang the bell, and Lolita's voice shouted from the kitchen. "Girls, that'll be your mum. Go open the door."

A moment later, I heard the patter of feet and the sound of chattering as they ran into the hallway.

"Hey, girls," I said when they opened the door.

"Mummy, I missed you," Lily exclaimed, launching herself at me and wrapping her arms tightly around my waist.

"Hi, baby, I missed you too," I laughed, ruffling her hair.

"Hi, Emily," I added, pulling her into my side for a hug.

Lolita entered with Cammy. "I was just finishing the breakfast dishes. The girls have all been fed," she told me.

"Perfect. So, who's ready for soft play?" I asked.

"Me!" Lily said, bouncing up and down.

"Me too!" Cammy added with a grin.

"And Emily?" I asked, smiling when she nodded eagerly.

"Well, grab your shoes and jackets, then we'll head out." They raced off, their giggles trailing behind them.

"I'll get mine too," Lolita said, disappearing into her bedroom.

I had just sunk onto the sofa to wait when my phone rang. Trigger's name lit up the screen, and my pulse kicked up a notch.

"Good morning," I answered, trying to sound casual despite the quickening of my breath.

"Morning, beautiful," his deep voice rumbled, sending a pleasant shiver down my spine. "What are you up to today?"

"Taking the girls to a soft play centre, then for a picnic in the park," I said, cradling the phone between my ear and shoulder. "Lolita's coming too, but she's planning to sneak off and shop for Cammy's birthday."

"Sounds like a busy day," he replied, his smile evident in his tone. "Soft play? You're a braver woman than me."

I chuckled. "It's usually pandemonium, but the kids love it. Keeps them entertained and burns off some energy."

"Still, I think you deserve a reward after surviving that. How about coming to see me play on Thursday? The band's got a gig, and I'd love to see you there."

The invitation caught me off guard in the best way. "Thursday? I'd love to. I don't usually go out on a school night, but since it's for something special, I'm sure Lola will babysit," I replied.

"That's great. I don't want to interfere with your routine

for the girls, but if you're okay with coming, I'd really like that," he said, and the thought that he cared about my routine made me melt.

"I don't mind at all," I reassured him, a smile spreading across my face.

"Brilliant. I'll text you the details," he said, and I could hear the happiness in his voice.

We chatted for a little longer, the conversation flowing easily, peppered with flirtatious banter that left me smiling long after the call ended. Trigger had a way of making me feel light and carefree, something I hadn't felt in years.

The soft play centre was a riot of noise and colour. Children squealed and laughed as they climbed through tunnels, slid down slides, and leapt into ball pits. I kept an eye on Lily and Emily, who had teamed up with Cammy to tackle the climbing wall.

"I'll be back in a couple of hours," Lolita said, slinging her bag over her shoulder. "Text me if you need anything."

"Don't worry about us," I assured her. "Go enjoy your shopping, I'll grab myself a coffee and try to read my book."

She flashed me a grateful smile and headed out, leaving me to supervise the girls. I purchased a coffee, grabbed a table near the play area, and settled in with my book.

Just as I opened it to start reading, Trigger's text came through with the gig details. The message brightened my mood even more, and I let out a quiet laugh, shaking my head at how something so simple could have such an effect on me. It had been almost a decade since I'd been to a live band performance, and the thought of it sent a rush of energy through me—not just at the prospect of seeing him again, but also at the idea of doing something different for a change.

"Mum! Watch me!" Emily's voice pulled me back to the present. She was at the top of the climbing frame, waving enthusiastically. I waved back, my heart swelling with affection. Moments like these were what I lived for.

The hours passed quickly, the kids expending their boundless energy while I chatted with other mums and occasionally helped settle minor squabbles over toys. By the time Lolita returned, the girls were ready to move on to the next adventure.

"How did it go?" Lolita asked as she joined me at the table.

"No major incidents," I said with a laugh. "The girls had a blast."

She glanced at my phone, which I'd left on the table. "So, how was last night?"

"Fantastic," I replied with a giggle.

"So, you're seeing him again?" Lolita asked.

I nodded with a grin. "He invited me to see his band play on Thursday. Can you look after the girls for me, please? If that's okay? I don't want to take advantage of you, Lola."

"Ooh, look at you, Miss Social Life!" she teased. "Of course I'll take care of the girls. They're no trouble and it's great to see you so happy. I'm really glad things are going well with him."

"They are," I admitted. "It's nice. He's nice."

Lolita's grin widened. "Nice? Come on, Sara, give me more than that."

I rolled my eyes, but couldn't hide my amusement. "Fine. He's charming, funny, and…" I hesitated, searching for the right words. "He makes me feel good about myself. Like I'm important."

"So, have you two done the deed yet. Or have I to lodge that complaint I told you I'd lodge on your behalf if you didn't get some action soon?"

I could feel my cheeks flush. "Lolita!"

"What? I need to know because I can't live vicariously through you without all the gory details," she teased.

"I am not going into details about my love life with you," I replied, trying hard to keep the amusement out of my voice.

"Oh, so you two haven't got down and dirty yet. Why the hell not? If a man like that was after me, I'd have jumped his bones ages ago," she giggled, and I rolled my eyes.

"Sara, seriously, you like him, he obviously likes you. What's the problem?"

I shook my head. "It's a bit too soon for anything serious. We're just getting to know each other."

"Mm-hmm," she said, clearly unconvinced, arms crossed and staring at me with an expression I knew only too well. The one that said she wouldn't drop the topic until she'd heard everything.

"Oh alright. I invited him in for coffee and he declined because he wants me to trust him more before we go further," I told her finally.

Her expression softened. "You deserve that. Trigger sounds like a really decent guy. Take whatever time you need, just don't let him slip through your fingers, and enjoy the guy's attentions while you can. If it works out, great, and if not, well, at least you'll have had some great sex. Because, honey, just one look at that man tells me he is going to be bloody fantastic in the sack," she said with a dirty grin.

Laughing, I nodded. She was right. I might not want to get serious yet, but that didn't mean I couldn't have some fun.

Just then Lily came bounding over with Cammy. "Mum,

can we go to the park now? It's too hot in here," Lily said, whining.

"Are you hot too?" Lolita asked her daughter, who nodded. "Okay, go and get Emily and we'll go," she told them before turning to me. "Come on, let's get these kids to the park before they start climbing the walls."

"Oh, they've already done that," I replied with a smirk, gesturing to the nearby climbing wall.

"Ha ha, you know what I mean, smart arse," she said with a chuckle.

―――

After the hectic soft play, the park was a welcome change of pace. The girls raced ahead to the playground while I carried the picnic blanket and food we'd brought. Lolita and I found a shady spot under a tree, close enough to keep an eye on the kids, but far enough to enjoy a bit of peace.

We chatted idly as the girls played, but after a while, I couldn't shake the feeling that we were being watched. I scanned the park, searching for anything out of place. Parents and children filled the space, laughing, chatting, and enjoying the sunny afternoon. Nothing seemed amiss, but the sensation wouldn't go away, prickling at the back of my neck.

"Everything okay?" Lolita asked, noticing my distraction.

I forced a smile. "Yeah, just daydreaming."

She didn't look convinced, but this time she let it drop. Still, I couldn't relax. I kept scanning the periphery of the park, taking in the trees and benches, searching for… I didn't know what. A shadow? A figure that didn't belong?

The afternoon wore on, and eventually, we packed up to head home. As we walked to the car, I caught a glimpse of someone from the corner of my vision. A man, standing by a tree. His back was to me, but something about his posture set my nerves on edge. I turned to get a better look, but he was gone.

"Sara?" Lolita's voice broke through my thoughts. "You're miles away."

I shook my head, forcing a laugh. "Sorry, just tired."

We loaded the girls into the car and drove home, but, even as I tucked the girls into bed that night, the uneasy feeling stayed with me.

Later, I curled up on the sofa to watch the TV. My mind wandered to Trigger and I wondered what he was doing and where he was. As if my thoughts conjured him, my phone vibrated with a text and his name flashed up on the screen. I scrambled to open the message.

Him: Hi darling, I have been thinking of you all day. How was the soft play?

Me: They loved it.

Him: I can't wait until Thursday night to see you again. Would you like to see a movie with me tomorrow night if you can get a babysitter arranged?

I paused, my hands hovering over the keys, unable to decide. It wasn't that I didn't want to go, it was just we'd said we were going to take it slow, and yet that didn't seem to be happening. Also, I meant what I'd said to Lolita, I didn't want to take advantage of her good nature or our friendship. Then there were the girls to think about. If we kept this up, I'd soon have to tell them about him, and I wasn't sure if I was ready for that. Or if Emily was. But then I remembered my discussion with Lolita earlier and decided to just go with the flow.

Me: I'm sure Lolita will do it.

I typed at last.

Him: Great you have a fantastic friend there.

I was pleased that he recognised the fact that Lolita was doing us so many favours.

Me: "I know it. Lola is fantastic. What movie did you want to see?

Him: Your choice. I'll pick you up after dinner and we can choose when we get there.

Me: Fantastic. It's a date.

Him: Can't wait. Got to go, I'm working. See you tomorrow, darling.

Me: Looking forward to it. Have a good night. x.

Him: Night darling. x.

By the time I climbed into bed, all thoughts of shadows in the park or being followed were forgotten. Instead, my thoughts were consumed by a long-haired, guitar-playing, sexy bodyguard with a mouth that promised trouble and a touch that made it impossible to think straight.

CHAPTER 14
TRIGGER
THE FOLLOWING DAY (MONDAY) – SIMPSON VS SARA

The faint aroma of coffee filled the SUV's cabin as I took a sip from my travel mug, trying to stay alert after being on night shift. Vlad sat in the driver's seat, cradling his own cup, staring at the house across the street. Simpson hadn't emerged yet, but we knew he'd be out soon—it was the start of the working week, and the weasel had to get to court.

It had been a long, boring, quiet night, broken up only by thoughts of my next date with Sara, while Vlad had napped on and off. I was looking forward to getting home.

A few minutes later, his front door swung open, and there he was—adjusting his tie with one hand and clutching a leather briefcase in the other. He glanced around the street briefly before heading toward the car parked in his driveway; a sleek black Range Rover that fit his carefully cultivated image of a successful London lawyer and family man. A carefully curated mask hiding the truth—a corrupt lowlife with a penchant for young men, drugs, and the very criminal activities he so often defended.

"Look at him," I muttered, setting my coffee down. "Like a rat pretending to be a bloody peacock."

Vlad smirked faintly as he watched the slimy bastard. "Focus. He's on the move," he said, his tone as measured as ever, but the smile tugging at his lips suggested he liked the analogy. It was a sort of game we played—or I did. Whenever we were trailing the weasel together, I'd come up with one analogy or another to describe the guy.

"I'm always focused," I replied, pulling out my phone to jot down the time. It was just that I enjoyed taking a dig at Simpson's expense. It gave an outlet to the anger that made me want to kill the pervert whenever I saw him. Yesterday's, was *a puddle of piss trying to pass as a fine whisky*. The day before it was *a cockroach in a tuxedo*. Not always very original, but I tried. Thinking up new ones helped break the monotony of the court days and the disgust of his weekend pursuits.

We followed the Range Rover at a distance, blending into the morning traffic. Simpson's route was mundane enough, weaving through familiar streets as he headed from his home into London, until he pulled into the car park of a coffee place on the outskirts of the city. Vlad found a spot a few spaces away. Unfortunately, it was too small a place for either of us to venture inside without being noticed, so instead, we settled in to watch.

"First stop, 7.45 am," Vlad murmured into the recording device we used to keep a record of the weasel's comings and goings, which were then passed to Marko at the end of each day.

I scanned the café entrance, noting two men arriving not long after Simpson. One was tall and broad-shouldered, moving with a heavy, deliberate gait. The other was shorter and leaner, his movements sharp and precise. Neither was much to look at, their sour expressions amplifying their already unpleasant presence.

"Recognise them?" I asked, raising my phone to snap a few discreet photos.

Vlad shook his head. "No. You?"

"Not a clue," I said, sending the images to Marko with a quick note.

Me: Any idea who they are? *picture attached*

The men joined Simpson at a table near the window. Their body language was calm, almost predatory, while Simpson fidgeted like a schoolboy caught with his hand in the biscuit tin. Their conversation seemed intense, though we couldn't hear anything, of course, from our vantage point. We had a good view of the scene. Simpson eventually slid an envelope across the table. The smaller man opened it, his sharp eyes scanning the contents before giving a curt nod. Simpson then handed over the briefcase with a strained smile, his unease clear in every stiff movement. What the fuck was he up to?

The men didn't open it, merely stood, shook Simpson's hand, and left the café. It looked like the little weasel had just supplied them with information and cash. Was he paying them to do a job for him?

"Well, that's not suspicious at all," I said, snapping photos of their vehicle as they climbed into a nondescript grey BMW parked farther down the street.

Vlad's grunt of agreement was barely audible.

I sent the images to Marko with another note.

Me: Got their car too. Run their plates, the weasel passed them an envelope and briefcase. The bastard's up to something. *pictures attached*

The weasel stayed for a few minutes longer, sipping at a cup of coffee before heading back to his car. We trailed him again, maintaining our distance as he drove towards the courthouse. As expected, he pulled into the nearby multi-storey car park. I checked my phone for his tracker's movement to see which floor he parked on as we idled nearby, watching the entrance.

Although Marko had placed a tracker on the weasel's car, we followed him anyway. The guy was a go-between for so many people, always meeting up with someone. He was a fountain of knowledge about what was going on in and around London, a great source of information, and the slimiest little weasel you could ever meet. Miki had been squeezing him for information on all of the human traffickers that had worked with Mathieson and the so-called clients of the hunts run by the MP. We were on him 24/7, and the fucking pervert sickened us all.

The door to the lift opened, and Simpson walked out, crossed the road, and headed into the court as I trailed him on foot. Once he was inside, I kept watch at the door until Boris arrived.

"Hey, how is the weasel today? Not banging any poor kids in the court toilets, I hope?" he stated with a disgusted sneer.

"Bloody hope not. He met with a couple of guys earlier at a café, no idea who, but I took some shots and sent them over to Marko. I'm sure he'll inform us later when he finds out who they are. Who's with you?" I asked him.

"Armen, he's back at our car waiting," he replied, and I nodded. Armen had been Sonia Rominov's bodyguard with Rolan while she was away at university, but now she was back and married to Romi, they were on the rota like the rest of us, fitting in other jobs between their main duties. Armen was a good soldier, loyal, and Bratva through and through.

"The weasel has a court case that's expected to go on for

the next few days, so he should be at court all day unless that changes. Have fun," I told him, patting him on the back as I headed back to meet Vlad in the car.

The drive back to the Rominov estate began in silence, both of us lost in our thoughts. But as the city faded into the background, the tension in the SUV began to ease.

"So," Vlad said, breaking the quiet. "How's Sara?"

I glanced at him, caught off guard. "She's good. Why?"

"You seem... happier lately. Less broody."

"'Broody?' I echoed with a laugh. "Did you seriously just call me broody?"

"Yes," he said simply, the faintest smile playing on his lips.

I shook my head, still chuckling. "She's great, actually. We're going to the cinema this evening."

"A date at the movies? How traditional."

"It's called being a gentleman, Vlad. You should try it sometime."

He snorted. "When I find a woman who can put up with me, maybe I will."

"That's your problem right there," I said, grinning. "You spend too much time in the boxing ring and not enough time in the real world. How are you supposed to meet anyone when you're too busy punching people in the face?"

"It's effective," he replied dryly.

"Yeah, well, women generally prefer flowers to black eyes," I joked.

Vlad's rare laugh was genuine. "I'll keep that in mind."

Not that he, or any of us, would ever hit a woman. That was one of the requisites of being in our Brotherhood and something I wholeheartedly agreed with. Women and children were to be protected and cherished, never harmed. I'd never understood a man who could do that. The thought dragged up what little I knew about the father of Sara's children—the bastard who'd been abusive. My hands clenched at the thought. If I ever met the fucker, I'd teach him a lesson or two.

"So, after the cinema date, if she doesn't kick your arse to the kerb, what else have you got planned to woo your woman?" Vlad's lips twitched as he asked.

"She's coming to see me play on Thursday night," I told him with just a hint of pride.

"Oh, god. Then she'll definitely dump your sorry arse after that," he said with a grin.

"Ha, fucking, ha!" I responded, and he chuckled.

The rest of the drive passed in a comfortable mix of teasing and camaraderie. By the time we pulled into the compound, the earlier tension of the day was a distant memory. As we parked and stepped out of the SUV, I clapped Vlad on the shoulder.

"One day, mate, someone's going to come along and knock your world sideways," I said.

He raised an eyebrow, his expression sceptical. "We'll see."

"You will," I said with a grin. "And when you do, I'll be the first to say, 'I told you so.'"

He rolled his eyes but didn't argue, and together we headed inside, ready to debrief and finish for a while.

―――

Later that evening, when I arrived to pick Sara up, she was waiting by the door in skinny jeans and a jumper that clung to her in all the right ways. Her hair was loose, and her smile brightened the dimming streetlights.

"Ready?" I asked, grinning widely, not caring to mask how thrilled I was to see her again.

"More than. I need a good film," she replied, slipping her arm into mine as we headed to the car.

By the time we got to the cinema, the lobby was alive with the chatter of families, couples, and groups of friends. The smell of buttery popcorn filled the air, and I glanced down at Sara as she scanned the details of tonight's showings.

"You picked that?" I teased, gesturing to the action movie poster. "There's a rom-com playing too, you know. Most women would have gone for that."

"I'm not most women," she shot back, her lips quirking into a smile. "I like action."

I leaned in, lowering my voice just enough to make it obvious. "You certainly aren't. In fact, I don't think I've ever met anyone quite like you before, Sara." Her smile softened, and for a moment, her eyes held mine. "Though, I'm starting to think that's a very good thing. And if it's action you want, I'll show you plenty of that soon, I promise."

She rolled her eyes, but her laugh came easily, and I couldn't help but grin as we made our way to the snack counter.

"Popcorn?" I guessed.

"And a bag of Maltesers," she added with a cheeky grin.

"A woman after my own heart." I ordered the snacks while she chose seats online. When entered on the screen, she led us up to the back row.

"Strategic seating?" I asked as we sat down.

"Obviously. No one blocks the view up here." Her innocent tone didn't fool me one bit. I chuckled. "Well, you did promise me some action," she whispered and my cock jerked.

Fuck!

The lights dimmed, and the previews started rolling. I wasn't sure what to expect from the action film, but Sara's excitement was contagious. Explosions and gunfire filled the screen, but I kept sneaking glances at her, watching her reactions more than the scenes unfolding. Her focus was intense, and I found myself drawn to the way she reacted to every twist and turn.

None of the noise bothered me. My PTSD wasn't tied to the chaos of battle—it was rooted in the silence that came after. The emptiness of loss and the burden of surviving when others didn't.

Somewhere around the third explosion, she turned to me, catching my gaze. "You're not even paying attention," she whispered, her lips curving into a smirk.

"I am," I protested, leaning closer. "To you."

Her cheeks flushed, and I didn't miss the way her breath hitched as I tilted her head, brushing my lips against hers. At first, she froze, but then her hand slid up my arm, and she kissed me back, soft and slow. The world around us faded—no awkward popcorn munching or laughter from the crowd, just her.

When we pulled back, her smile was dazzling. "You're a terrible distraction," she whispered with a pout, "we're supposed to be watching the movie. You're being very naughty." She was trying to sound stern while her lips twitched in a way that beckoned me to them again.

"You love it," I shot back, sliding my arm around her shoulders, pulling her close and planting another kiss on those lips. She turned into me and deepened the kiss, her hands snaking into my hair the way mine did hers. Our tongues danced together in a precursor to what I knew was soon to come between us. The next stage of our relationship was inevitable, the only question was how long I could hold off. If I didn't stop now, it wouldn't be long.

Reluctantly, I pulled away, placing my forehead against hers as I tried to slow my breathing. When I could finally speak again, I whispered, "Darling, any other action will need to be confined to what's on screen, otherwise, I can't be held responsible for taking you right here in the back row."

She giggled and snuggled into my side. I released a long, slow breath despite the discomfort in my nether regions, as contentment filled me.

The film played on, but the story unfolding between us felt more compelling. We whispered and stole kisses, her laughter mingling with mine. By the time the credits rolled, my cheeks hurt from smiling.

As we stepped out into the crisp night air, Sara tugged her coat tighter around her. "So, what did you think?"

I shrugged, stuffing my hands into my pockets. "It was... alright."

Her mock gasp made me laugh. "Alright? You're impossible, Hugh Scott. That was brilliant, and you know it."

"Maybe I'll admit it was decent," I conceded, enjoying teasing her.

She rolled her eyes, but linked her arm through mine as we walked back to the car. As we got to it, I grabbed her and pushed her against the side, kissing her passionately, the way I'd been longing to do all night but held myself back.

Gasping for air, I opened the car door for her. She slid into the passenger seat and without a word I sped off, my breaths coming in short, sharp gasps.

I needed her. Trying to hold back was too much torture. Deep down I wasn't sure if she was ready for more despite how willing she appeared. I wanted her to fully trust me before she gave herself completely, but that didn't mean we couldn't take things up a notch.

But heading directly to her flat wasn't an option—it was too far, and I needed Sara now. Besides, if I took her there, I might not have the strength to stop things from going further than I intended. So, as unromantic as it was, I pulled into a supermarket car park and parked as far from the security cameras as possible. No matter what we did here, there was no way anyone was getting a show.

"I'll take you home soon darling, but, right now, I need to kiss you again," I told her, taking her smile for acquiescence.

Unbuckling my seatbelt, I turned to her, my eyes searching hers to ensure I wasn't mistaken. Her small, shy smile flickered, then grew as she nodded, her eyes locking with mine in silent agreement.

My lips smashed down on hers, desperate and heated. Her soft gasp mingled with my breath as I deepened the kiss, my hands finding her face to pull her closer.

We kissed and touched each other, making out like a couple of horny teenagers. It was a whole load of fun, but not nearly enough to satisfy the urges of a grown man.

"I want more, darling. Will you let me touch you?" I asked my hands slipping down to her thigh.

She licked her lips and nodded.

"Are you sure you're ready for that? We can head home immediately if you're not," I asked, determined to ensure she didn't feel pressured to do anything she wasn't ready for.

"Touch me, Hugh," she whispered.

Opening her jeans, I lifted her hips enough to slide them down her hips before slipping my fingers inside her sexy lace knickers.

She was so wet.

My fingers moved over her folds, teasing them, and she

moaned, her hips lifting almost involuntarily. I smirked and kissed her as I moved to her clit. I mimicked the movement of my tongue in her mouth, swirling, probing, and twirling it until her breaths came quickly and she shook beneath me.

God, she was so responsive. My cock throbbed painfully against the tight restraint of my jeans, desperate to be let loose. But that wasn't going to happen. Not yet. The trust I was building with Sara far more important than a momentary release. That would wait. Things were going well and there would be time for my cock to play later. Tonight, I would enjoy satisfying my woman and that would be enough.

"You feel so good, darling," I whispered in her ear before kissing it. Nibbling on the lobe, I pulled it into my mouth and sucked on it, wishing it was her clit, but there was no room for that here. Another time soon, I promised myself as she groaned.

"Hugh," my name was a gasped cry that was a balm for my battered heart. "I want you," she pleaded.

"Soon, Sara. Tonight is for you, darling," I told her as my fingers moved faster.

She was close, I could feel it. Her hips rising and falling, rocking maddeningly against my fingers. I slipped two fingers inside her and she bucked more frantically, riding them, her breaths ragged while I trailed kisses all over her face and down her neck.

Finally, she came, shaking with her release. My cock leaked pre-cum, its hardness so bloody painful. My breaths were as ragged as hers as she came down from her high. I loved how she looked, lying there, eyelids closed, mouth swollen and slightly open, chest heaving.

"Fuck, darling, that was amazing. You felt so fucking good coming all over my fingers. I can't wait to have you come on my cock," I whispered into the side of her neck.

She chuckled. "Trigger, that was fantastic and if that's what your fingers can do in a confined space, I can't wait to see what you can do when there is more room."

I grinned. "Darling, that was just a little taster, to get you hooked," I said with a cheeky wink.

"Oh, I'm hooked," she replied, licking her lips. "So, hooked, I want to reciprocate," she said with a wicked smirk as her hand brushed the front of my jeans. My cock jerked in response to her slight touch, and I groaned in painful pleasure.

"Darling, as much as I'd love that, you don't need to," I told her, my voice straining with the effort to talk.

"Oh, but I want to. I really want to," she grinned mischievously as she pushed me back into the driver's seat. "Now, be a good boy and get them off," she gestured to my trousers.

I raised my eyebrows. "Are you sure?"

"Please, Hugh, I want to taste you," she pleaded, her voice taking on a sultry, seductive quality.

Well, there was no way I was denying a request like that.

My jeans were around my ankles in seconds.

"The boxers too, babe," she murmured, and I rushed to comply, my eager cock bouncing to stand to attention as her hand enclosed it.

She gave me a long stroke and my eyeballs rolled back. Her touch was so bloody great. I'd never felt anything like it.

She huffed a small laugh as she gave me another tug. I couldn't look at her or I was going to spill everything now, and I really wanted this to last at least a bit longer.

"Her tongue flicked over the head of my cock, and I jumped under her, the shock making me grab onto the side of the car and the roof. "God, darling, keep that up and I won't last a second."

She chuckled, the sound vibrating down my length as she took me into her mouth.

"Fuck, fuck, fuck!" the words slipped unbidden from my lips with each jagged breath.

Gasping for air, I placed one hand on the back of her head while the other gripped the steering wheel so tightly I thought I might snap it.

She hummed as she slid up and down my length, sucking deeply before licking the tip and then sinking that sweet mouth down again.

"Darling," I groaned, the sound a plea, but I wasn't sure if it was for her to keep going or slow down. I didn't want to finish yet, but my release was building, like a dam on the verge of bursting.

She squeezed my balls, and that was it, game over. My release shot into her mouth, taking us both by surprise at the intensity of it. But she didn't pull away. I tried to tug her up by the hair, but she wasn't having it. She remained with her mouth wrapped firmly around my cock, her throat working hard to swallow every last drop of my seed.

I threw my head back and roared as another wave of cum shot out.

When she finally removed her mouth, my breathing was slowing down. She gave the head of my cock a few licks to clean it off and the caring gesture made my heart clench. In that moment, I knew that I was lost to this woman forever. I would do anything to keep her. No matter what it took, I was going to make her mine. I could never give her up.

We sat back in our seats and just breathed, matching smug grins on faces.

Eventually, Sara leaned over.

"It's late," she said, "I told Lolita I'd be home by half past ten."

"You're the one who kept me tethered to my seat with that wicked mouth of yours. You're a bad influence," I told her, grinning like a fool.

"I'll take that as a compliment." Her grin was mischievous, her mood light.

The silence between us was easy, comfortable as we drove back to her place. For once, I wasn't thinking about surveillance or missions. I wasn't analysing every detail or planning the next move. I was just… present. With her.

When I dropped her off, she hesitated at the door, looking up at me with a soft smile. "Thanks for tonight."

"Anytime," I said, brushing a strand of hair from her face. "I'll call you tomorrow."

She nodded, standing on her toes to press a quick kiss to my cheek before slipping inside. As I walked back to the car, I couldn't stop the grin spreading across my face.

By the time my head hit the pillow, I felt utterly spent, content, and at peace in a way I hadn't felt in years. Sleep claimed me quickly, and for once, the darkness was kept at bay, replaced by thoughts of soft kisses and a smile that lit up my world.

CHAPTER 15
SARA
THURSDAY – BAND DATE

I sat behind the counter, the hum of the shop almost soothing in the quiet afternoon. The last few weeks had felt like a blur—busy, but in a good way. My design business was thriving, my shop was steadily growing, and for the first time in a long time, I could feel the heaviness of the past lifting. It wasn't gone entirely, but it wasn't the force it had once been. Things were good. No, scratch that. Things were better than good.

With that thought, my lips kicked up into a grin. Part of the reason things were so good was Hugh. Meeting the guy had done wonders for my confidence, and our heavy petting session the other night had been an incredible rush I couldn't wait to experience again. He'd promised me some action, and he'd definitely delivered. Hopefully, tonight after his gig, we'd each get some more.

My thoughts turned back to the shop as a customer entered to collect her mother of the bride outfit I'd altered.

"That's great. Thanks, Sara," she said after paying.

"Enjoy the wedding. Have a great time," I called after her with a smile.

Another satisfied customer. It was always a good feeling, knowing I was getting things right.

Lolita was in the back room sorting through stock. I could hear the occasional rattle of hangers as she worked, and the rhythmic sound was oddly comforting.

"Hey, boss!" Lolita's voice rang out from the back. I looked up from the sketchpad in front of me, the designs I was working on for Melissa's photoshoot dancing in my mind.

"Hey, you okay back there?" I asked, standing up to stretch.

"Totally! Just dreaming about my own Trigger," she teased, emerging from the storeroom, her arms full of fabric rolls.

I laughed, shaking my head. "You're a menace, Lol."

She grinned, tossing a roll of denim onto the counter. "Well, if the universe is handing out bad boys, I'll take one." She leaned over the counter. "But seriously, Sara, things are going so well, right? I mean, look at you. The business, your man... I need a piece of that."

I glanced at her, amused. "You want a Trigger of your own?"

"Definitely. Can't be the only one around here who doesn't have a badass by her side. When you see him later, ask him if he's got any single friends he could hook me up with." She winked, making her way back to the backroom.

I chuckled, though there was something in the comment that made me pause. I still couldn't believe how things had fallen into place with Trigger. We'd both come from places of pain and mistrust, our pasts full of heartache, but somehow, here we were. Taking it slow. And yet, it felt right. His patience, his understanding... everything about him made me feel safe. The way he didn't rush, didn't push, didn't assume things—he respected the boundaries I'd put in place, and I respected his.

But there was something more than that. It wasn't just his understanding or his gentle approach. It was the way he made me feel alive in ways I hadn't thought possible. The simple moments—walking into the shop with him, the quiet mornings with coffee, him beside me at the counter, his laugh as it filled the space—those were the moments I treasured the most.

"Yeah, things are good," I muttered to myself, smiling.

I should've known better than to think my life had at last hit that sweet spot of normal. The phone rang, snapping me out of my thoughts. I glanced at the screen and sighed.

It was my lawyer. I picked up the phone with a little more force than necessary.

"Hello?"

"Hi, Sara, it's James. Just wanted to give you a quick update."

I pulled the phone away from my ear to glance at Lolita, who was now humming and rolling fabric. "I'm listening."

"We still haven't heard from Adam regarding the divorce papers," James said, his tone even but laced with frustration. "We've been trying to track him down, but his whereabouts are… uncertain, to put it mildly."

A sigh escaped me. "Of course he's playing games," I muttered, running a hand through my hair. "What now?"

"We're working with a private investigator to get more information. We're not giving up on this, but it's taking longer than we hoped. I'll keep you updated as soon as we make progress."

I closed my eyes for a moment, the weight of the situation crashing down again. Adam hadn't signed the papers. He hadn't even responded. It wasn't a surprise, but that didn't mean it didn't sting. The idea of him dragging this out was maddening. I thought I was done with him. But, of course, he had to prove me wrong.

"Thanks, James. Just… keep me in the loop," I said, my voice a little colder than I'd intended.

"Of course, Sara. We're on it."

The call ended, and I slumped back into the chair, exhaling loudly. Lolita came over, sensing the shift in my mood.

"What happened?" she asked, placing a hand on my shoulder.

"It's nothing," I said, shaking my head. "Just that damn divorce. Still no word from Adam. It's like he's intentionally dragging it out."

"Arsehole," Lolita muttered. "What a fucking bastard."

I let out a small laugh, though it was tight. "Yeah, tell me about it."

Just then, the bell over the door jingled and in walked Melissa, her eyes lighting up when she saw me. Behind her, Marko loomed, a smile on his face.

"Look who's here," I said with a grin, standing to greet them. "What's up, guys?"

Marko gave me a quick nod, his grin wide as ever. "Just bringing Mel round to catch up with her favourite designer."

Melissa stepped forward, her heels clicking on the polished floor. "Are you still up for making the costumes for my next photoshoot?"

"Absolutely, when do you want to start on the designs?" I asked grinning, excitement chasing away my earlier upset.

"Now, if you can fit me in?" she beamed eagerly.

"Definitely," I told her, just as eager to get started. "You still want a 1930s Chicago gangster type shoot, with everyone dressed to look the part?"

"Yes. Are you're ready to make some magic happen?" She grinned, rubbing her hands together with glee.

"Oh, you know I'm always ready for that." I gestured toward the office where we could sit and chat. "I've got some ideas for you already."

Marko raised an eyebrow. "That was fast."

"It's a fun concept, and I can't wait to work on something a bit unusual for a change," I told him as I began pulling some of my sketches for her next shoot.

I'd been working on a set of outfits for Melissa's upcoming campaign, and I was excited about it. Fashion design had always been my passion, and being able to create custom pieces for people like Melissa felt like the perfect way to push my business into new territory.

"I'm really excited about these pieces I've designed for you. I hope you like them, but we can change them or tweak them to suit your vision," I said.

Taking out my sketchbook, I flicked through the various designs, explaining them in detail as I went as Melissa and Marko inspected them closely.

"Wow, they are brilliant, just what I was hoping for," Melissa gushed as we finished discussing the last one.

"Are you keeping the photographs black and white or will you be doing some in colour?" I asked, feeling the thrill I always did when my designs were praised.

"Well, I was initially just thinking about black and white prints but now I see your designs I think it would be good to get some colour shots as well," she confirmed.

"Okay, I will think about making sure we have some vibrant colour when I select the materials. I'll send several samples over with my draft designs in a couple of days. You can have a look and let me know what you like and if you have any changes you want me to make, or other ideas you want to incorporate," I told her, feeling delighted at the chance to work on this project.

Mel threw her arms around me, obviously as thrilled with this concept as I was.

"You really know how to bring a person's dreams alive," she cried.

Her words hit me with a wave of pride. It felt good to hear. It felt right. "Thanks, Mel. It means a lot to hear someone say that.

"Seriously, you're going to be my go-to designer forever. Although at the rate your popularity is growing, you soon won't be able to fit me in," she laughed.

Marko chuckled as he leaned against the wall. "Melissa's right, Sara. You're going to need a bigger team soon if you keep growing like this."

I nodded, already planning. "I think so. I've been considering bringing in a couple of new staff members. With the commissions I've had recently, it makes sense."

"Well, we need to head out, I'll look forward to getting your samples soon," Melissa said, before kissing me goodbye.

As I waved them off, my mind flickered between the work at hand and the future. Marko was right—at the rate my business was growing, I'd need to hire more staff sooner than I expected. It made me realise it was time to talk to Lolita. I'd intended to wait until everything with Adam was sorted, but with his whereabouts still a mystery, who knew how long that would take? I couldn't wait any longer.

At the end of the day, I found myself pulling Lolita aside as she was organising fabric rolls.

"I need to ask you something," I said.

Lolita looked up, a curious smile on her face. "What's up?"

I hesitated, doubts about my ability to grow creeping in. Adam's voice echoed in my mind—his cruel words about how useless I was—but I forced them out. That bastard would never hold me back again.

"Would you consider becoming my partner in the business? I know we've been talking about growth, and you've been here through it all. But I want to take this to the next level, and... I can't do it alone."

Lolita's eyes widened. "Wait, really?" Her face broke into a grin. "You want me to be your business partner?"

I nodded, my pulse quickening. "Yes. I trust you, Lola."

"You really believe I can do it?" Lolita bit her lip, a look of vulnerability that I understood all too well. She'd once been beaten down in life herself and although most of the time, you would never know, every now and then, it showed.

I nodded. "Of course. You've been more than just an assistant all these months, Lola. You've been a driving force in making this place what it is, and I couldn't think of anyone else who would make a better partner."

She blinked back tears, then her smile widened. "You've got yourself a partner, Sara. And just so you know, I've been thinking of enrolling in a business course. I want to be able to pull my weight—really contribute."

My heart lightened at her enthusiasm. "You're perfect for this."

"Hell yeah, I am." Lolita chuckled, her energy infectious.

Beaming, I explained my vision for the future. As I did, Lolita's eyes grew wider and her excitement more palpable. "This is going to be amazing."

Yes, it was. The future looked bright. Business was booming, my relationship with Trigger was going well and the girls were happy. Life was good. The only downside was the lack of response to the divorce papers from Adam.

Frustration filled me at the delay to my divorce. But I wouldn't let Adam win. I'd been through enough, and the life I was building was too good to be overshadowed by him.

The taxi Trigger had sent for me pulled up outside the venue where his band was playing. The Spring night air had a crisp bite to it, but it felt good against my skin as I stepped out and walked up to the entrance.

Nervous excitement made my hands shake and my insides flutter as Trigger appeared at the door, his eyes scanning the crowd waiting outside. I took a second to admire him. He looked as incredible as always, his dark, worn leather jacket fitting him perfectly, his hair falling loosely around his face. When he caught sight of me, a grin tugged at his lips, that dangerous grin I'd come to crave.

He pulled me close, his lips brushing mine in a kiss that left me breathless. "Ready to see me rock?" His voice was low and smooth, a teasing challenge in the way he said it.

"I'm always ready for you to rock my world," I blurted, the words slipping out before I could even think to stop them.

He raised an eyebrow, a smirk curling the corner of his mouth. "I'll remember that. And I'm glad I do. But you might want to brace yourself. I'm a whole different kind of dangerous up there," he murmured, his breath warm against my ear, sending a rush of heat through me.

I swallowed hard, my heart thundering against my ribs as if it wanted to leap out and into his arms. The air between us seemed to crackle with an electric pull, a silent understanding passing through the tension. Oh, this guy was definitely dangerous. The kind of dangerous I wanted to dive headfirst into.

Before I could come up with something clever to say, he took my hand and pulled me along.

"We're about to go on," he said, his words sending a thrill through me.

As we pushed our way through the crowd, my heart raced. The gig was in one of those small, dimly lit bars where the thump of the music echoed in your chest and the crowd bounced in time with the rhythm. The kind of place I hadn't been to in years. It was packed, and the whole vibe made me feel immediately young again.

We made our way to the side of the stage, where the band was finishing setting up.

"Will you be okay here?" he asked, and I nodded.

"Yeah, I'm fine. I'll hang out here or go to the bar if I need a drink. You just go do your thing and don't worry about me," I reassured him, trying to sound casual, though my heart was already racing at the thought of seeing him play.

Trigger gave me a brief kiss before turning and striding to the stage. I followed his movements. I still wasn't quite used to his dangerous charm, the way he moved with that effortless confidence that made everyone around him take notice.

After a brief nod to the other guys, he grabbed his guitar with that same casual confidence. The lead singer was good-looking, the rest of the guys weren't unattractive either, but none of them stood out like Trigger.

The singer launched into the opening chords, and Trigger, without missing a beat, picked up the rhythm. Then everything faded, and all I heard was the music, all I saw was Trigger. He was every bit the seasoned rocker.

I watched him, mesmerised by the way he handled the instrument, the way his fingers moved effortlessly across the strings, the intensity in his posture. I couldn't stop staring. The way his hands worked the fretboard, the way he threw himself into the music—completely lost in it. There was a rawness to his performance, a vulnerability beneath the sharp edges of his usual persona. And it made me want him more. I moved to the rhythm, my pulse racing in time with the beat, my chest tight with an unspoken need.

His eyes flicked over the crowd, but every now and then, they landed on me, his gaze hot and hungry. And I could feel it—the connection. Like he was pulling me into his world.

When the band launched into a slower song, one of those deep, smoky ballads that seemed to speak directly to my heart, I caught Trigger's eyes again. This time, he didn't look away. Instead, he stepped toward the edge of the stage, his gaze never leaving mine. As if the rest of the crowd didn't matter. Only me.

When the song ended, he grabbed the mic from the singer. "This next one's for someone special," he said, his voice rough and dark, filled with promise. I felt the heat in those words, and the way the crowd responded—cheering, yelling, urging him on—only made the moment feel more intimate, more personal. It was like he was playing just for me.

The night wore on, the music flowing seamlessly, and every glance, every smile between us felt charged. When the final song ended, the applause was deafening, but all I could hear was the beat of my own heart. Trigger's bandmates were packing up, and he stepped offstage, wiping his brow, a grin still playing on his lips as he approached me.

"Damn, you make it hard to concentrate when you're looking at me like that," he said, his voice rougher now, the passion of the performance still crackling in the air.

"You were amazing," I said, the admiration slipping out before I could stop it.

"Yeah, well," he smirked, pulling me close. "I had a pretty good incentive."

Trigger grabbed the back of my head and kissed me fiercely. The feel of his body, the thrum of his energy, and that sexy grin—and I was hooked.

Like he'd said, he was dangerous, but the kind of dangerous every woman secretly longed for. The kind of man who would make you lose yourself completely if you let him. My breath was ragged when we finally pulled apart.

Before I could even think about it, he led me outside and the cool air hit me like a jolt of reality. The moment we stepped into the alley behind the venue, away from the eyes of the crowd, he pulled me against him, his lips crashing into mine. This kiss was no slow burn—no careful exploration. It was desperate, hungry, as if neither of us could wait any longer.

His hands roamed to my hips, pulling me flush against him. I could feel the roughness of his touch, the tension in his body, the need he could no longer contain. There was no holding back now. My breath hitched as he kissed me deeper, his tongue slipping into my mouth, demanding, asserting. The world around us disappeared, leaving just the two of us.

"Trigger..." I gasped, pulling away just enough to speak, my body already trembling with desire.

"Shh," he murmured, his lips trailing down my neck. "I just want to kiss you, darling."

Just kiss me? Oh, hell no. Whether it was Trigger, the music, or the rare freedom of a child-free night, I felt wild—uninhibited. For once in my life, I wasn't going to hold back.

"I want you," I breathed. "Now."

"Not in the alley babe," I chuckled.

"Then where? I don't want to wait, I need you now," I cried tugging at his hair as I pulled his lips back up to meet mine.

"Fuck, darling, you make it hard for me to keep in control," he murmured against my lips.

I rubbed my self against him, "That's the point," I smirked when he groaned, the tone amused.

A fresh gush of wetness made me squirm. It had been a very long time since I'd been with a man, and even longer since I had wanted one, but I'd never wanted anyone as badly as I wanted him. And I didn't want to wait any longer.

"I need to feel you, Hugh," I murmured, frustration evident in my voice as I reached down to cup his erection through his jeans.

"Are you sure?" he asked, his voice strained as his cock reacted to my touch.

I didn't respond, just squeezed him. He groaned, his resolve snapping as he took my hand and led me to the side of the building, where the band's van was parked. The door slid open with a low creak, and he glanced over his shoulder to make sure we were alone.

"Inside. Now," he growled.

I didn't need any more encouragement. The band's van was cramped, the air thick with the scent of leather, and the faint remnants of cigarette smoke. But as soon as the door slammed shut behind us, Trigger was on me again and nothing mattered but him. His hands pulled at my clothes urgently, as if he couldn't get them off fast enough.

He yanked my t-shirt over my head and bent to take my nipple into his mouth. He groaned, "God, I've imagined doing this so many times," his voice was thick with lust, making me shiver.

My bra was quickly unhooked, and his hands were on my breasts before I could catch my breath. I moaned as he rolled one nipple between his thumb and forefinger while sucking hard on the other. My back arched as I pushed myself against him.

The tight space of the van made everything feel even more intense, the heat of his body against mine, the roughness of his touch. My breath came in shallow bursts as he tugged me closer, lifting me so I straddled him, my legs wrapped around his waist. I could feel the hardness of him against my centre, and it made me wild—like I needed him, needed this, in a way I couldn't explain.

"God, you drive me crazy," he muttered, kissing me with fierce intensity. I felt a thrill shoot through me, like a spark igniting deep in my chest. His hands were everywhere—my back, my thighs, my waist—before sliding between us to undo my jeans. His fingers were swift, desperate, as he undid the button and zipper, dragging them down just enough to expose me to his touch.

His lips trailed down to my neck, biting and sucking gently, as one of his hands slipped between us, finding my clit, his thumb pressing firmly in circles. I gasped into his mouth, the sensation building rapidly. His fingers worked me with expert precision, making me tremble beneath him, but just when I thought I was about to break, he pulled away, leaving me aching for more.

He shifted his focus, pulling off my jeans and knickers, leaving me bare. The cool air of the van hit my exposed skin, a contrast to the heat of his body, but it only heightened my desire. His hands roamed down, sliding over the smooth curves of my body, before his fingers worked quickly to remove the last of my clothing, leaving me completely naked in front of him.

He paused, taking in the sight of me fully exposed, his breath quickening as he ran a hand over his face. A grin spread across his features, rough and filled with hunger.

"God, you're perfect," he muttered, voice thick with desire. He moved closer, his hands tracing over my bare skin, as if absorbing every curve. "I can't wait to feel you, to have all of you."

A shiver ran through me at his words, my breath catching. My skin tingled under his touch, every movement of his hands sending waves

His fingers slipped into me, their intrusion filling me up so well. I cried, rolling my hips towards him as he leaned in for a kiss. My hands flew to his T-shirt. I tugged at the bottom, desperate to feel his skin against mine. He helped me remove it, only breaking our kiss long enough to pull it over his head and toss it aside. He pushed me back onto the top of a large speaker and sunk down between my knees.

Hoisting my legs over his shoulders, he dipped his head. His tongue stroked through me in one long motion. I gasped and clutched at his head as the sensation overwhelmed me. He continued licking for a second before pushing his fingers back inside me and taking my clit in his mouth.

"Trigger," I cried, his name sounding like a prayer.

His tongue and fingers worked their magic and soon I was racing towards the finish line.

"God, you taste so good," he murmured against my folds before ramping up the pace. My eyelids fluttered as I came, my juice flooding his tongue.

"That's my girl," he said, and the approval in his voice sent a fresh rush of liquid into his mouth.

Lord, help me, that man was an absolute sex god. But I needed more. My pussy throbbed, delighted with what had occurred but at the same time needing to be filled more fully.

"Trigger, I need you," I sobbed, desperate to have him inside me.

"I've got you, darling," Trigger mumbled, his voice strained.

Without another word, he shifted, and suddenly, I was bent forward, my hands gripping the side of the van for support. I heard the faint rip of foil as he prepared, the brief pause heightening the anticipation before he entered me from behind. The angle, the intensity, everything felt heightened—raw, real, primal. My body arched instinctively, and I gasped as he thrust into me, each movement sending waves of pleasure crashing through me. The van rocked slightly with each of his thrusts, the music from inside the venue muffled but still there, a distant reminder of the world we'd left behind.

"You feel so damn good," he murmured, his voice a low growl, his breath hot against my neck. And it was like a dam had burst—everything I'd been holding back, everything I'd been resisting, poured out of me. I moved against him, urging him deeper, faster, needing more, wanting more.

I felt like a part of his world now, like I was a wild, untamed thing—just another part of the chaos, of the music, of everything that was *him*. And I loved it. My body responded to his every movement, the rhythm of his thrusts syncing perfectly with the pounding in my chest.

The release came in a rush, like an explosion of light, and for a moment, all I could do was cling to him, my body trembling beneath his. Trigger wasn't far behind, his grip tightening on my hips as he drove into me one last time, finding his release with a low growl that sent shivers through me.

We stayed there for a moment, both of us trying to catch our breath, the only sound the faint hum of the city outside and the rush of our own heartbeats.

Finally, Trigger pulled away, his fingers brushing my hair out of my face. He gave me a crooked smile, still panting.

"Damn," he muttered, eyes dark with something I couldn't quite place. "That was fucking perfect."

I grinned, feeling like I was floating, like everything was *right*. And for the first time in a long time, I didn't care where the night would take me. I was just glad to be with him.

———

We returned to the venue, the night still vibrant with energy, and spent the rest of the evening lost in each other. Flirting, kissing, dancing to the beats of the DJ who took over after the band finished. Every moment felt like it was just us, nothing and nobody else intruding as we shared quiet, stolen touches and heated glances.

But eventually, the night had to end. Trigger drove me home, the car ride silent but comfortable, both of us processing the events of the evening and the deepening of our relationship.

"Thank you for tonight," I said softly, my voice barely above a whisper as we stood outside my door.

He smiled at me, a tender expression that made my heart flutter. "The pleasure was all mine, Sara. I had a great time."

We remained there in the silence, both of us unsure of what came next, caught in that in-between space where words failed. Then he reached out, his hand gently cupping my cheek, his touch tender enough to steal my breath.

"Sara," he whispered, his voice barely audible against the rapid beat of my heart. "When can I see you again?"

"Whenever you want," I murmured, not minding if I sounded needy or desperate. I was both—and I didn't care.

A smile spread across his face, his eyes dark with an

intensity that made my pulse race. Before I could say another word, his lips crashed down on mine in a kiss that burned with the promise of more.

Passion flared, I melted into him, hands tangled in his hair, letting myself lose track of time in the sweetness of our kiss. It felt like coming home after a long journey, like finding solace in someone who understood me in ways no one else ever had.

When we finally pulled apart, breathless, dizzy with desire, I found myself lost in the depth of those stormy blue orbs again. A silent promise passed between us in that glance. This was only the beginning of things to come. Beautiful, terrifying, and full of everything we both needed.

"I'll call you in the morning," he said softly, "and we'll arrange something."

He reached for my door, holding it open as I stepped inside.

I turned to him, a small smile curving my lips. "Goodnight, Hugh."

"Goodnight, darling." He grinned, winking, before turning and heading down the stairs. He waved over his shoulder, and I couldn't help but watch him disappear, already looking forward to what tomorrow would bring.

As I stepped into my flat, my heart still racing from the moment I'd shared with Trigger, an unexpected sight brought me up short. A large white envelope lay on the floor, obviously having been pushed under the door.

My breath caught, dread creeping over me. I bent to pick it up, turning it over in my hands. It was blank—no name, no markings.

A chill ran down my spine as I opened it, my fingers trembling. Inside was a stack of photographs, some recent, others older and dredging up memories I'd fought hard to bury.

Fear tightened its grip, but anger soon followed. Adam had found us. After everything I'd done to escape, he'd managed to track us down and invade our lives again.

But I wasn't the same woman I'd been back then. I refused to let him win, refused to let fear dictate my life any longer.

Clutching the photographs, I forced myself to think. I needed a plan. Contacting the authorities was logical, but deep down, I knew the reality. Without a clear threat or evidence tying the photos to Adam, the police might not be able to help.

My pulse quickened as memories of his threats resurfaced. If I ever left, he'd make me pay. He'd make the girls pay. That promise had kept me trapped for far too long.

He wouldn't trap me again.

I tightened my grip on the envelope, my mind racing. The police might not act—but I knew someone who might.

Biting my lip, I hesitated before picking up my phone.

CHAPTER 16
TRIGGER
LATER THAT NIGHT – THROWN OFF COURSE

The drive home felt different—not the usual quiet that followed a good night, but one charged with thoughts of her. Sara. My knuckles tightened on the steering wheel as I replayed every second: her laugh, the way her eyes lit up when she caught me looking, how my whole body came alive under her touch. Those kisses... they'd wrecked me in the best way.

I'd told Vlad that one day a woman would come along and knock his world sideways. I knew exactly how that felt. It was like my whole life had been thrown off course, just like when I left the army—but this time, it wasn't frightening. The road ahead wasn't filled with darkness and nightmares. No, this one was bright, full of hope and possibilities I'd never dared dream of. And for the first time in years, I wanted to sprint headlong into it.

We'd taken a big step forward tonight, but it wasn't enough. I wanted more. Not just the mind-blowing sex—though hell, that was incredible—but everything. Sara had sparked something in me I didn't even know I wanted: love, a family. Now, that fire burned hotter than ever.

The next step would be meeting her girls. Sara had made it clear they came as a package, and I was more than ready to accept that. I pictured two little girls with her smile, and my heart clenched. I wasn't sure how they'd take to me, but I'd do whatever it took to win them over.

I chuckled, knowing I was rushing things, but I couldn't help myself. My head was in the clouds, caught up in her and how she made me feel. Tomorrow, I'd arrange another date and bring up meeting the kids. If she wasn't ready, I'd respect that—but I couldn't help thinking that what we had was something special.

As I sped along the motorway, different ideas of how our first meeting might go played out in my mind. Just as I settled on one I liked, a trip to the zoo, my phone rang.

I cursed under my breath—until I saw the name.

It was Sara.

With a smile, I pressed answer. "Hey, are you okay?"

"I'm not sure," she said, and the uncertainty in her tone made my heart rate spike. "I got in to find an envelope with photos of me and the girls inside. I think I'm being watched… and I think I know who it is."

That hit me like a punch to the gut.

"Where are the girls?" I asked, my voice low, already thinking about how I'd handle this.

"They're with Lolita next door," she said, and I could hear the fear in her voice, the hesitation. She was trying not to panic, but she couldn't hide it from me. I knew better.

"I'm not far away. I'll come back. I'll be there soon," I said quickly, hanging up before she could protest.

My mind raced, calculating how fast I could get back to her and how much time I had before whatever threat was lurking could close in.

I floored it, speeding back down the road, grateful it was late at night and the motorway was nearly empty.

Sara had made it clear from the start that she was done with her ex. They'd been separated for around five years without a word from him. She'd told me she'd sent him divorce papers, but then he'd vanished. I'd offered to get Marko to trace the bastard, but she hadn't wanted to involve me. I'd understood at the time, but I wasn't about to sit back and let him frighten her now—if it was him.

Although, who else would want to upset her? Anger flared in me. Was this just another way to hurt her before he signed the papers? Or was there something more sinister?

I let out a sharp breath, frustration gripping me. Whatever his game was, it was clear—he wasn't going to let her go easily.

Had he been the one watching her? Or was someone else doing his dirty work?

Sending photos anonymously was a classic intimidation tactic. I understood it all too well; we'd used similar methods ourselves. But he wouldn't get away with it. He thought he could scare Sara, but he hadn't counted on her having an ace up her sleeve: me.

I wanted to find the bastard and make him pay for every ounce of fear he'd caused her. But I couldn't let my anger cloud my judgment. He might be a cruel, abusive pig, but he was still the father of Sara's daughters. Whatever happened, I'd have to keep a cool head when I dealt with him. And I would deal with him.

Taking a few deep breaths, I forced myself to focus.

When I pulled up outside her building, I barely took the time to park properly, my concern still gnawing at me.

"It's me, darling," I said after pressing the buzzer. The

outer door clicked open, and I rushed up the stairs two at a time.

"Trigger," Sara said, her voice trembling as she opened the door. She looked so damn small standing there, like the weight of whatever was happening was crushing her.

"You didn't have to come all the way back tonight. I just wanted to ask if you could get Marko to help find Adam. I don't want to drag you into my mess," she said, her expression a mix of apology and worry.

"Let me in, Sara." My voice was firm, leaving no room for argument. "I know you don't want to involve me, but it's too late for that. I was involved the moment I saw you."

She hesitated for just a moment before stepping back to let me in.

The flat was too quiet—the kind of silence that felt heavy, like the air itself was holding its breath. It made everything seem fragile, like it could all shatter with the wrong move. I wouldn't let that happen.

I followed her to the table, where an envelope lay waiting.

She opened it slowly, like the contents might explode in her hands, and pulled out the photos. One look was all it took to send another surge of anger through me.

There were pictures of Sara and her daughters at the park, the café, walking down the street. Someone had been following her, watching her every move. But there wasn't a single picture of me. Why not?

"You're sure it's him—Adam?" I asked, keeping my voice steady despite the fury bubbling under the surface.

"I think so," she replied softly. "It has to be Adam. He's the only one who would do this. I thought I was being followed, especially the other day at the park, but when I didn't see anyone, I brushed it off as paranoia."

I took a deep breath, forcing myself to stay calm.

"Sara, darling, you should have told me," I said, stepping closer to pull her into my arms.

"I know," she admitted, her voice cracking. "But I thought I was just being silly."

She looked up at me. "Adam's been quiet since the divorce papers were served. His lawyer's been trying to reach him, but… nothing. I figured he might be stalling to get under my skin, but I didn't think, after all this time, that he'd actually do anything. And now this. I don't know what he's playing at."

I tightened my hold on her, a silent reassurance.

"Don't worry about it. I'll handle this. I'll get Marko on it, find him, and make sure you and the girls are safe."

She nodded, her gaze drifting back to the photos.

"Trust me, Sara. I'll deal with this. I promise."

A tentative smile tugged at her lips, her face shadowed by worry, but a glimmer of relief was there too.

"Thank you," she whispered, her voice barely audible.

I kissed her then, a soft, lingering kiss meant to reassure her. She kissed me back, her fingers threading through my hair, the sensation helping to calm me further.

When we finally pulled apart, she leaned into me, her face pressing against my chest, and I held her tightly.

"I'm calling Marko. He'll find out where that bastard is, and we'll make sure he signs the papers and stays out of your life," I told her firmly.

She nodded, and I was grateful for the trust she was placing in me.

With a reassuring smile, I stepped into the kitchen to make the call.

"Trigger, what do you need?" Marko answered, his tone alert.

"I need you to find Adam Carruthers, Sara's husband," I

said, my voice tight with anger. "Her lawyer sent divorce papers weeks ago, but he hasn't signed them and isn't at his old address. Someone's been following her. She came home last night to an envelope with photos of her and the girls. I'm sure it's him."

"That fucking prick," Marko growled. "Don't worry—I'll find him. We'll make sure he doesn't get another chance to mess with her."

"Thanks, Marko. Let me know as soon as you have anything. I'm staying with Sara tonight. She's not going to be alone," I replied before hanging up.

When I returned to the living room, Sara was still staring at the photos, worry creasing her brow as she bit her lip.

Gently, I took the photos from her hands and slipped them back into the envelope, then pulled her into my arms.

"I'll make sure nothing happens to you," I murmured, my voice low but resolute. "You and the girls are safe with me."

She smiled faintly, her face shadowed by worry, but I saw a glimmer of relief too.

And then, before I knew it, she pulled back just enough to kiss me again, this time with a hunger that matched my own. I couldn't get enough of her. The kiss deepened quickly, the heat between us flaring up again. Her hands roamed over my chest, tugging at my shirt as though trying to erase the distance between us.

"Stay the night?" she asked.

"Yeah, darling, I'm not leaving you alone. I'll sleep on the couch," I told her, brushing a soft kiss on her forehead.

"Or you could join me?" she whispered, biting her lip.

I grinned. Hell yeah! I hadn't expected an invitation into her bed, but I sure as heck wasn't going to turn it down.

Pulling her back into my arms, I lifted her, and without thinking, carried her towards a bedroom.

"This one?" I asked between kisses.

She nodded, and I kicked the door open, crossed the room, and threw her onto the bed.

She giggled as I pounced. "Eager?" she asked coyly.

"Darling, you have no idea."

CHAPTER 17
SARA
THE NEXT MORNING – MEETING MY GIRLS

The soft light filtering through the curtains gently stirred me from sleep, its brightness coaxing my eyelids open. For a moment, I allowed myself to bask in the peaceful embrace of the morning, the calm settling around me. I stretched, feeling the pleasant ache in my muscles, a reminder of the night before. A smile tugged at my lips as I relished the feel of being held in Trigger's arms.

His chest rose and fell beneath me, strong and steady, and I inhaled the deep, masculine scent of him. The roughness of his morning stubble brushed against my cheek as he shifted slightly in his sleep, and I allowed myself to savour the comfort of his embrace, feeling safe and cherished.

The softness of the sheets contrasted with the solidness of his body and I closed my eyes, letting the intimacy wash over me. I could have stayed there forever, simply enjoying the closeness between us.

But then, the reality of the day pressed in. I couldn't let myself stay here forever, no matter how much I wanted to. It would be time to go get the girls soon. A soft sigh left my lips as I shifted, careful not to disturb him as I eased out of his hold.

I stood, pausing as to look at him. His features were softened in sleep, his lips slightly parted, and I was drawn in, but with a reluctant sigh, I turned and crept away. I snagged his T-shirt on the way out, slipping it over my head. The scent and smell of him still so close made leaving him a little more bearable.

The floor creaked slightly as I padded toward the kitchen, the morning silence broken only by the quiet hum of the refrigerator. My fingers brushed over the countertops as I grabbed the eggs, the coldness of the carton grounding me in the present. I cracked them into the pan, the sizzle of the bacon filling the quiet air. The smell wafted through the room, rich and savoury, wrapping around me like a blanket. It wasn't just breakfast I was making; it felt like the start of something bigger, something better.

Before I could get the toast started, I heard a groan from the bedroom, followed by the sound of feet shuffling on the hardwood floor. I smiled to myself as Trigger appeared in the doorway, his hair messy, wearing only a pair of boxers and a lazy smile on his lips that made my heart flutter. What a gorgeous specimen of a man.

His eyes were still half-closed with sleep, and I couldn't help but feel a rush of affection for him, rivalled only by the rush of lust.

"Good morning, sleepyhead," I said softly, my voice still a little rough from sleep.

Trigger's smile deepened and he stretched, his movements slow and languid as he walked over to me. His voice was hoarse with sleep when he spoke. "Morning, beautiful." He wrapped his arms around me from behind, his chest pressing to my back. His warmth was like an anchor, and I leaned back into him, closing my eyes as his lips brushed against my shoulder.

The scent of him—clean and fresh from sleep, with just a hint of musk—made something inside me tighten. I could still taste him on my lips from last night, the memory of our kiss lingering like a sweet secret.

"Are bacon and eggs okay with you?" I asked, turning my head slightly to look up at him.

"Sounds perfect to me," he murmured, kissing the top of my head. "Do you have any plans for the day? If not… I was thinking…" He hesitated, deliberating over his words. "I was wondering if I could meet your girls?"

I blinked in surprise, not expecting him to say that. His request took me off guard, but I liked the idea. "That sounds wonderful, Trigger." I found myself smiling, my heart swelling at the idea. "I'm sure they'd love to meet you."

"I'm glad you think so," he replied, his tone low, almost shy. But then he grinned, pulling me closer.

Those stormy orbs I loved to lose myself in softened with something unspoken, and for a brief moment, I sensed the invisible thread between us tighten, drawing us closer together. There was undeniable care in the way he looked at me, as though he was contemplating more than just the present. If I wasn't careful, I'd let myself fall completely—and that might not be such a bad thing at all.

My heart fluttered at the thought of seeing him with my girls. The image of him fitting so seamlessly into my world made everything feel more real, more grounded. He wasn't just a guy I was dating; he was someone already considering my daughters and me, someone who wanted to be part of our lives.

I wasn't sure when I'd started trusting him this deeply, but I knew, deep down, it wasn't just the attraction or the physical connection. It was something more. Something I wasn't quite ready to name yet, but I could feel it growing in the space between us.

We finished making breakfast together. The sound of sizzling bacon, the soft clink of plates being set on the table, and the quiet rhythm of our movements as we worked side by side brought an unexpected calm.

When we finally sat down to eat, a rush of gratitude washed over me. I wasn't just sharing a meal with someone who made my heart race. I was sitting across from someone who was becoming far more than I'd ever expected—someone who didn't just show up for the good moments, but was ready to stand by me through the bad as well.

As we ate, the sunlight from the bright spring day streamed in, casting a golden glow across the table. It seemed to lend the world a brightness full of endless possibilities. I smiled at the imagery, which seemed to reflect the growing brightness of my future with Hugh.

Despite the worry over what Adam was up to, my life felt like everything was finally falling into place.

"So, after you collect the girls, what are your plans for the day?" he asked.

"We're going to the zoo," I told him. "Remember, I mentioned Emily loves it there?" He nodded. "Well, today they have a special petting day where the kids can pet the smaller animals."

"Sounds fun," he replied.

"And you? Are you working?" I asked, my stomach fluttering with nerves. He'd asked to meet the girls, but did he mean right away?

"No, why?" he asked.

"Would you like to come with us?" I asked, my voice a little tentative. The idea of bringing Trigger into my world, into the one I shared with my girls, felt like a huge step. But there was something about him that made me think he would understand, no matter how big or small the role he played in our lives.

"Meet your girls?" he blinked, gulping hard. Oh god, maybe he really hadn't meant quite yet when he'd suggested it. I was about to tell him it was okay if he felt it was too soon when a grin spread across his face.

"I'd love to, darling. I really would." His voice softened, and there was something in the way he said it that made my heart flutter. He didn't sound hesitant. He sounded certain.

I leaned in, pressing a soft kiss to his lips. Just as I kissed him, his phone rang.

He groaned, pulling away to look at the screen. "It's Marko," he said.

"Okay, I'll finish clearing up," I told him. He brushed his lips against mine and swiped to take the call, sauntering off into the living room. And if I tracked the way his bum moved under the soft fabric of his boxers, or salivated over the muscles in his back as he walked away… well, I was only human after all. Good God, the man was built! A giggle threatened to erupt as I realised that the Adonis I was happily ogling, was mine, and I couldn't wait for another chance to get my hands on that body.

CHAPTER 18
TRIGGER
THAT SAME DAY – A DAY AT THE ZOO

As I walked into the living room, I could feel myself being watched. Sara. I added a little more swagger to my step and squared my shoulders to emphasise my muscular frame. The woman was mine in my mind, but I still had to seal the deal and I was going to do whatever it took to make that happen. Including resorting to every possible seduction technique I could think of.

"Hey, what have you got for me?" I asked Marko, trying to keep the smirk out of my voice.

"I haven't located the bastard yet, but I know he's a heavy gambler, got himself in debt to a loan shark, some guy known as Big Al Draycott, who works out of the East End. A slimy fucker named Goran. The guy's been looking to get his money back, and it seems that's why Adam Carruthers has gone into hiding. He's been staying on and off at a girlfriend's place, but isn't there right now. I've got Rolan watching her place, and Boris and Armen are digging into the loan shark for more details on the debt. I'll keep you informed. Do you need someone to cover Sara, or are you okay with that?" he asked.

"I'm spending the day with her and the girls. I'll let you know if I need any cover later," I replied, smiling.

I hung up and went to back into the kitchen. Sara was just finishing drying the dishes. I slipped my arms around her and nibbled her ear.

She giggled, setting the last plate down before turning in my arms to face me. "So, when does this day start? Or do we have time for me to take you back to bed and devour you the way I just devoured that breakfast?" I asked, waggling my eyebrows suggestively.

She chuckled. "You'll have to keep the devouring for some other time, Casanova. We need to get dressed, then go get the girls."

"Go get showered, I'll jump in after you," I told her. "Unless you want me to join you?" I added with a wicked, and probably slightly hopeful, grin.

"Nice try! But if you do that, we'll be late and you know it," she laughed.

"Can't blame me for trying!" I winked and smacked her on the bottom as she hurried to the bathroom.

"Oh, now that was fun," she said, casting a sultry look over her shoulder before disappearing into the bathroom, leaving me with thoughts of all the other things we could do that she might consider fun.

Shifting uncomfortably, I groaned. I was about to meet her girls. Doing so with a hard-on would not be the right impression, I reminded myself, pulling my thoughts out of the gutter.

"I'm done. You can get your shower now," Sara called about ten minutes later, and I hurried to comply.

After I'd finished and dressed, I made my way back into the living room. My breath caught at the sight of Sara looking as effortlessly beautiful as ever in tight jeans, a jumper, and her hair styled in a messy bun. God, how was it, no matter how much effort she took with her appearance, the result was always stunning?

She walked over to me, looking thoughtful.

"I was thinking..." she started, biting her lip as if unsure of how to phrase it. "When I introduce you to the girls, I'm going to simply call you my friend. If you don't mind. I don't want to rush anything. I want them to get to know you first, to see you as someone who's important to me, before I tell them how deep this goes. If that makes sense?"

I gave her a reassuring nod, knowing what she meant.

"I'm on the same page," I said, my voice steady. "I don't want to push you or them. We'll go slow, and I'll let you take the lead. I want to get to know your girls in a way that feels right for all of us."

She smiled, her eyes softening. "I think they'll really like you, Trigger. I do, too."

I reached for her hand, squeezing it gently. "I really like you too, darling. So, let's take this next step and see how it goes."

"Okay, let's do this," she said, gulping but trying hard not to look nervous.

I nodded, and we walked over across the hall to Lolita's flat.

Lolita opened the door to greet us after Sara knocked.

"Good morning you two, I trust you had a great night," she said with a wink.

"We did, thank you," I told her with a smirk.

Her grin widened. "Girls! Mum is here," she shouted over her shoulder before moving away from the door to let us inside.

Two gorgeous little versions of Sara came rushing out of a

room and straight into her arms. She laughed and hugged them close.

"Morning. Did you have a good time?" she asked as I stood behind her and observed the scene.

"Yes," the younger one said.

The older one was already looking at me with a cautious, yet curious expression.

"Girls, I'd like you to meet my friend, Hugh, but everyone calls him Trigger," she said, biting her lip and looking at me with a question in her eyes.

"You can call me either, Hugh or Trigger, whichever you prefer," I told them.

"And Trigger, these are my girls, Lily and Emily," Sara said, placing her hand lovingly on the back of the head of each girl as she introduced them, her pride in them obvious.

"Nice to meet you, girls," I said, trying to keep my voice steady while nerves suddenly tightened in my chest. This wasn't going to be easy. I didn't spend much time around kids, didn't know how to be with them, but I really wanted the girls to like me. "So, I believe you are going to the zoo today. Is that right?" I questioned.

"Yes, and I can't wait. I want to pet the rabbits," Lily squealed excitedly. Emily didn't respond, just met my eyes with her quiet, steady gaze.

I bent down beside them. "Well, do you think it would be alright if I joined you?"

Lily nodded happily, throwing her arms around me with another squeal, "Yes, we are going to have so much fun."

My heart leapt at her easy acceptance of my presence. My gaze moved to Emily. "Would that be alright with you, Emily?" I asked, praying she said yes, but knowing if she didn't, then I'd back off and we could reintroduce me another time.

She stared at me hard before letting her eyes roam over me, slow and assessing. I met her stare head-on with a small smile, waiting for her to assess me. Respect for her caution and her overall guarded nature drew me to her even more than Lily's exuberant nature. After a moment, she slowly nodded, and I let out a relieved breath and grinned at her.

Turning, I caught sight of another girl about the same age as Emily. "And who is this young lady?" I asked.

"This is my daughter, Cammy," Lolita said, ushering the girl closer.

"Nice to meet you, Cammy," I said with a smile.

"Do you and Cammy want to come with us?" I asked Lolita.

"No, thank you. We're visiting my cousin for a few days. She just had a new baby, so Cammy is very excited to see her," she replied, and Cammy nodded enthusiastically.

"Well, maybe some other time then," I said to Lolita before turning to Sara and the girls. "Ready?"

"Yey!" Lily shouted excitedly and grabbed my hand. I looked down at where our hands met, noting how small her hand looked in mine, and something about the gesture, the size difference, made me feel fiercely protective and tender.

I grinned at her and then met Sara's eyes. She was grinning too, holding Emily's hand.

"Thanks for looking after the girls again, Lola. Enjoy your trip. See you in a few days," Sara told her friend before we left.

As we walked together to my car, I felt a tightening in my chest, at the unfamiliar sense of belonging and it felt good. Very good, and suddenly I was looking forward to the trip more than I'd looked forward to anything in a long time.

The cool day and overcast sky didn't dampen our spirits as we made our way toward the zoo. The prospect of a day filled with fun and laughter the only thing on my mind. Sara walked beside me, close but not too close, while Emily and Lily chattered a few steps ahead, their youthful energy contagious. I couldn't help but smile.

As we approached the entrance, a rush of eagerness surged through me. This was exactly what I'd imagined for our first meeting; a trip to the zoo. That they were coming here today and Sara had invited me along felt poignant.

When I'd first thought about meeting the girls, I'd wanted to take them somewhere we could not only forge new bonds, but also create memories in a place that was special to me. I didn't know when I'd become so eager to be part of something like this, but I was, and it felt right.

The girls' faces lit up as we entered the gates and headed to buy our tickets. Emily, the more reserved one, took everything in with a quiet, measured curiosity that I couldn't help but admire. But it was Lily who truly stole my attention. Her pure joy was infectious, her eyes glowing as she tugged at Sara's hand, eager to reach the animal enclosures. The sight made my heart swell.

I leaned down toward her. "What's your favourite animal, then?" I asked, keeping my tone light.

"All of them!" she giggled, bouncing on the balls of her feet.

I laughed, ruffling her hair. "Fair enough."

"What about you, Emily? I hear you love the zoo. Your mum said animals are your thing. Do you have a favourite?" I asked her.

She stared at me, her eyes cool, assessing, before flicking towards her mum. This little girl understood more than anyone gave her credit for, it seemed.

"I like the lions the best," she said after a moment, her voice quiet and thoughtful.

"How about we start with the lions, then? They're pretty badass and they just so happen to be my favourites too." I told her, although she didn't look as if she really believed me. She was cautious, and I understood why. Still, I hoped she'd let me in, eventually.

Lily nodded enthusiastically, grabbing my hand. "Yes! The lions. Can we see them first?"

"Of course. Lead the way."

Emily glanced over at me with a sceptical look. She reminded me of myself at her age—guarded, a little too aware of everything around her. But as we made our way toward the lion enclosure, I could feel her interest stirring. She crept closer, zoning in on the big cats, studying them as they paced in their habitat. It was sad to see such magnificent animals caged, but I knew the zoo only housed those that couldn't survive alone in the wild for one reason or another. Still, as I watched them, I was awed by their sheer power and grace.

"Do you know anything about lions?" she asked, her voice cautious but carrying a spark of curiosity—and maybe even a hint of challenge.

I grinned. "Do I know anything about lions? I've spent hours watching them, Emily. In fact, I know a guy who works here. He's a keeper. Want me to introduce you?"

Her eyes flickered, just for a moment, before she nodded. "Yeah, sure."

When we reached the lions, I waved over one of the staff members. Tom had been with the zoo for years, proud of being the longest-serving lion keeper. I'd met him one day when I was first homeless, wandering the streets aimlessly, and he'd let me in for free. He'd done that whenever I needed to break the monotony of life on the streets. I'd always been drawn to the lions. There was something about those caged, regal beasts that had felt comforting.

He gave me a warm smile as he approached, his hand running through his messy hair. I couldn't help but feel a sense of comfort around him. The zoo had always been a refuge for me, a place of peace in the chaos of my life.

"Trigger, it's good to see you. It's been a while. You're looking good, son," the old guy said.

"Good to see you too, Tom," I replied, catching the tiny gasp of surprise that escaped Emily as she saw I knew the lion keeper.

"These are my friends," I said, nodding toward the others. "Sara and her daughters. This little cherub here is Lily," I added, ruffling her hair, making her giggle. "She loves all animals—no favourites," I said with a smile. "And this is Emily." I gestured to her. "She's got a thing for animals, wants to be a vet someday, but especially loves lions."

Emily's cheeks flushed with pride, though she tried to play it cool. "Yeah, maybe," she murmured, clearly not wanting to seem too eager.

"Well," Tom said, looking down at her, "I've got a free spot for an extra hand with feeding an orphaned baby lion, if you'd like to help with him. I think you'd do great."

Emily's eyes widened. "Really? You'd let me do that?"

"Of course. I'm sure you'll be a pro."

Her smile was small but genuine, and it made my chest tighten with hope. This was good for her, I could tell. She needed something like this. As Tom walked off, she turned to me, her expression softening. "Thanks," she said.

"No problem," I replied, tapping her on the shoulder.

"Why don't we do that now if you have time?" Tom turned back and asked.

"Well, we were going to the petting event to pet the

smaller animals, but that's not for another hour, so I guess we have time. What do you think, Emily?" Sara asked.

Emily's eyes widened in delight. "Yes, please, I'd love that," she replied.

"Yay, can I help too?" Lily asked, excitedly, jumping up and down.

"I don't see why not, but you'll have to promise not to be too loud and startle it. Kendra is just a baby, only a few weeks old," Tom said, gesturing for us to follow him.

"I promise," Lily vowed solemnly, and I smiled at how quickly she calmed, taking her vow seriously.

A few minutes later, we were sat in a small room near the lion enclosure that housed the poor little mite. Tom lifted it and placed it into Emily's arms. It was so small, it fit into them easily.

Handing her a baby bottle, Tom showed her how to feed the cub. My heart clenched at the look of pure joy on her face. Sara reached over and squeezed my hand, her eyes full of unshed tears.

It was Lily's turn next, and she was a good girl, quiet and careful as she fed the cub.

About a half hour later, we left the lion enclosure, the enjoyment of the experience still giving the kids a glow, and said goodbye to Tom.

"You girls come back and see me anytime," he said, waving at them, and Emily whispered, "Can we, Mum?"

"The next time we're at the zoo," Sara replied. "After all, it would be rude not to," she grinned, and Emily beamed back.

"Right, I believe we have some little animals to pet now too," I said, ushering them toward the area where the event was taking place.

The girls ran on ahead, giggling and chatting excitedly.

"Thank you, that really made their day. Especially Emily's," Sara said, squeezing my hand again.

Just as she did, Emily looked back and caught the gesture, glancing between us, cocking her head, before giving me a shy smile. "Come on, slowpokes," she called, and we laughed and hurried to catch up.

"It looks like you're making an impression," Sara whispered.

"Well, they are certainly making one on me. Your girls are lovely, Sara. But then I knew they would be. They are a reflection of their mother, after all." I winked at her, and she blushed.

Lily darted from one enclosure to the next, determined to pet every animal she could. Emily moved more slowly, watching the keepers at work and choosing a few animals to spend time with. She seemed especially drawn to the rabbits and snakes, her quiet fascination evident.

The girls' laughter was infectious, and as the afternoon went on, I found myself more at ease in their company. They seemed to relax around me too, especially Emily, her initial shyness giving way to easy smiles and playful chatter. Sara looked more relaxed too, her expression softening as she watched her daughters.

When the petting event was finished, we wandered through the rest of the zoo, marvelling at the playful monkeys, the majestic giraffes, and the sleek cheetahs. I'd been here plenty of times before, but this time felt different. Sharing the experience with a family made it so much better. The day wasn't just fun—it felt like an adventure.

Lily stayed close, laughing at my silly animal jokes and asking me questions about the creatures she found the most fascinating. The bond between us was instant, as if we'd always known each other. She loved the animals, and I loved how much joy they brought her. With every moment, I fell into step with her, ready to support her however she needed.

Emily, though clearly passionate about animals, was harder to read. She'd started off distant, only speaking to me when necessary. But as we moved through the zoo, there were moments when her guard slipped—when that quiet curiosity of hers reminded me of myself at her age. I knew Emily needed time, but I could see she was softening. Today felt like a small step in the right direction, and I looked forward to taking more.

CHAPTER 19
SARA
TWO DAYS LATER – STANDING MY GROUND

The tinkling of the bell above the door announced an arrival.

I looked up and froze as he stood there, a menacing figure in the doorway, and a shiver ran down my spine. Adam, my husband, stood there, and his gaze slowly swept around the shop before settling on me, cold and calculating.

For a second, time seemed to stand still, I blinked, unable to move, my whole body feeling locked in place as a familiar panic blossomed inside. My breaths came short and shallow, cutting through the silence.

He looked me over, a sneer of a smile lifting the edges of his mouth. Then, without a word, he strode toward me, his expression dark with anger and resentment.

"Sara," he said, his voice a low growl.

I swallowed hard, my heart pounding in my chest, but my body's fight-or-flight response kicked in and I rushed to put the workbench between us, gripping the wood as I steeled myself for whatever was coming.

He saw my discomfort and smirked. "It's so good to see you again."

"What do you want?" I managed to choke out, my voice barely above a whisper.

He moved closer, invading my personal space with a predatory gleam in his eyes. "You know damn well what I want. I want you to come back home, where you belong. And if you know what's good for you and your precious little girls, you'll do as I say."

A chill ran through me at the way he said "belong," as if I were some possession he could reclaim at will. But that wasn't the worst of it. No, that wasn't even close. It was the threats to my girls, his daughters, that made my blood boil even as terror threatened to grip me. But I refused to let it. Pushing the fear back, I let my anger surge, sharp and unyielding, as I met his gaze with a steely resolve of my own.

"I'll never go back to you," I spat, my voice laced with defiance. "Leave now! Lolita?" I shouted, hoping the thought of someone else witnessing his behaviour would make him leave.

He laughed, the sound cold and bitter. "I know she isn't here, Sara. She's gone away for a few days. I'm not a fool. I've been watching you, for a very long time. Did you think I would ever let you go so easily? No, I've been biding my time. I see how well you've been doing, Sara," he added, his voice laced with something like amusement but with a darker edge. "You've built quite a nice little shop here. But you know what? You didn't do it alone. You're still my wife. I'm entitled to a share, don't you think?"

The bastard wasn't just trying to control me again; he wanted to control my success, my independence. There was no way in hell I'd let him. Not this time. "You've lost any power you once had over me. I'm done living in fear."

His eyes narrowed, a dangerous look flashing in them as he took a step closer, his breath hot against my skin. "You don't get to decide that, Sara. You belong to me, and I'll do whatever it takes to make sure you remember that."

But I refused to back down, refused to let him intimidate me again. "You think you can scare me into coming back to you? You think I'll just roll over and let you walk all over me? Well, you're wrong. I've had enough of your threats and your abuse. If you so much as lay a finger on me or my girls, I'll go straight to the authorities. And believe me, they'll be very interested to hear what I have to say."

For a moment, he seemed taken aback by my boldness, his eyes widening in surprise. But then, the mask of rage returned, and he lunged toward me, his hands reaching out to grab me.

I stepped back quickly, instinctively moving towards the counter. There, sitting on the ironing board in the corner, was the iron I had been using to press a garment. Without thinking, I grabbed it, the metal still hot from earlier. Hefting it, I brandished it in front of me like a shield.

Adam froze for a moment, his eyes flicking between the iron and my face. His expression faltered for an instant, but the fury in his gaze remained, sharpening. "You think that will stop me?" he sneered.

I tightened my grip on the iron, my breath quickening, adrenaline flooding my veins. "I've had enough," I said, my voice low but steady. "You're not welcome here. And you're sure as hell not getting anything from me—not my business, not my money, and certainly not me. Not anymore."

His expression twisted as he took a step forward, but I didn't budge. The iron felt solid in my grip, a reminder that I was no longer the person he could push around. "One step closer, and I'll make you regret it," I warned.

For a long moment, we stared each other down, the tension so thick I could taste it. His body practically vibrated with fury, trembled with my attempt to hold back the panic desperately trying to break free.

"This isn't over, Sara. You'll be the one to regret this. You and those little bitches—this isn't the last you've seen of me."

Lifting my chin in defiance, I held my ground, refusing to give in to the fear. "Leave now, Adam. Before I make you."

"You'll be hearing from me. This isn't over, Sara." With one last glare, he turned on his heel and stormed out of the shop, his footsteps heavy and filled with venom.

As the door swung shut behind him, I exhaled sharply, the adrenaline still coursing through me.

Running over to the door, I locked it, my hands shaking badly as I turned the sign to closed before finally setting the iron down.

My breathing was ragged as I hurried into the office and slumped on my chair. Tears came, falling in great big drops, as all my past fears, humiliations, and the sense of powerlessness that had defined so much of my life came flooding back.

The burden of it all was crushing, but I refused to let it break me. I'd fought too hard to let the past claim me again, no matter how deeply it had scarred me.

Adam's words echoed in my ears, but I refused to let them take root.

I might not know what the future held, or how this would all play out in the end, but one thing was certain: I refused to live in fear of him any longer. He wasn't scared of the police, but I knew who could scare him. Opening my bag, I took out my phone.

"He's gone. I'm fine, just a bit shook up," I told him, sniffing and trying to calm my racing heart.

"I'll be right there, darling," he said, his voice steady and reassuring, and I closed my eyes, letting the sound of it soothe me. Whatever happened next, I wouldn't have to face it alone and while I was fully prepared to stand my ground, that fact filled me with relief.

CHAPTER 20
TRIGGER
THE SAME DAY – CONFRONTING THE EX

I knocked loudly on the shop door, feeling a rush of relief when Sara appeared from the back. Despite her telling me that her fucking husband had left, and she was alright, I'd still been frantic, needing to see for myself that she was okay.

The moment she opened the door, I pulled her into my arms and held her tightly. It was as if the floodgates opened at the motion, and she began to cry. I held her, letting her sob into my chest. "That's it, darling, let it all out. You're safe now, I won't let him near you again," I murmured, gently rubbing her back.

She hiccupped, sniffing. "I'm sorry," she whispered through her tears.

"Don't apologise, darling," I replied softly, pressing a kiss to the top of her head. I guided her into the office, sitting down on a chair and pulling her onto my lap, wiping the tears from her cheeks with my thumbs.

"Now, Sara, tell me what happened," I said once she'd calmed a little.

She poured out all the details about their interaction, and

my blood boiled. I was going to fucking beat the shit out of Adam Carruthers. It was bad enough him upsetting Sara but threatening her and the kids was enough to make him a marked man in my eyes. It galled me that I couldn't kill the fucker, but I couldn't risk losing them for a moment of satisfaction. The guy was an arsehole, but he wasn't worth that.

After making Sara a cup of tea, she'd rallied enough to want to get back to work.

"Okay, darling, if you're sure you are up to it," I told her, kissing her on the cheek.

"I'll stay here and call Marko again," I said, grabbing my phone. She nodded before returning to the main shop.

———

"Marko, Sara's husband was at the shop threatening her. Have you located him yet?" I asked, my voice gruff with annoyance.

"Yeah, I was just about to call you. He's been staying in a cheap hotel in Hackney since his newest girlfriend threw him out. What do you want to do about him?" he asked.

"Call Brad. I want a contract made up. Once he's got it prepared, get Boris to pick it up and bring it to me, along with a copy of the divorce papers from Sara's lawyer. He can watch over Sara and the girls. I'm going to go see the fucker and make him sign the divorce papers," I told him, my mind racing with what needed to be done.

"Do you want help? It might be quicker if you turn up with a show of force. You don't want to actually hurt the fuck too much if you can help it. We don't want him citing coercion at a later date," he said.

"Yeah, a show of force will be good. I'd love to throttle

the fucker. He's only going to live because he's the father of two little girls I've come to adore. I'm not averse to sending a stronger message if necessary, but hopefully, we won't need to exert any real pressure. The bastard wants money, so I'm going to pay him off," I told him.

I outlined the details of my plan. "Okay, I'll get it arranged. In the meantime, I'll send Vlad over to locate the bastard and keep an eye on him until we're ready. When Boris arrives, head over to the hotel, and I'll meet you there," he said before hanging up.

A few hours later, after picking up the girls from school with Sara and then dropping them home, with Boris keeping a discreet watch from outside, I met Vlad and Marko outside the hotel where Adam Carruthers was staying.

"We need to get him out of there," I said.

"I'll handle it," Vlad replied, his tone all business. "You two wait here. I'll bring him out. Then we'll take him for a drive somewhere quiet and sort this."

I nodded, watching as Vlad strode inside. A few minutes later, he emerged, gripping Adam Carruthers firmly by the arm. The bastard's pale face twisted in a mix of fear and indignation. Vlad dragged him out like he weighed nothing, and the sight brought me grim satisfaction. The guy looked like he'd pissed himself, and judging by the smell, he probably had.

Vlad shoved him into the SUV, slotting him between Marko and me. Carruthers' head darted around, his wide eyes scanning the interior as though searching for an escape, but there was nowhere for him to go.

"Please… please, let me go. I didn't mean it. I'll leave Sara alone, I swear," he pleaded, his voice trembling.

I leaned back, folding my arms, watching him as he squirmed. He was drenched in sweat, his hands trembling as he sat between us.

When his gaze landed on me, his eyes widened, and whatever false bravado he'd been clinging to fell apart in an instant.

"You!" he cried, his voice cracking as panic set in.

I raised an eyebrow. "Ah, so you know who I am?"

He gulped, his lips trembling. "You're the arsehole who thinks he can fuck my whore of a wife," he spat, venom dripping from every word.

Before he could get another syllable out, I hit him—hard. My fist connected with his face, splitting his lip and sending blood trickling down his chin. The satisfying crack of the impact was like music to my ears.

Carruthers let out a strangled cry, clutching his face as he winced in pain.

I leaned in close, my voice low and cold as ice. "Talk about Sara like that again, and I'll put you in the ground. Understand?"

He nodded quickly, his wide eyes filled with fear.

"What do you want?" he asked, trying to regain some control.

I didn't answer immediately. Marko let out a low, mocking chuckle, and Carruthers flinched, his unease deepening.

"We're going for a little drive," I said, keeping my tone flat. "Then we're going to talk. You're going to be a good little arsehole and do exactly what you're told, or things will get very unpleasant for you. Got it?"

Carruthers nodded rapidly, wiping the blood trickling

from his lip with a shaky hand. He looked at me, then at Marko, and back again, desperation flickering in his expression as he tried to gauge just how bad this was going to get. He didn't have any leverage here, and he damn well knew it.

The drive was silent, the tension thick enough to cut with a knife. Carruthers sat rigid, his fear palpable in the confined space. When Vlad finally pulled onto a deserted stretch of road, the SUV rolled to a stop, and we got out.

I yanked the fucker out of the vehicle by his arm. He swung at me—clumsy and desperate—but I dodged and slugged him hard for the attempt. He stumbled slightly, dazed, but I wasn't about to give him a moment to collect himself.

"What's this?" Carruthers asked, his voice barely a whisper as I thrust some documents into his hand.

"Sign it," I said, holding out a pen.

I let him scan the first bit of paperwork—the divorce applications.

"I'm not signing anything. That bitch is my wife, and she stays mine," he said, though the weakness in his voice betrayed his words.

Without hesitation, I stepped forward and punched him again, right in the gut, knocking the wind out of him. "You'll sign," I growled. "Or I'll make you wish you never fucking met Sara."

His hands shook as he grabbed the pen and squiggled a signature as he gasped for air.

Marko peered over my shoulder at the scrawled mess. "No fucking way. Write your signature properly or it will be the last thing you ever do," he growled.

"Trying to play games?" I asked, "Good job we've got several copies. But I guess you still need a lesson in obedience," I tutted in annoyance before punching him again.

He sank to his knees with a grunt, but I hauled him back to his feet.

"Now, sign the bloody form!" I thrust another copy into his hands.

With a strained sigh, he grabbed the pen and signed his name, using his correct signature this time. "There," he said, looking up at me, his voice barely audible. "Are you're happy? Will you let me go now?"

"Not yet, you've more stuff to sign." I told him as Marko handed him another set of paperwork.

"What the fuck is this? I'm not giving up custody of my daughters for one hundred grand. They belong to me," he shouted, suddenly finding some courage.

For a second, I thought it was because he actually cared about them.

"They're worth way more than that!" he scoffed.

"You care about them?" I asked, unable to keep the shock out of my voice.

"Care? Hell no, those wee bitches were always a pain in my arse. Always demanding their mum's attention. Stupid bitch was always running after them. No, I meant there's no way I'm giving over my rights to them for only one hundred grand," he sneered.

Bile rose in my stomach, and I saw red, lunging at the bastard and knocking him out. Unfortunately, I only got a couple more hits in before Vlad pulled me off.

"Get a grip on yourself, Trigger, or you'll kill the bastard —and you said you didn't want to do that," he barked, his tone sharp enough to cut through my rage.

I nodded and turned to stalk away from the car. Stopping a few feet away, I dragged air into my lungs with deep breaths, counting my breathing in the way I'd learned to calm myself.

By the time I returned, the guy was conscious again.

"This says you agree to a one-off payment of one hundred and fifty grand, an increase of fifty from the first offer, to relinquish all fatherly rights over the girls and stay the hell out of their lives—and Sara's," Marko told him, thrusting a new set of paperwork into his hands.

The bastard remained quiet and didn't look at me as he read the document.

"It's all you're going to get. Take the deal and walk away for good. You really don't have a choice," Marko added as he stepped closer, his voice menacing, his presence looming like a dark cloud.

Carruthers' face paled, and his hands shook as he grabbed the pen. I could see the internal battle in his eyes—he didn't want to lose his daughters so cheaply, but he also didn't want to suffer whatever punishment we had planned for him. He knew we weren't fucking around.

I grabbed the paperwork and checked it over before nodding to Marko, who transferred the money into Carruthers' account.

"Now," I said, grabbing the guy by the throat. "If you ever come near Sara or either of the girls again, I will kill you. Do you understand?"

His face was tight with fear as he nodded quickly. "Yes… yes, I understand."

Satisfied, I gave Marko a nod, and we shoved Carruthers back into the SUV as Vlad climbed into the front.

"Take this fucker back to his hotel," I said, my voice flat with finality.

The guy didn't say a word as we drove and I hoped his silence meant he wouldn't be a problem anymore. He'd learned the hard way that some people—like us—weren't to be fucked with.

We dropped him off without another word, and I couldn't help the small smile that tugged at the corner of my mouth as the SUV disappeared down the road.

"Good riddance," I muttered under my breath.

Marko chuckled beside me. "You enjoyed that a little too much, didn't you?"

I shrugged, feeling the satisfaction of the moment settle into my bones. "Some people need to learn the hard way. He was one of them, and I was happy to teach him."

———

The drive back to Sara's flat was quiet, each mile stretching longer as the reality of what had just unfolded settled in. She was free now. I'd done what I promised I'd do. I'd got those papers signed, secured her girls, and finally put an end to Carruthers' shit.

When I stepped into her flat, it was late, the place dimly lit, but the quiet warmth of her space settled me. The girls were in bed, and Sara was sitting on the couch, a cup of tea in hand as she stared out the window, lost in thought.

I walked in and didn't say anything at first. I just watched her, the way her shoulders seemed to relax when she saw me, the way her eyes softened.

"Everything's taken care of," I said, breaking the silence as I pulled the papers from my jacket.

She looked up, her brow furrowing. "What do you mean? What happened with Adam?"

I handed her the signed documents. "It's all there," I said. "The divorce papers, the deal he signed handing over full custody of the girls to you. It's done. He agreed to everything."

She took the papers, her hands trembling slightly as she flipped through them. Finally, she looked up at me, first with disbelief, then relief.

"You—" she started, her voice cracking slightly, "You did it. You really did it."

I nodded, stepping closer. "It's all going to be okay. I promised you, didn't I? He won't bother you or the girls again."

Tears welled up in her eyes, but she didn't cry. Instead, she just smiled, a real, genuine smile that made everything I'd just done feel worth it.

"Thank you," she whispered, her voice thick with emotion. "It's so good to be free of him."

I cupped her face gently, my thumb brushing her cheek. "I know," I said softly. "He's gone now and you can move on with your life. You and the girls. I won't ever let anyone hurt you again, I promise."

Leaning in, I kissed her, sealing the vow.

CHAPTER 21

SARA

A FEW DAYS LATER – AN EXHILARATING RIDE

"Come on, darling. You'll love it, I promise," Trigger said as I eyed the motorcycle warily.

Trigger's bike, his pride and joy, sat before me like some terrifying predator, its sleek and dark frame menacing. The sun glinted off the black metallic surface in a way that should have been pretty, but instead evoked images of fire dancing in the darkness of hell.

I was being ridiculous, I knew, but I couldn't help it. I'd never been on a motorcycle before. The thought of riding one had never even crossed my mind, but today I'd promised to give it a try. We were heading for that lunch I owed him. The one I'd planned being a nice relaxing drive in the country to a romantic pub. Not a scary ride as a pillion passenger on the back of a demon bike.

Reluctantly, I forced myself to step forward, one step, then the next. My hands shook, and I swallowed hard, my heart thudding in my chest, as I finally stood at the side of his bike, watching Hugh adjust his gloves and throw me that knowing look. "You ready for this?"

Taking a deep breath, I nodded, despite the knot in my stomach.

Trigger smiled in that effortless, confident way he always did when he was in his element. It made me feel like I should be fearless, too.

Feeling foolish for being so worried, I squared my shoulders. Trigger would never take me out on the bike if he didn't think he could take care of me. He wasn't the type of man to do anything stupid just to try to impress me, either. If my man said I'd love it, then I would.

"Okay," I said, my voice a little unsteady as I stepped even closer to the bike. "Let's do it."

The idea of straddling a motorcycle, the open road ahead, and the wind rushing past me felt both exhilarating and terrifying. But the chance of spending this time with him, being so close, made me push past my fears.

"Safety first," he said, handing me a helmet. I shoved it on my head, and then he reached up, fastening the strap for me.

When I was set, he grinned. "Hop on then."

Gulping hard, I swung my leg over the seat, settling behind him. I hadn't considered how intimate it would feel—how close we'd be. The feel of my thighs pressed against his, the subtle tension in his muscles as he readied the engine—it had me holding my breath. His scent—leather, cologne, and something uniquely him—wrapped around me. Gripping his waist, I could feel the hard lines of his body beneath the jacket. Though I tried to seem casual about it, my pulse quickened.

"You good?" he asked, his voice low as he glanced back.

"Yeah, just don't go too fast," I said, my nerves creeping back in.

He chuckled. "Don't worry, I've got you."

Then the engine roared to life beneath us. The vibrations coursed through me, and before I knew it, we were pulling onto the road. As we picked up speed, the scenery blurred around us, and I clung to Trigger as if he were the only thing keeping me grounded. There was freedom to it—wild and unrestrained, like breaking free from invisible chains.

Thoughts of the girls, the shop, and everything waiting back in my world faded. For the first time in what felt like forever, those worries seemed distant. All that mattered was the thrum of the engine, the open road, and the man in front of me who made me feel like I could do anything.

Trigger kept a steady pace—never too fast, never too slow—as we rode through the countryside, rolling hills and open fields stretching out before us. It was peaceful, exhilarating, everything I hadn't realised I was missing.

When we neared our destination, Trigger signalled to pull off. Guiding the bike to a small parking area behind the pub, he killed the engine, and I already regretted that the ride was ending.

"Come on, let's grab a bite," Trigger said, flashing a grin as he took off his helmet.

I removed mine, my hair now a tangled mess but feeling strangely free.

As we walked into the pub, comfortable decor and the smell of hearty food greeted us. We found a quiet corner and settled in. After ordering, Trigger leaned back in his chair, his posture relaxed.

Just as I opened my mouth to ask about his morning, his phone buzzed. He pulled it from his pocket, glanced at the screen, and his whole demeanour shifted.

"Shit," Trigger muttered under his breath.

"What is it?" I asked, leaning forward, sensing the shift in his mood.

"Vlad needs me," he said, shaking his head. "I have to cover his shift watching Simpson."

My stomach dropped a little. Simpson, I had no idea who that was, but if Trigger had to watch him, he couldn't be anyone nice.

"Sorry, darling, duty calls. I'll drop you home," he added quickly, but I wasn't quite ready for the day to end.

"I want to go with you," I blurted without thinking.

Trigger looked at me, his brows furrowing in confusion. "With me on a job?"

"Yeah," I said, surprising myself with how quickly the words left my mouth. "The girls are at school, Lolita's handling the shop, and she's going to pick them up later and take them to a movie, anyway. So…" I paused, unsure how best to explain my curiosity, "I want to understand more about you, about… what you do. I know you're a Bratva soldier, and I accept that, but I don't fully get it."

Trigger didn't say anything, but was obviously thinking over my request as he waved to the waitress and asked to make our food to go. He was quiet for a moment, eyes scanning my face as if to assess my seriousness.

Then, with a sigh, he nodded. "Alright, I suppose since you've let me fully into your world, it's only fair I do the same. So, let's do this then. It's likely to be incredibly boring though," he warned. "Although having you there will definitely brighten things up."

His sexy smirk went straight to my core and I quickly closed my legs, slamming down on all thoughts of sexiness. Instead, I let my mind wander to whatever it was I was about to find out about the man I was fast losing my heart to.

A few minutes later, he grabbed my hand and led me back out to the bike. I stuffed the food containers into the small backpack I'd brought and we headed off again.

I wasn't sure what the next few hours would bring, but before I could allow myself to fall any further for Hugh, I had to know what that would mean. Not just for me, but for my girls. They'd lived a life of fear and uncertainty before, I didn't want to bring them into another life like that without being absolutely sure I understood everything first.

———

Less than an hour later, we parked the bike and walked towards an SUV sitting further along the road.

"Sara, you remember Vlad?" Trigger asked by way of a reintroduction.

I nodded, "I certainly do," I said, smiling at the handsome big guy I knew to be Hugh's best friend.

"It's a pleasure to meet you again," he replied, before gesturing to Trigger.

"Just a minute, darling," Hugh said, turning to follow his friend.

They stopped a few feet away and chatted quietly before Vlad returned to the SUV and climbed in.

Trigger removed a holdall from the boot before returning to my side as the guy drove off.

"Okay, darling. You are definite you want to do this?" he asked again.

"I am," I replied with a smile.

He nodded and grinned. "Okay, then come on."

"Where are we going?" I asked as he pulled me into an alleyway.

"Up there," he replied, pointing to the rooftop.

My eyebrows raised, and I couldn't stop a grin from spreading as I looked up. I was filled with a sense of exhilaration. As a child, I'd always wanted to be a police officer, imagining myself on a stakeout, or following some shady character, and here I was about to get a little insight into what it might actually be like in real life.

We climbed up a fire escape and reached the rooftop. The view was breathtaking. I peered over the edge of the building and swayed a little as vertigo hit. Heck, in my enthusiasm I'd forgot that I didn't really like heights. Yet, I was still thrilled by the sights before me.

"You alright?" Hugh asked, his voice low as he came up behind me and slid his arms around my waist.

"Yeah," I replied, turning around to face him. "Just… a little scared at being up so high… and kind of excited at the same time."

He chuckled, giving me that small, reassuring smile that always seemed to make me feel like I was right where I needed to be. Leaning down, he brushed a kiss to my lips. "Let me set up my scope and check on Simpson and we can talk. I know you have questions, and as long as we don't let the guy slip out unnoticed, we can talk things through. Stay here for now."

"Okay," I said, observing as he moved through a routine that seemed second nature to him.

A short while later, we were sitting on his jacket tucked out of sight. The camera he'd set up showed the front of Simpson's house.

"How will we know if he goes out another way?" I asked as I looked at the live footage on his phone.

"We have cameras placed permanently in the trees behind his garden, which will activate if there is any movement, and that will send a ping to my phone," he explained.

"So, Sara, you had questions?" he asked, placing his arm around my shoulders and settling me into his side.

"Yes," I began, looking out at the sunset as I snuggled closer. "What exactly is your role in all of this?"

Trigger leaned back against the wall and looked down at me and for the first time I could feel his uncertainty. Was he afraid to tell me? Did he worry I'd judge him harshly and end things? Or did he have to hold back information for my own good? If it was the latter, I should probably be concerned about that. The strange thing was, I really wasn't.

"I'm a soldier. I take orders, I do what's necessary," he said eventually.

"Necessary?" I echoed, glancing at him. "Like what?"

He hesitated for a beat, before answering, "Like making sure people like Simpson don't get away with what they're doing. Like making sure the people I care about stay safe."

"And what does that mean, exactly?" I asked, leaning my head on his chest, my hand gently rubbing his abdomen in what I hoped he'd take as a sign of reassurance, that whatever he told me, things between us would be okay.

It must have worked because, for the next couple of hours, he talked. I asked a few questions here and there, but mostly, I just listened, taking it all in. He was candid with me. His life had its dark side—he made that clear—but it was more than that. There was duty, protection, and responsibility woven into everything he did. Trigger's loyalty to the Rominov family, to Vlad, and even to me was unwavering. But I couldn't ignore the thought—it had to come at a price.

"Does it ever bother you? The cost of all this? Being a Bratva soldier?" I asked softly.

His expression darkened slightly, but it wasn't anger. It was something harder to read, a quiet understanding. "Every day," he said, his barely a whisper now, "I think about it."

There was a long pause, and I knew that we were both considering how much we had shared, how much we had revealed to each other. The silence felt heavier than the stars above, but it wasn't uncomfortable.

"And do you ever have to do things you don't want to do?" I asked, my voice trembling with emotion as I leaned back to see his face.

"No, I wouldn't do anything that didn't sit well with me. The guys would never ask that of me either," he replied, but I could tell he was looking for the right words to explain more.

"Like I explained already, if someone is our enemy, we have ways of dealing with them. We try legitimate means first, or methods of persuasion that don't involve killing." He paused for a moment, his expression firm as he continued. "However, if that doesn't work, we will resort to whatever is necessary to put an end to any threat they pose."

His tone shifted slightly, deeper now, as he added, "Even so, we have a code. We're not complete monsters. We never hurt a woman or child, and we don't tolerate that behaviour in others."

He drew in a breath, tugging me closer into his side, the intensity of his words clear. "So, you never have to worry about either myself or any of us hurting you or the girls. On the contrary, we'd die to protect you. I'd die to protect you."

The conviction in his words settled the worries I'd buried deep inside. He was a dangerous man, a killer even, but he was a man of honour, regardless. A man who would never bring harm to me or mine, but instead would do everything in his power to keep harm from us. That was all I needed to know, as my heart swelled with love. There was no escaping it, I was well and truly smitten.

———

Later, as the night stretched on, Trigger pulled out the food we'd taken to go. We sat there, under the stars, eating in quiet companionship.

"Looks like the weasel has headed off to bed for the night," Trigger murmured and my eyes flicked to the screen where I saw that all the lights in the house were off.

And then, without warning, Trigger leaned in. His lips brushed against mine, soft and slow, and my heart jumped, thudding hard against my chest. For a second, time seemed to stand still, and I felt a rush of emotions—desire, affection, the deepening bond between us that seemed to grow stronger with each passing moment.

The kiss deepened, and I felt him, truly felt him, in every part of me. It was more than passion. It was love, deep and real, and it made my heart sing.

When we finally pulled away, I smiled at him, breathless. "I'm glad I came with you tonight," I whispered.

"Me too," he murmured, pulling me into his lap and kissing me again beneath the stars. His hands slid to my waist, his touch gentle yet firm, as though he was afraid to let go.

I melted into him, my fingers brushing against his jawline before tangling in his hair. The kiss deepened, slow and intoxicating. His lips moved against mine with a tenderness that stole my breath, each kiss deepening the bond I felt down to my very core.

When he pulled back slightly, his forehead rested against mine, his warm breath mingling with my own. "You're incredible, you know that?" he whispered, his voice low and full of something I couldn't quite name but felt all the same.

I smiled, my heart racing as his fingers traced lazy circles along my back. "I'm starting to believe it," I whispered back with a teasing smile before taking his lips in another searing kiss.

There, beneath the endless night sky, with his arms wrapped around me, I felt like the world could wait. Nothing else mattered but this—him and me, together. It was perfect. But were things too perfect?

A flicker of unease brushed against my mind, but I pushed it aside, determined not to let anything ruin the moment.

CHAPTER 22
TRIGGER

SEVERAL MONTHS LATER – BECOMING A FAMILY

A childish giggle drew my attention, and I smiled as I watched Lily running around being chased by Marko, Melissa, and Vlad who she'd badgered into playing a game of tig with her.

The months slipped by easily after we'd put Adam behind us. Sara and her girls had settled into my life more seamlessly than I could have imagined. My Bratva family loved them. The girls had found a special bond with the Rominovs who doted on them, while Sara had easily slipped into their hearts.

We'd spent the day at the Rominov estate with Lolita and Cammy, celebrating Maria's birthday. Maria, the Rominovs' housekeeper and everyone's surrogate grandmother, was known as Nonna, and adored by all of us.

The estate had been alive with laughter, the air filled with music and the clink of glasses. Nonna, ever the vibrant matriarch, had made sure everyone was well-fed and well-loved, no small feat considering the size of the family.

I searched around for Sara and found her talking with Sonia. No doubt discussing fashion. It was a passion of Sonia's and she'd recently commissioned several outfits from the '*Simply Sara*' brand, which was fast becoming the talk of London. My chest swelled with pride at how well Sara was doing. Her shop was still in the same location, but soon she'd have to look for bigger premises. Once she'd taken on more staff. She was determined to employ and train up a couple of new people first.

Emily ran up to Sara, Cammy following closely behind. They were full of joy, two happy little girls, as they giggled at whatever she said and ran off again.

I watched them go, with a sense of contentment that I was becoming used to. Emily was still a little guarded, not yet ready to fully open up, but I could see her softening little by little. It made me feel more and more honoured to be a part of her world.

Sara and the girls had filled a space in me I hadn't even realised was empty. Slowly, we were becoming a family, and I found myself enjoying every minute of it.

Vlad, of course, had immediately placed them all under his protection. He was already playing the role of surrogate uncle to the kids, even babysitting for us when he could. Emily seemed especially taken with him, ever since he'd brought a dog to visit—one he was looking after for a friend. Now, all she talked about was getting a dog of her own. Unfortunately, neither mine nor Sara's flat allowed pets. If it were up to me, I'd have got her one in a heartbeat, just to see that smile.

One day, I wanted to ask Sara to be mine completely. I could picture us in a house of our own, the girls happy, and—hopefully—a dog or two. It was a future I could imagine, and I wanted it more than I'd expected.

I caught myself. *My girls.* That's what I was starting to think of them as. It felt right, but I knew I had to move slowly.

One step at a time! I reminded myself. Emily was warming up to me, but I knew I couldn't rush things. Patience wasn't always my strong suit, but I'd wait as long as it took.

I smiled as Lily ran up to me, "Trigger, look," she cried, holding out a new doll. "Uncle Marko gave it to me. It looks just like a real baby and has a bottle and…" she beckoned me close to whisper in my ear, "it can pee and everything," she giggled and I laughed.

"Well, that is special," I replied, "can I hold her?"

"Oh dear, maybe later, Molly just went pee pee," she giggled again.

I chuckled. "Looks like you'd better go change her nappy then," Sara said, coming up beside me, amusement lacing her voice.

"Your family are spoiling them," she said with a soft smile as she watched her daughter run away.

"They tend to do that," I replied, pulling her close and kissing her neck.

"I can't believe they hired horses so Emily and Cammy could learn to ride," she shook her head. "This is meant to be Nonna's day."

"You know nobody can resist the kids, especially Nonna. It was her idea," I laughed, pointing to where Nonna was standing beside Lolita, clapping as they watched the girls being walked around on the back of the horses.

"I'd better go cheer them on," Sara said, "are you coming?"

I kissed her again, a light brush on the lips. "I'll be over soon," I told her, my eyes shifting to where Vlad was standing alone, watching but not engaging. This was unusual. While he was generally stoic when working, he always had a smile or a soft expression around the girls. Something was off with him. It had been for a few weeks now.

"Everything okay?" I asked him once Sara had left.

He nodded, but there was a heaviness in his posture. "You're lucky. All of you are. The Rominovs, Luca, Anton, and you. I hope you know that." His voice carried a quiet intensity, the look in his eyes almost wistful.

"I do, and I'm grateful for every second I spend with them," I told him, meaning every word. There was a pause, and I took a moment to study him. "When are you going to let love into your life?" I asked, the question slipping out as I realised how much of himself he seemed to hold back.

"If I'm ever lucky enough to find what you guys have, I'll grab on to it with both hands and never let it go," he murmured. I glanced at him, there was a look in his eyes I couldn't read, but I smirked. Vlad was carrying a secret, and if I wasn't mistaken, it was one he was going to have to spill soon because it looked like it was desperate to get out.

"Hey, guys," Boris said, breaking into my thoughts.

"Boris, thought you were watching Simpson," Vlad said.

"I was, but Armen has taken over. I was just updating Miki. He had another meeting with those guys again," he said.

"The ones from the café months ago?" I asked.

"The very same. Turns out they are Polish, nothing to do with Glowacki. They come over from Poland every few months to meet with the weasel and spend a day or two here before returning home," he replied.

"Does Marko know who they are?" Vlad questioned.

"Yeah, some lowlife criminals working out of Wroclaw. Not anywhere near Glowacki's hometown or the area his father-in-law runs," he replied, his eyes tracking the girls on the horses before shifting to the women cheering them on.

"Any idea what they're doing here and why they're talking with the weasel?" I asked, intrigued.

"Nope, but Glowacki's in the office with Miki now, and we've passed the information to him. He's going to look into it. It might have something to do with the new tensions in his council. He needs to clean house once and for all—those fuckers can't be trusted. It's time he ran his brotherhood without them, save himself from watching his back against enemies within as well as outside," he said, frustration sharpening his voice.

"Yeah, I agree," Vlad said. "But he has to make that decision himself. You know Glowacki will see the necessity to dismantle the council in the end."

"As long as he doesn't wait too long. With Marta pregnant now and the unrest becoming more obvious, sooner would be better than later," I added.

Ever since Marta and Glowacki announced they were expecting, the council that ran the Polish Mafia, with Glowacki at its helm, had been making waves—always causing trouble. The Brotherhood had been on edge since Glowacki's wife died. She was the daughter of the man who ran the Mafia in Poland and had married Glowacki as part of an arrangement, her father having never trusted the council to manage the UK operations. Since her death, Glowacki had been battling nonstop to hold his ground and protect his family.

"These constant meetings between Simpson and those Polish guys spell trouble, and it's only a matter of time before it ends up at our door, Glowacki's, or both," Vlad said, and I nodded in agreement.

"And we've only just got rid of that fucking MP and his crazy lover," I said, shaking my head at the prospect of more trouble on the horizon.

Sighing heavily, I pushed the thoughts aside. I'd dwell on

them another day. Today, I wanted to bask in the love of family and friends.

"Who's the Hispanic-looking bird beside Sara?" Boris asked, his eyes glued to Lolita.

I smirked. "That's Lolita. She's a single mum, that's her daughter, Cammy, on the black horse, next to Emily. And if you're interested, she's looking for, and I quote "a bad boy of her own," I told him with a wink.

He raised his eyebrows at me before turning his gaze back to the woman. "Is she now? I wonder if she'd like this bad boy," he smirked.

"I'm going to cheer the girls on in their lesson. Come and I'll introduce you if you want," I said, keeping my face neutral.

"Damn right I do," he said with a grin.

I chuckled. Lolita was going to eat him alive.

―――

When we got home later that night, the girls were still buzzing with excitement from the party, talking over each other about their favourite parts as I tucked them in.

Once they were asleep, Sara and I settled into the living room. She poured herself a glass of wine and handed me a beer, and we curled up on the sofa, the TV casting a soft glow around us. We snuggled into each other, savouring the rare peace between us. Then her phone buzzed on the table.

Sara reached for it absentmindedly, her fingers grazing the screen, and for a moment, I wondered if she'd even noticed the message. But then her expression shifted, ever so slightly. Her brows furrowed, and the small crease between them deepened as she read.

"Everything okay?" I asked, voice low, not wanting to intrude but unable to ignore the change in her mood.

She didn't answer immediately, just stared at the screen for a moment longer before exhaling a shaky breath.

"It's from Clara," she said, her voice soft but sharp with something I couldn't quite place.

"Who's Clara?" I asked, tilting my head, trying to gauge her reaction.

"An old friend, and one of Lolita's cousins," she replied quickly, then hesitated. "She helped me escape... from Adam."

My fists clenched automatically at the sound of Sara's ex-husband's name. I leaned forward, elbows on my knees. "What's going on?"

Sara took a deep breath before showing me the message on her phone.

Clara: Sara, something's going on. Your old place was burned down yesterday. Then today, some tough-looking guys were asking about Adam. They didn't know the house had been repossessed. I think he's in deep trouble. They asked about his wife, and I told them you were divorced, that I had no idea where you were. I don't know what mess he's got himself into, but I wanted to warn you to be careful. I'd hate for him to drag you into any of his shit again.

Her hand tightened around the phone, her fingers trembling slightly. She didn't need to say anything for me to understand what was going through her mind. I could see it in her eyes—the remnants of fear, the gnawing doubt that always lingered in the corners of her thoughts when it came to him.

I pulled her into my lap, holding her tightly against me, offering the quiet support I knew she needed without words.

"Do you think he's involved in something bad? Maybe gambling again?" she asked, biting her lip.

Yes, I wanted to answer. It was a logical conclusion, but I didn't want to worry her more than necessary. "I don't know," I said finally, squeezing her shoulder.

"I know you paid him a lot of money, but what if he's already burned his way through it?" she questioned, her voice cracking with a mix of frustration and worry. "What if Clara is right and these men come looking for me?"

"I'll get Marko to check him out again. But remember, whether he's in trouble or not, it's not your problem, and I won't let him or anyone else drag you into it," I told her, tilting her chin up to look into her eyes. Fear lurked underneath the surface, mingling with uncertainty.

"Let's take things one step at a time," I said gently. "We'll find out what's going on and then deal with it if we need to. Okay?"

She nodded, her lips pressing into a thin line as if trying to gather strength. "Okay," she whispered, her voice quiet.

I gave her a reassuring smile and kissed her gently, but my gut churned with worry. Whatever was going on, it was obvious that something was brewing, and I wasn't sure I could stop it from spilling into our lives.

CHAPTER 23
SARA
THE FOLLOWING DAY – KIDNAPPED

"It's perfect, Sara. You're a miracle worker," my client gushed, spinning in front of the mirror, her laughter light and carefree as she admired herself. The deep burgundy fabric of the dress clung to her curves, the intricate beadwork along the neckline shimmering as it caught the overhead light. It was subtle, yet radiant, a perfect balance of glamour and elegance, not too much, but just enough to make an impression.

I stepped back, feeling a soft, satisfied smile tug at my lips. "I'm glad you like it. You've got the perfect figure for it. It'll turn heads for sure."

Her grin widened as she continued to smooth down the fabric, the soft rustling of the dress against her fingertips almost melodic. She gave one final glance at her reflection before turning to me. "You're a genius. Thank you."

"Of course," I said, my voice carrying a hint of pride. As I helped her out of the dress, the fabric slid smoothly over her skin, leaving behind the faintest trace of perfume. The gentle scent, sweet and floral, mixed with the crisp, clean smell of my shop.

I carefully hung the dress on its padded hanger, smoothing the fabric as I adjusted it. Just as I finished, my phone buzzed on the counter.

"Excuse me for just a moment," I said, as I reached for the phone.

"No problem, I've got to get changed anyway," she said, closing the door to the changing room.

The name "Lolita" flashed across the screen. She should have been at the school by now, picking up the kids. A knot of worry formed in my chest as I swiped to answer.

"Lola?" I asked, my voice laced with concern.

"Sara!" Her voice crackled through the line, sharp and frantic, sending a chill racing down my spine. The panic in her tone was unmistakable, and it made my heart stutter. "The girls—they're gone!"

My throat went dry, and my heart stopped for a beat. "What do you mean they're gone?"

"I went to the school to pick up Cammy and the girls," she rushed on, her words tumbling over each other, "but when I got there, the teachers said the girls had already left. With their father."

"What?" The word barely left my mouth before it caught in my throat. I froze. My pulse faltered for a moment, my mind unable to make sense of it. *With their father?* No, that couldn't be right.

"That's not possible. He wouldn't... He couldn't." I shook my head in denial, but I knew that it was true. The thought of him taking them—after everything—hit me like a punch to the gut. I forced myself to breathe, though the air in the room was suddenly too thick, too suffocating. My chest felt like it was caving in, every breath a struggle as I tried to focus on what Lola was saying.

"He told them you'd been in an accident," Lolita cut in,

her voice trembling, her breath shallow. I could almost hear the frantic pace of her heart. "He said he was taking them to the hospital to see you. The teachers believed him, Sara."

"Oh god," I cried, panic clawing at my chest as tears blurred my vision. "I told them to call me if anything happened. Why didn't they check with me?"

"I don't know, but apparently Emily didn't want to go at first, then he said you needed her, and she went with him. I'm sorry, Sara," Lolita cried, her voice breaking. "If only I'd got there sooner. I was running a bit late because of the traffic and just arrived in time, if I'd been there a bit earlier, I might have seen them and stopped him."

My stomach dropped like a stone, my pulse thundering in my ears. "It's okay, I should have known he wouldn't leave us alone so easily," I replied. I couldn't believe I'd let myself think it was all over. He'd warned me it wasn't, I should have listened to that warning. I'd let my guard down and now my girls were paying the price.

"When did he take them?" I asked, my knees threatening to buckle beneath me. I gripped the edge of the counter for support, the cool wood rough under my palms.

"Just a few minutes before they were supposed to finish. But by the time I got there, he was gone, and so were the girls. I called you straight away. What do we do, Sara? Do we call the police, or Trigger?" she sobbed, desperation colouring every word.

"Is Cammy okay?" I cried as a terrible thought occurred to me. There was no reason to think he'd take her too, but the teachers knew they always went home together. What if they'd sent her with him?

"Yes. He said I'd be coming to collect her. She's here in the car with me," she replied, and I could hear the relief mingled with guilt in her voice, along with a child's cries in the background.

"Thank God. Don't do anything. Go straight home and wait for me there. Lock the doors. I'll call Trigger. We'll figure this out."

"Okay," she whispered, but the fragility in her voice made my heart ache. "I'm so sorry, Sara."

"It's not your fault," I said, though I wasn't sure if I was trying to comfort her or myself. The phone slipped from my ear as I ended the call, my mind spiralling. My thoughts were a blur, a storm of what-ifs and fear, but I knew one thing for certain: I had to act quickly.

I turned to face my client, her expression one of growing concern and curiosity.

"I'm so sorry, but I have to close the shop," I said, my voice tight but controlled, despite the chaos of emotions churning inside me. "There's been an emergency."

She nodded quickly, her eyes wide with concern. "Of course. I hope everything's all right."

The words were a blur as she paid and left, the door clicking shut behind her with a finality that echoed in the emptiness of the shop. I locked it, the key turning with a faint, metallic click, and flipped the sign to Closed. My hands were trembling, and the weight of what had just happened pressed down on me like a vise.

I dialled Trigger's number, my fingers slipping slightly over the screen. The phone rang twice before he picked up.

"Sara? Everything okay?" he asked, his voice betraying his surprise to hear from me so soon after we talked just prior to my client arriving.

"No," I said, my voice cracking under the strain of not screaming my heart out, making each word feel like it was being pulled from me. "Adam has taken the girls."

CHAPTER 24
TRIGGER
THE SAME DAY – KIDNAPPED

Anger coursed through me as I sped towards Sara's shop, every bump in the road making my jaw tighten further. Adam had taken the girls. The panic in Sara's voice when she told me was enough to set every nerve in my body on fire.

I couldn't believe the nerve of the fucker. We'd obviously not taught him enough of a lesson if he thought he could pull this shit and get away with it. If he touched a hair on their heads, I was going to kill the bastard with my bare hands.

When Sara had called, I hadn't been far away from her shop, but every second of the drive felt like a bloody lifetime. I finally pulled up, thanking God there was a parking spot right outside for once. I slammed the car door shut, my boots hitting the pavement with a hard thud as I made my way to the entrance.

Sara opened the door almost immediately, her face pale, eyes wide, the kind of look that could gut a man's soul. Her phone was pressed to her ear. "It's Adam," she said, her hand pressed over the mic, her voice barely above a whisper as she spoke. She put the phone on speaker as her breath hitched, and she said, "How much?"

"A quarter of a million," the slimy fuck said. Sara swayed on her feet, clutching at the workbench, before slumping onto the stool beside it.

My stomach sank. The bastard had the audacity to ask for money in exchange for the girls. I wasn't sure what made my blood boil more—the thought of him holding them hostage or the fear they must be feeling.

"I'll get the cash," Sara said, trying to sound calm, though I could hear the tremor in her voice. "Where do I bring it?"

I moved closer and slipped my arms around her, holding her in a tight embrace. For a heartbeat, she remained rigid, before leaning into the quiet comfort I offered. No words were needed—just the reassurance that I wouldn't let her face this alone.

"I'll handle it," I whispered, my voice cold and precise. "Give me the phone."

She hesitated for only an instant before handing it over to me.

"Listen, you fucker. I'll get you your money, and you'll return the girls to me, but then you'd better leave the UK and never return, or I swear to God I will find you and gut you alive. If you touch one hair on their heads, I'll do it anyway," I growled, every word dripping with menace.

He laughed. "You won't do shit while I have the girls, and I won't hand them over until I've got the cash and am out of the area. I'm no fool," he sneered. "How long before you can get the cash together? And don't lie, I know who you and your Rominov friends are. You're good for the cash. More probably, but I don't have time to fuck around, so a quarter of a mill will do."

I glanced at Sara, wanting to stall, but knowing there was

no way I could leave the girls in the hands of the bastard for any longer than necessary. "About two hours."

"Good. I'll be in touch with a location in about an hour," he said before hanging up.

The moment the call ended, a heavy silence fell over the room. My body was on edge, but now, it felt like I could physically feel the heat of my anger radiating through me.

My mind raced, already piecing together a plan. Time was slipping away—every second we wasted brought those girls closer to danger. The guy had people chasing him, and he was unpredictable, desperate. Who knew what he'd do if things didn't go his way?

I called Vlad first. He'd be my right-hand man in this, no question. He answered on the first ring.

"Trigger?"

"Carruthers has the girls. He's asking for money, a quarter of a million," I said, my words clipped, my anger simmering just beneath the surface. "I need the cash within the next couple of hours, and you, Boris, and Marko. We're going in to get them back."

"I'll sort it," Vlad said without hesitation. "I'll let you know when we are set," he said.

"Okay, I'm going to take Sara home. Meet me there when everything's set. The fucker is going to call back in twenty minutes with a location," I added, feeling the pressure of every passing second.

Sara cried silently all the way back to her flat, and I let her, knowing that no words I could offer in that moment would ease the pain. My anger smouldered, the thought of tearing Adam Carruthers apart consuming me. His arrogance was what made me want to end him, but it was the girls that spurred me on. Nothing mattered more than bringing them back safely.

Lolita rushed to Sara as soon as we entered, the two women clinging to each other, both overcome with emotion. Little Cammy came over to me, and I pulled her close, feeling her tiny body tremble in my arms as tears streamed down her cheeks. I bent down, keeping my voice controlled despite the rage inside me.

"It's going to be okay. I'll bring your friends back. I promise."

She nodded, her little body shaking but trusting.

"I believe you, Uncle Trigger," she said, and her faith in me fuelled my resolve. I would not fail her. I'd never fail any of them.

We sat together in the small living room as Lolita made tea and a sandwich for Cammy. The minutes dragged on like hours, each one seeming longer than the last as Sara's emotions fluctuated. At times, she went silent, fists clenched, her gaze distant, while other times, her tears flowed freely. She wiped at her face, as though trying to suppress everything inside, but it wasn't working. After what felt like an eternity, the phone rang.

Sara's breath hitched as she answered. It was Adam.

"Bandstand, Hampstead Heath. One hour," he said, before abruptly hanging up.

I didn't hesitate calling Vlad. "Hampstead Heath, six o'clock. Have you got the money?" I asked.

"Yeah, Marko's got it and we're on our way over to Sara's now. We'll meet you outside in five," he replied.

Relief washed over me, so glad I had Bratva friends who kept large amounts of cash at home, otherwise trying to come up with that amount of cash at such short notice would have been even more of a nightmare.

I grabbed Sara's head, pulling her in for a deep kiss. She

clung to me, a sob escaping her as she tried, unsuccessfully, to hold herself together.

"You stay here. Keep the phone on. I'll get them back."

She didn't argue. I could see the trust in her eyes, but also the fear. Fear for the girls. And fear for what I might have to do to get them back.

"Watch her for me," I told Lolita, who nodded, her face pale but determined. "I'll call as soon as they are safe."

"Be careful. Bring them home," she replied.

"I will," I promised. "I'll have Boris watch your building from outside, just to ensure the bastard doesn't come here and try to do anything even more stupid," I told her, and she nodded.

Lolita closed the door behind me as I stepped out, my mind already focused on the mission ahead. Every step I took brought me closer to those girls, and I wasn't going to stop until they were back in Sara's arms.

We pulled up at the entrance to Hampstead Heath in record time. The fucker had sent a text to Sara's phone with specific instructions for the handover, and she'd forwarded it to me. Vlad and Marko piled out of the car with me, boots echoing through the quiet park as we made our way towards the bandstand.

He'd picked a time when there were still a few stragglers around—some joggers, a couple of dog walkers—but not too many. A public place for the handover, but one where we wouldn't draw too much attention. Still, we had to tread carefully. Whatever happened, we couldn't afford to involve the police. Marko's sudden appearance with that much cash would raise questions, and Carruthers had hinted at knowing who we were. Who knew what he might tell the authorities if given the chance?

A feeling of dread gnawed at me. He'd asked for two hundred and fifty thousand pounds, even though he probably thought we could deliver more. What if this wasn't the end? After we handed over the money, would he really leave us alone, or would he keep coming for the girls—hell, for Sara—and try to extort more from us?

I couldn't stop thinking about the money he'd already been given him. It had probably gone straight into his gambling habit, his bad choices. The man had ruined his own life, but I wasn't going to let him drag us into the mess he'd made. And I sure as hell wouldn't let him remain a threat. But there was still one thing I couldn't ignore: he was the girls' father. A shit father, but their father, nonetheless. It wouldn't be right to kill him myself. Not unless he left me with no choice.

Once this was over and the girls were safe, I'd have the Bratva track him. At the first sign of trouble, I'd have someone else take him out.

I was already preparing for the inevitable when Carruthers met us outside, a smug look on his face as he held Lily by the arm, her eyes wide and terrified.

"Trigger, I want my mummy," she whimpered, struggling to get to me.

"It's okay, baby, I'm going to take you home to Mummy in a minute," I told her, offering a smile that I hoped seemed reassuring.

"Where's Emily?" I asked, my voice low, dangerously calm.

Carruthers grinned, and that's when I knew, this was not going to be a simple exchange.

"I've kept her," he said, his voice thick with self-satisfaction. "You gave me a hundred and fifty grand, but it wasn't enough to cover my debts. Big Al increased the interest after I took out another loan. So now I need more, and he won't just take the cash. He wants compensation, and Emily's the perfect solution. He can sell her on the dark web for far more than I owe him."

The rage inside me flared, but I kept it contained. Barely.

"You think you can just keep her?" I growled. "Sell her like some damn commodity?"

Carruthers laughed. "She's my daughter. My property. I can do what the fuck I want with her."

My lip curled in disgust. "Not anymore. You lost that right when you signed over custody to Sara for money," I snarled. "And she's a person, a beautiful, kind, loving little girl. Not a fucking possession!"

"Money? That pittance? I should have asked for more, much more. Hell, if I'd known who you were, I would have," he sneered.

Lily stared at her father in shock, tears streaming down her pretty little face. The knot of rage squeezed my chest, my fists clenching so hard the leather of my gloves creaked. The urge to lunge at him was barely held back, the need to keep her safe the only thing stopping me.

"You're only getting off so lightly this time because I don't have time to mess around. Big Al's chomping at the bit to be paid, and I need cash to get the hell out of here after I pay him off. I'll barely have enough to scrape by on what's left," he spat, his voice rising with desperation.

Lily began to cry in earnest.

I wanted to tear the man apart right there, but I held back. Emily's life mattered more than Carruthers' existence.

"We need to find her." My voice was an urgent whisper to the guys.

Vlad nodded, his eyes scanning the area. Marko stepped forward, a device in his hand, and motioned to it. I hid my smile. Two bright dots bleeped on the screen, one right on top of where we stood. Lily's and the other a short distance away. The trackers he'd put in the necklaces I'd given the girls for Christmas. I watched Marko's fingers move quickly over the buttons, and within seconds, he had the coordinates.

"She's not far," Marko whispered. I nodded.

"Okay, Carruthers, send Lily to me and I'll give you the bag," I told him.

"No chance, the big guy there," he gestured to Vlad, "can bring it over. once I have it I'm going to my car and taking Lily with me. When I'm at the entrance to the heath, I'll drop her off and you can pick her up from there."

Lily cried harder, and I knew I had no choice.

I nodded to Vlad, who walked over with the bag, every step deliberate.

"That's far enough," Carruthers said, "drop it and back away."

Vlad did as he was told. My hands twitched, and I wished I had my rifle to shoot the bastard between the eyes, but I couldn't—wouldn't—kill him, not in front of the girls. They'd both be traumatised by this enough.

Carruthers forced Lily to walk with him, but she started to struggle, and he cuffed her around the head. She cried out, and I lunged, but he yanked her in front of him, pressing a knife to her throat.

"After dealing with you guys last time, you didn't think I'd come prepared, did you?" he laughed.

Lily cried harder, and the bastard snapped, "Shut up, you annoying little bitch," as he grabbed the bag with his other hand, hoisted it up onto his shoulder and dragged Lily towards the car.

"Trigger," she cried, her little hands stretching towards me. My heart fucking broke. Right then, I vowed Carruthers wouldn't live to enjoy the money for even a second. Once the girls were free, I'd hunt him down and make him pay for every moment of fear, every tear he'd caused.

"You're doing so well, sweetheart. Just get in the car, and I promise this will all be over in a few minutes. I'll meet you at the entrance," I said gently, my voice steady, though the storm inside me was about to break. She sniffed and nodded.

As soon as they were in the car, Carruthers slammed the engine into gear and roared off.

We didn't waste any time, turning and jumping into the SUV. The hunt was on. I was getting both girls back no matter what I had to do. And Carruthers? He'd feel my revenge with his last breath, and then he could rot in hell for all I cared.

A minute later, we arrived at the entrance to Hampstead Heath, and there was Lily, crying by the side of the road.

I jumped out and pulled her to me. "It's alright, sweetheart. You're safe now," I murmured, my voice low as I held tight to her trembling form.

"What about Emily?" she asked, her voice thick with tears.

"We'll go get her now," I said, lifting her and putting her into the back of the SUV. Once her seatbelt was fastened, I kissed her on the top of the head, climbed in beside her, and held her hand.

"Let's go," I told Vlad.

"How are we going to find her?" Lily asked, her voice thick with worry.

Marko leaned towards her, "Uncle Marko put a little device in your necklaces," he said, pointing to the small dots on the screen. "This one is you, and this is Emily."

"Wow, are you a spy, Uncle Marko?" she asked, awe filling her voice.

"A spy? What makes you think that?" he asked, a smirk tugging at the corner of his lips.

"Well, in *Spy Kids*, the mummy and daddy have all sorts of spy gadgets like that," she explained.

"Oh, I see," he said, amusement lacing his voice.

"No, he's just a nerd," I told her.

She giggled, then leaned in with an exaggerated whisper. "It's okay, Uncle Marko. Nerds are sexy. That's what my mommy and Aunt Lolita say about Henry Cavill. And he's Superman."

"Your mum likes Henry Cavill?" I asked without missing a beat, feeling an uncharacteristic pang of jealousy.

There was a second of silence before Marko and Vlad burst out laughing.

"It's okay, Trigger. Mummy likes you more," she said with a grin, giggling again.

"How do you know?" I asked, genuinely curious.

"She said so. Aunt Lolita asked if she'd rather have Henry Cavill or you, and she said you. I heard her," she said, nodding and patting my hand. I grinned at her reassurance. She was a funny little thing.

"Emily's only a few feet away—in that building," Marko said, breaking the moment.

I glanced at the screen, then at the house. It was a small end-terrace, worn down but not quite derelict. The windows were old, the frames peeling, and the front garden overrun with weeds. A faded pink bicycle leaned against the wall, rust blooming on the handlebars.

"That place is owned by a woman named Janine Baxter," Marko added.

"Probably Carruthers' latest fling. She's a petty criminal—shoplifting, a few scams—nothing major, but she's no angel."

I nodded. "Stay with Lily. We'll handle this," I said, my voice low and firm.

Marko turned in his seat, flashing Lily a reassuring smile. "Don't worry, sweetheart. I'll keep an eye on you while Uncle Trigger and Uncle Vlad go get your sister back."

"Okay," she whispered, clutching the necklace around her neck like a talisman.

Vlad and I stepped out of the SUV, crossing the road with purpose. The front door was a dull green, chipped paint around the edges, and a brass knocker hanging loosely.

I knocked hard, my fist striking the wood. After a moment, the door creaked open, revealing a dishevelled woman in her mid-thirties. Janine Baxter had bleach-blonde hair pulled into a messy ponytail and wore a leopard-print dressing gown over leggings. Her eyes narrowed, suspicion written all over her face.

"Yeah? What do you want?" she snapped, her voice sharp.

I didn't answer. Instead, I shoved the door wide open, pushing my way inside with Vlad close behind. She stumbled back, cursing.

"Hey! You can't just—"

"Where's the girl?" I cut her off, my voice ice-cold.

"What girl? I don't know what you're talking about!" she protested, but her eyes flicked toward the stairs, betraying her.

Vlad moved past me, bounding up the stairs two at a time,

while I kept her pinned with a lethal glare. "Don't move," I warned, my tone leaving no room for argument.

From upstairs, I heard a door slam open, followed by a muffled cry. My chest tightened as Vlad called down, "I've got her!"

Moments later, he appeared at the top of the stairs, carrying Emily in his arms. Her face was tear-streaked, her small body trembling as she clung to him.

"It's okay, sweetheart. You're safe now," I said as Vlad reached the bottom of the stairs. Emily's wide eyes locked onto mine, and she sniffled, nodding, still clutching Vlad's jacket.

Janine tried to protest again, but I shot her a hard look. "If I ever find out you're involved in anything like this again, you'll regret it. Understand?"

Her mouth opened, then quickly snapped shut, and she nodded, fear flickering in her eyes.

Without another word, we left the house and hurried back to the SUV.

The moment the door opened, Lily launched herself at Emily, wrapping her arms around her sister. "Emily!"

"Lily!" Emily sobbed, clutching her sister desperately.

"Let's go," I said to Vlad, sliding into the front passenger seat.

Marko nodded, his usual cheeky grin replaced by a hard determination as he started the engine.

I glanced in the backseat, where the two girls clung to each other. For the first time in hours, I let myself exhale.

We weren't out of danger yet, but I had my girls back. Now it was time to find that bastard Carruthers and make sure he never hurt anyone again.

CHAPTER 25
SARA
LATER THAT NIGHT – REUNITED

The flat was unnervingly quiet, save for the soft tick of the clock on the bedside table, reminding me of how precious time was and at the same time how one single second could feel like a lifetime when someone you loved was in danger.

After hours of coaxing, I'd finally managed to settle the girls into the same bed. Emily clung to Lily like a lifeline, too terrified to let go, and I couldn't blame her. It had taken far longer than it should have, soothing her with quiet reassurances until their breathing evened out.

Now, standing in my pyjamas at the bedroom window, I watched the darkness beyond, my arms wrapped tightly around myself, trying to soothe the ache in my chest. The creak of the door caught my attention, and I turned. There he was—Trigger. His hair was a mess, as though he'd been running his hands through it in frustration. Shadows clouded his expression, and he looked utterly exhausted, but he gave me a small, lopsided smile as he stepped inside.

"They're asleep," I said softly.

He nodded, crossing the room in a few long strides to pull

me into his arms. I sank into him, burying my face in his chest. The rhythmic thrum of his heartbeat steadied my frayed nerves, finally calming the panic that had refused to release its grip since the moment I realised the girls were missing.

"They're safe now," he murmured, his hand trailing gently down my back. "It's over."

I pulled back just enough to look up at him. "What happened? How did you find them?"

Trigger sighed, guiding me to the edge of the bed where we sat. His fingers intertwined with mine, the touch of skin on skin grounding me further. He began to speak, his voice tight, as though each word cost him something.

"Carruthers handed over Lily in exchange for the money, but he kept hold of Emily. He planned to sell her to pay off a debt," he said, his voice strained with restrained anger.

A violent shudder ran down my spine at the thought of what Emily might have gone through if Trigger hadn't found her. My stomach churned, a wave of nausea rising in my throat as I pictured Emily, alone and scared, enduring something I couldn't even begin to imagine. My mind spun with a thousand terrible possibilities. How could anyone treat a child like that?

"How did you get her back?" I asked, my voice barely a whisper, as if speaking too loudly would shatter the fragile moment of safety we'd found.

"Remember the necklaces I gave them with the little trackers inside, like yours?" he asked, and I nodded. "Well, she was wearing it, thank God, and we tracked her to a house and got her out."

"What had he done to her?" I cried, fear lacing my voice, yet unable to stop myself from asking.

"Nothing. Just locked her inside. She was scared but unharmed," he said quickly, squeezing my hand.

Relief flooded through me, and I exhaled shakily. "I don't know how to thank you, Trigger. You saved her—both of them."

His lips quirked into a wry smile. "You don't have to thank me, Sara. They're my family too."

I felt the subtle brush of his rough stubble against my fingertips as I cupped his face and pressed a kiss to his lips. "Yes, they are. We are," I murmured into his mouth.

"What about Adam?" I asked after we broke apart.

Trigger shook his head, his features tightening with frustration. "He wasn't there, but Marko is looking for him. We'll get him and when we do, I swear to you I will make him pay. Do you understand what that means?" he asked me, and my stomach churned.

I nodded, the weight of his words sinking in.

"Good, because I can't let him continue to hurt you or our girls," he said.

Emotion welled up, and I leaned into him again, brushing my lips against his jaw. He turned his head, capturing my mouth with his. It was gentle at first, a reassurance, but it quickly deepened, a desperate need to feel alive after the horrors of the day.

Trigger's hands slid up my back, drawing me closer until I was straddling his lap. His lips trailed down my neck, leaving a line of fire in their wake. My fingers tangled in his hair, holding him to me.

"Trigger," I murmured, my voice trembling with more than just desire.

He pulled back just enough to look at me. "You okay?"

I nodded, cupping his face. "I just need you right now. All of you."

A low growl escaped him, and he turned, lowering me onto the bed. His touch was deliberate yet tender, his hands roaming over every inch.

Those stormy blue orbs didn't leave mine as he leaned over me. The soft light from the bedside lamp flickered across his face, highlighting his features in a way that made my heart squeeze. Lord, the man was beautiful.

His fingers trailed along my skin, slow and sure, as if learning every curve, every inch of me in the dim, intimate glow. I shivered at his touch, the tenderness of his caress sending a ripple of desire through me. There was no rush, no urgency—just the quiet desire to be close, to reassure each other that they were safe.

My hands reached for him, slipping under his shirt, feeling the taut muscles of his back, the warmth of his body against mine.

He lowered himself down beside me, his breath tickling my neck as he pressed a soft kiss there, his lips lingering for a moment longer than necessary. I melted into the sensation, the stress of the day slipping away with each brush of his lips, every light touch. His hand found mine, fingers intertwining, holding me as if he never wanted to let go.

When our lips finally met again, it was a gentle exploration—soft, sensual, and filled with the love neither of us had spoken out loud, yet In that second, I knew—the time to confess my feelings was now.

"I love you," I whispered into his lips.

He froze, a shudder wracking him. I stiffened at the reaction. Didn't he feel the same? A flicker of panic consumed me and I pulled away, wondering how I could have got things wrong.

Hugh pulled me back into his embrace. "God, Sara, you don't know how long I've been desperate to hear those words. I love you too, and the girls, so goddam much it hurts," he said, gulping hard, the vulnerability in him sending a rush of love and affection through me. I smiled, a small laugh escaping as I leaned in and kissed him deeply.

His hands moved lower, cupping my bum as he rubbed me against his erection. I let out a low hum of approval at the sensations that tore through me with the feel of his hardness.

My fingers slid into his hair and I tugged him off my mouth, "Get your clothes off, lover boy, it's time I showed you just how much I love your sexy ass!" I said, my voice filled with lustful promise. "I need to taste you."

He grinned and tugged off his T-shirt as I shifted to undo his jeans. Lifting his hips, he pushed them down, along with his boxers, eager to bare himself to me. I giggled before lowering myself and taking him into my mouth. His taste made me moan, as it always did. No matter how often I did this—and it had certainly become one of my favourite indulgences recently—I couldn't get over how incredible he tasted.

Other men had been far too salty, their flavour something I endured as a necessary evil of the act. But with Hugh, it was entirely different—a perfect mix of salty and sweet, like the best kind of popcorn, making the experience unexpectedly enjoyable. I licked the head, taking him deeper before slowly dragging my mouth back up his length.

Trigger shuddered, his hands tangling in my hair as he held me to him. My tongue swirled around the head before sliding lower, tracing down to the base of his shaft. I shifted, letting my lips graze his sack before taking it gently into my mouth.

"Fuck," Trigger groaned, the sound low and guttural, his jaw tightening as he fought to keep his voice down.

I chuckled softly, delighting in the raw response I could

pull from him. My hand joined the motion, working in perfect sync with my mouth, tongue, and throat, pushing him closer to the edge.

"Darling, if you don't stop, I'm going to come down that pretty throat of yours," he rasped, his voice strained with need.

I pulled back slightly, licking my lips as I looked up at him. "That's exactly what I want, babe," I said with a wicked grin.

Although I'd done this countless times, he'd never let himself release in my mouth, always preferring to finish buried deep inside me. But this time, I wanted to give him something different, something just for him—and for us.

"Please, Hugh," I murmured, my words barely audible with my mouth so full of him.

"God, Sara, love," he gasped, his breath coming fast and ragged. "I can't deny you anything."

That was all the encouragement I needed. I ramped up the pace, my mouth and hands working together to push him over the edge. His muffled roar sent a gush of wet heat pooling between my thighs. The sound alone was enough to send waves of desire crashing through me.

My pussy clenched desperately, the emptiness inside making me squirm with need. But it had been worth it. The salty-sweet taste of him spilling into my throat was more than worth it.

When he was spent, I licked him clean, savouring every moment before he pulled me back into his arms. Straddling him again, I pressed my body against his, our mouths colliding in a deep, unhurried kiss. My sensitive nipples brushed against his chest, the friction sparking twin moans from us both. His cock twitched against me, already stirring back to life.

I smirked, knowing the night was far from over.

Trigger's hands slipped beneath my top, cupping my breasts and squeezing them gently before pulling the fabric over my head. He tossed it aside, letting it join the pile of discarded clothes on the floor. His head dipped, and he caught a hardened peak between his lips, suckling with an intensity that made me gasp.

My core clenched again, a ripple of pleasure coursing through me as I shifted, dragging my wet heat over his groin. His cock jerked beneath me, responding to my touch as if it had a will of its own.

I clutched him tighter, arching into his mouth as I ground against him. "Your tits are gorgeous, darling," he murmured, his deep voice vibrating against my already sensitive nipple. The sensation sent a shudder of delight straight to my core, making me moan in response.

"That feels so good, babe," I murmured, my voice trembling as his lips moved to my other breast. He squeezed them together, alternating between licking one taut peak and the other, each flick of his tongue sending jolts of pleasure straight to my core.

I couldn't take much more. The pressure inside me was building rapidly—I was on the verge of coming just from his attention there. But I needed more.

"Hugh, I need you," I whispered, my voice breaking as I spoke. "Deep inside me. Now."

He flipped me onto my back, his hands firm as he climbed over me. Lowering himself between my legs, his tongue darted out, trailing a slow, deliberate path through my folds. I cried out, my hips instinctively bucking up toward him, desperate for more. He moaned, the sound vibrating through me, and I bit my lip, shivering at the intensity of the sensations that coursed through my body. He continued, licking and kissing me with an aching sweetness, then twirling my clit between his fingers as his tongue pushed deeper inside me.

The pressure was building with each stroke, each flick of his tongue, until I was lost in the sensation. I couldn't stand it any longer. "Inside me, please, babe," I begged, my voice trembling.

He wasted no time, his mouth claiming mine as he slid inside me, filling me completely.

"God! Yes!" The cry tore from my throat, muffled by his kiss. His movements drove me wild, and though the house was quiet, we both knew we had to be careful. Two little girls under this roof meant we couldn't always let go as we wanted. But I promised myself that soon, we would steal away—just the two of us—for a break. No more whispers, no more restraint, just us, letting go completely.

Afterward, we lay tangled in the sheets, his arm draped protectively over my waist. His breathing slowed, deepening as he drifted into sleep. I listened to the rhythm of his heartbeat—solid, comforting—and knew, without a doubt, that it belonged to me. To me and my girls. Love filled me, wrapping me in warmth and safety, even as my thoughts turned to the man who could still destroy that peace: Adam.

Just thinking his name sent a wave of revulsion through me. Once, I'd never have wished him dead—not even after all he'd done to me. The bruises, the lies, the suffocating fear that had consumed me for years. I'd convinced myself that walking away was enough, that he wasn't worth the stain of hatred in my heart.

But now? After tonight?

My stomach twisted with a fury I hadn't known I was capable of. He hadn't just hurt me—he'd hurt my girls. He'd taken them, used them as pawns to save his own miserable skin. And what he'd planned for Emily... My hands clenched into fists at the thought. If Trigger hadn't found her in time...

A shudder rippled through me, but I forced myself to take a slow breath. The man I'd once feared so deeply no longer deserved the space he'd occupied in my mind. Adam had crossed a line, and for that, I wouldn't just wish him dead. If I had the chance, I'd do it myself.

The realisation hit like a freight train—no fear, only grim clarity. I would do anything to protect my daughters. No one would ever hurt them again—not Adam, not anyone. And if that meant becoming the kind of person who could take a life to keep them safe, or sit by as someone else did, then so be it.

But at least for now the girls were safe. I was safe. Trigger was here. And I knew, no matter what, I could count on him to keep us that way.

I closed my eyes, letting sleep finally claim me.

CHAPTER 26
TRIGGER
THE NEXT DAY – RETURNING TO NORMAL

The sound of the girls' laughter pulled me from a restless haze as I sat by the window, nursing my second cup of coffee. Sara was in the kitchen, making sandwiches for lunch, while Emily and Lily were playing a board game at the table. It was a simple, ordinary scene, in stark contrast to the events of the day before.

The girls seemed fine this morning, but I knew from personal experience how deeply trauma could affect someone—and how lasting the impact could be. Determination filled me. I wasn't going to let either of these girls suffer the way I had. Not if there was anything I could do about it.

I stood, stretching the tension from my shoulders. Slipping into the living room, I pulled out my phone and dialled my therapist's number.

"Hi, Doctor Webber, it's Trigger," I said when she answered.

"What can I do for you? Are you okay?" she asked, concern clear in her voice.

"I'm fine, and I'll see you for our usual session on Friday. But I was hoping you could send me details of someone who specialises in child psychology. A friend of mine's children might need their services," I explained.

"Certainly, I'll text you the details," she replied.

"Great, I'll see you Friday," I said before hanging up.

Feeling satisfied that I'd taken care of one part of my plan, I turned my attention to the next. We needed to get the girls back into normal life as soon as possible. I knew Sara might want to shield them, but that wouldn't be good for any of us in the long run.

"Right, troops," I called out, my voice light as I ruffled Emily's hair on my way to the counter. "Get your shoes on. We're going out for a bit."

"Where to?" Emily chirped, already halfway to the door.

"It's a surprise," I replied with a grin.

Sara glanced up at me, her brows knitting with concern. I moved closer, lowering my voice. "Their favourite park, for a picnic. It'll be good for them to get some fresh air. Somewhere familiar. Take their minds off yesterday and bring back some normality."

She opened her mouth as if to protest, but I pulled her close, my voice quiet and for her ears only. "They need this. You need this."

After a beat, she exhaled softly and nodded. "You're right. I guess I'll pack the lunch then."

The park was quiet, a hidden pocket of greenery surrounded by rows of neat houses. The girls sprinted ahead, their shoes slapping against the paved path as they chased each other toward the swings. Sara and I followed behind at a slower pace.

"Do you think Adam or this Big Al will try to snatch

Emily? I mean, if Adam still needs to pay the loan shark off, he might be desperate enough to try. And if not, this Big Al might want the compensation he thinks he's due," she asked, her voice low and filled with worry,

"It's possible," I said, scanning the tree line. "But I've got Marko keeping tabs on Big Al, I'm with you and Vlad's a call away. We won't let anything happen to either of the girls. That includes you, darling," I told her, tugging her into me.

She didn't look entirely convinced, but she didn't argue either. Instead, she brushed her fingers lightly down my cheek—a small gesture, but it spoke volumes.

We stopped near a picnic bench, and I leaned against it, watching the girls climb onto the swings. Emily waved wildly. "Trigger! Look at me!"

"I'm watching!" I called back, running over to give her a push.

Sara did the same with Emily. "Mum, I don't need a push, I'm a big girl now," Emily said with a giggle as Sara cried, "Okay then, I'm on this one," before jumping on to the swing beside them.

"Trigger, go give Mummy a push, I can go high all by myself. Mummy needs help. She's too old," Lily said, laughing at Sara.

Sara gasped in mock horror as a laugh escaped me, too. "I can manage myself young lady, and I am not too old. I can swing way higher than you. Cheeky madam!" she said her voice laced with a mix of shock and amusement.

"Well, Trigger can push you now, anyway. Aunt Lolita said it's romantic for a daddy to push a mummy," she said, the innocence in her tone suggesting she'd no idea what she'd just inferred. But Sara had got the connotation, her legs faltered, and the swing slowed. I stopped dead and blinked as a wave of emotions engulfed me. Releasing the breath I hadn't even realised I was holding, I looked at her, then Sara, a slow smile spreading across my face. Sara grinned. It had always amazed me how easily Lily had accepted me as part of their lives, but it was obvious that she now saw him me as a father figure.

I turned to look at Emily. She was watching me intently, but looked away when she noticed me staring. Sara's eldest was still a little cautious around men and I didn't blame her, but lately I was sure she was getting past that. Sighing heavily, I slowed the swing to let Lily clamber off. Yesterday had definitely set her back.

Emily slowed and jumped off her own swing before walking towards me. "Race you to the top of the climbing frame," she said, her voice tinged with challenge.

A grin split my face. "Last one there has to do the dinner dishes," I cried, setting off at a run. But Emily was already halfway there. She laughed loudly as she made it just seconds before me. "Ha, you're doing the dishes!" she said, climbing up the frame like a spider monkey.

I laughed loudly as I followed her up. When we got to the top, I held up my hand, wondering if she would leave me hanging. She smirked and then high fived me before climbing back down again. I followed her again, this time at a more leisurely pace, as I relished the memory of that moment. After what Lily had implied, it felt significant. Like Emily's own way of acceptance and it made my heart swell.

Spying a nearby picnic table that looked clean, I grabbed the bag with the food from where I'd left it next to the swings and walked over to it.

As I was laying out the food, Sara sank onto the bench beside me, her gaze flicking between me and the girls. "You're good with them," she said softly.

"They're great girls, and I enjoy spending time with

them," I replied, my eyes fixed on the girls. Emily was pushing Lily on the merry-go-round as Lily shouted, "Faster, faster!" giggling when Emily complied. The sunlight glinted off their blonde hair, creating a halo-like effect and giving the pair an ethereal beauty that matched their sunny dispositions.

The sight of them laughing and having fun together was heartwarming. Maybe the thing with Adam hadn't had such a worrying effect after all.

"After yesterday, it's good to see them so happy," Sara said quietly, her voice tinged with both relief and concern.

"They deserve to be happy. And safe," I replied.

She smiled, but it didn't quite reach her eyes. "I don't think any of us really will be safe or happy, not with Adam or this Big Al person continuing to be a threat." She sighed heavily. "But at least we're all okay—for now."

"I'll make sure somehow that things remain that way," I promised, my voice firm.

She didn't respond, just leaned into me and kissed my cheek. Maybe she wasn't fully ready to hope just yet, but she was willing to take that step with me.

CHAPTER 27
SARA
TWO WEEKS LATER – IT'S NOT OVER YET

I could see the concern in Trigger's eyes, even though he tried to mask it with that familiar stoic expression. The way his brows furrowed as he glanced between me and the door told me everything I needed to know—he wanted to stay. But I wasn't about to let him.

Ever since Adam had taken the girls, Trigger had barely left our side. When he wasn't working, he was with us, and when he couldn't be, Boris or one of the others kept watch. But things needed to move forward. He had a job to do, and the Bratva had been tied up with an MP who had caused them trouble for years. They needed him more than I did right now.

"It's fine, babe. Boris will be here soon. Go do your thing, and we'll see you later," I said, nudging him towards the door. Trigger paused, but I added quickly, "Look, Adam's long gone. You said Marko tracked his car to the airport weeks ago, and Adam booked a flight to Las Vegas. Right?"

He nodded.

"The stupid man will be living it up in Vegas, trying his luck with whatever he has left after paying off Big Al.

Hopefully he'll stay there and we'll never have to deal with him again."

"I know but—" he went to speak, but I stopped him with a finger to his lips.

"He's a gambler, babe. It makes sense. And since we've not heard anything from the loan shark, it looks like he's decided to cut his losses. He probably wanted nothing to do with Adam's stupid plan, anyway. We'll be fine." I wasn't sure I fully believe what I was saying, but we couldn't live in limbo like this, watching over our shoulders all the time, forever.

His gaze softened, but there was still a flicker of reluctance. "I'll just wait for Boris. He said the traffic's heavy coming into London, but he won't be long."

"No," I insisted, walking over to the workbench where I had a project waiting. "Go. You've got your own things to handle. I'm fine. Besides," I added, glancing at the bench where we'd spent far too many moments of passion recently, "you're distracting."

He smirked sexily before sighing. "Fine," he said, making it clear he was only doing so under great duress.

He dropped a kiss on the top of my head, before heading to the door. "Bye, girls. See you later," he shouted to them.

"Bye, Trigger!" they chorused from the office, their voices light and carefree.

The bell above the door jingled as he gave me one last look before slipping out of the shop. I locked it behind him, securing it with a firm click. The sound was reassuring.

I really did have work to do. The shop had a steady stream of customers now—far too many for me to continue to handle alone. My lips curled into a grin, a feeling of pride blooming deep in my chest. Everything was falling into place.

The shop was thriving in a way I'd only imagined when I first took the leap.

The pile of applications on the counter me made me pause, my fingers grazing over them. I needed to hire more help—someone fresh out of training for the alterations and a more seasoned hand for assisting with my designs. I picked up the stack of C.V.'s, my grin widening as I thought about how far things had come. The designs I'd created were finally being noticed, and custom orders were rolling in from people I never thought would consider me. It was humbling, overwhelming at times, but all worth it.

Heading to the office, I placed the applications on my desk, the girls still in the background, laughing over their game. It was an in-service day for the teachers, which meant not school for the girls. So, they were here, playing a board game on my desk. Lola had taken Cammy to the dentist and then had some errands to run, so for now, it was just the three of us—until Boris showed up.

"You girls be good now. I'll be out in the shop working if you need me," I told them.

They nodded too engrossed in the game of Monopoly to take much notice of me.

I made myself a coffee then sat down at my workbench. I could hear the girls in the background, their laughter and squabbles over a board game filling the space. The normality of it made me laugh as I started on my first task, sewing a hem on a dress that was almost finished. The rhythmic hum of the sewing machine was soothing until I heard the soft creak of the back door. A sense of dread washed over me, I didn't need to look up to know who it was.

"Sara." His voice, rough and frantic, sliced through the air.

I froze, my hands gripping the edge of the sewing table.

Slowly, I turned my head. He stood in the doorway, wild-eyed and dishevelled, his clothes torn and streaked with dirt and bruises. He didn't look like the man I used to know—he looked like a stranger.

"You need to leave," I said, forcing my voice to stay steady even as fear coiled tight in my chest.

"Where are they?" His eyes darted to the office door. "Where are my daughters?"

"They're not your daughters," I snapped, shaking my head. "They never were."

He took a step forward, his breath ragged. "I'm their father. You might have divorced me, you little slut, and that fucking arsehole you're shagging might have made me sign over custody, but it doesn't change the truth. Nothing will." His lips twisted into something that might have been a grin if it weren't so cold. "I want them back, Sara. Both of them."

My stomach turned. "Adam, you don't get to do this. Not after everything you've done."

He ignored me, a manic gleam lighting up his face as Lily's laugh drifted from the office. He started toward the door.

Panic shot through me. "Don't you dare," I warned, stepping into his path. "If you think for one second—"

"Shut up!" His voice cracked like a whip.

Before I could react, his hand was on the office door. He shoved it open, and the girls' startled voices filled the air. My heart slammed against my ribs as I lunged forward.

Emily and Lily stood frozen, their board game forgotten. "Daddy?" Emily whispered, her voice barely audible.

Adam's gaze locked on her, his expression shifting into something darker. "Come here, sweetheart," he coaxed, his voice almost soft. "We're leaving. It's the only way out of this mess."

He reached for her, his hand trembling.

"No!" I screamed, grabbing his arm. "You're not taking them! Not now, not ever!"

His eyes snapped to mine, his face twisted with rage. Without warning, he slapped me across the face. The force sent me stumbling back, pain exploding along my cheek as I tasted blood.

"Better," he muttered, wiping his hand on his trousers.

I barely had time to recover before he grabbed my arm, yanking me toward the back of the shop. My knees buckled, and I hit the floor with a hard thud. His boot caught my side, driving the air from my lungs.

"Get up," he growled, dragging me upright.

I struggled, but his grip was iron. He shoved me into the office and slammed me into a chair, the impact stealing my breath.

"You're going to sit there," he hissed, pulling a length of rope from his jacket. My arms ached as he tied my wrists, the coarse fibres biting into my skin. "Lily! Emily! Be good girls and come to daddy now," he said his tone frantic.

They huddled together, peering at him in fear, but didn't come closer.

"Come to daddy or you'll be punished!" he shouted angrily. The girls flinched at his tone.

"Adam, please," I cried, my voice cracking. "You don't have to do this. Don't hurt them. Please."

He ignored me, his focus shifting to the girls. They huddled in the corner, their wide eyes glistening with fear.

"You're coming with me. You need to pay off my debts," he said, his voice breaking as he looked at them.

Tears streamed down Emily's cheeks as he stepped closer, his trembling hand reaching for her.

Oh god. Why did I send Trigger away? I was a bloody

fool and now the girls would pay for my stupidity. If anything happened to them, I would never forgive myself. I pulled against the ropes, desperation surging through me. "Adam, stop!"

But he didn't hear me. His world had narrowed to the terrified little girls in the corner. As I struggled helplessly in the chair, I prayed that someone would come—before it was too late.

CHAPTER 28
TRIGGER
THE SAME DAY - ENDING THE THREAT

As the door clicked shut behind me, sealing Sara and the girls inside the shop, I forced myself to turn and walk towards my bike parked further up the street. Every fibre of my being screamed at me to stay. But Sara was right—we had to live without the shadow of Carruthers looming over us.

Even so, until I knew exactly where the bastard was and what he was planning, I wouldn't be able to relax. Not that I ever really did. Years in the army, the streets, and the Bratva had made sure of that. My PTSD might be a hell of a lot better these days, even after everything with Carruthers and the girls, but letting my guard down completely? That wasn't in my nature.

Sara and the girls grounded me in a way I'd never experienced before. Their presence was my anchor, calming the storm inside me like nothing else ever had. The thought of losing them, of failing to protect them, sent ice through my veins. If anything happened to them, it wouldn't just break me—it would destroy me.

I swung my leg over the bike and gripped the handlebars.

Kicking the engine to life, I felt the vibrations rumble through me. The sound was a familiar balm, but even as I revved the throttle, a nagging unease gnawed at my gut. Forcing the feeling aside, I turned towards the motorway, intent on the meeting with the Irish Mafia. Miki had said they had a job they wanted help with and thought I should assess whether it was something I could handle.

I tried to focus on the task, but the unease wouldn't shift. With every mile I rode, the feeling only tightened its grip. Sara and the girls being alone—unprotected—left a knot in my chest that refused to loosen. What if Adam wasn't in Vegas like we thought? What if he was just waiting for the right moment?

My knuckles whitened on the handlebars. This wasn't like me, letting my imagination run wild. But I couldn't shake the sense that something wasn't right.

Cursing under my breath, I gave in. Swerving into the next lay-by, I swung the bike around and headed back the way I'd come.

When I parked outside the shop, I pulled out my phone. A missed call from Boris flashed on the screen. Tension coiled in my chest. Without hesitation, I hit redial.

"Trigger, thank fuck. Where are you? I just arrived at the shop—Adam's inside with Sara and the girls," Boris said, his voice taut with urgency. "He looks completely unhinged. The front door's locked, but we need to get in there. Now."

A cold spike shot through me as the words hit. The urgency in Boris's voice matched the pounding in my head. My legs were already moving. Every second wasted was a second too long.

"I'm a block away. I'll be there in a minute," I replied, my voice steady despite the storm brewing inside me.

As I reached the shop, Boris hurried to meet me, his expression grim.

"He was already here when I arrived," he said quickly. "I was about to knock when I saw him dragging Sara into the office. The girls are in there too. The front door's locked. I was going to break in, but he's got a knife. I didn't want to risk them getting hurt."

"Does he know you're here?" I asked, keeping my voice low and measured.

"No, I've stayed out of sight," he replied.

"Good. That gives us an edge."

We crept towards the shop's front window. Inside, I caught a glimpse of Carruthers standing at the office doorway, his back to us. Fury flared in my chest, but I clamped down on it. I couldn't afford to lose my focus now.

"We'll go in through the back," I said. "That's probably how he got in. Once we're inside, we play it by ear, but no matter what, make sure Sara and the girls are safe."

Boris gave a sharp nod, his jaw tightening.

We moved quickly, circling to the back of the shop. The lock on the door was broken, the frame splintered and left ajar. Slipping inside without a sound, we stepped into the dimly lit storeroom, every nerve on edge.

Voices carried from the front. Carruthers' frantic, angry tone rose above the rest. I didn't care what he was ranting about; my only thought was getting Sara and the girls out of there.

Boris stayed close as I led the way through the cramped storage area. Reaching the narrow hallway, I could see into the main space. Carruthers' voice was clearer now, sharp and erratic.

"Come to daddy or you'll be punished!" he shouted.

"Adam, please," Sara cried, her voice cracking. "You don't have to do this. Don't hurt them. Please."

The sight of her stopped me cold. She was bound to a chair, her wrists red where the ropes dug into her skin as she fought against their hold. Despite her pleading tone, defiance burned in her eyes. Emily and Lily were huddled close, trembling as they stared at their father, whose face twisted with desperation and fury.

Sara tugged at her restraints, her voice breaking. "Adam, stop!"

The sound sent a sharp ache through me. I moved quietly, each step calculated as I tried to get into position. But then Lily spotted me. Her gasp broke the fragile balance.

Carruthers spun, grabbing Lily by the arm, his grip rough enough to draw a frightened cry from her.

"Get away from her," I growled, my voice low and laced with menace. I stepped closer, every muscle in my body coiled and ready.

"Stay back!" he snarled, jerking Lily in front of him like a human shield. The gleaming blade of his knife pressed against her neck, the sight snapping me back to the last time this bastard had her in his grip.

I froze, forcing calm into my tone. "Adam, listen to me. If you hurt her—if you hurt any of them—I swear I'll make sure you don't leave this room alive. Put the knife down and walk away while you still have a chance."

Sara twisted against the ropes, her face tight with determination as she fought to free herself. Out of the corner of my eye, I caught a glimpse of Emily edging closer to her mother, scissors clutched tightly in her small hand. Our eyes met, and I gave her a slight nod. She understood.

Adam's voice cut through the tension like a blade. "I'm

not leaving! Not until I get what's mine. I want both girls this time."

My hands curled into fists. "That's not going to happen," I said, my voice a lethal calm. "Put the knife down now, or you'll face the consequences." I shifted slightly, drawing his attention to me and away from Sara and Emily.

His eyes tracked my movements, the knife moving a little lower and in that split second, Lily acted. She sank her teeth into his hand, hard enough to make him roar in pain and shove her to the ground.

Sara, freed by Emily, threw herself over Lily, shielding her with her body.

Carruthers still had the knife. In a heartbeat, he lunged at Sara, his rage wild and unrestrained. My stomach dropped as the blade moved toward her, but Emily acted faster. She darted forward, driving the scissors into his side with a ferocity that startled even him.

Howling in pain, Carruthers spun toward Emily, his face contorted with fury. I moved to intercept him as he went to grab her, but he lashed out. The knife glanced off my arm, leaving a burning sting in its wake. I ignored it, staying focused. I wasn't letting this bastard hurt anyone else. I braced to attack when a voice from behind stopped me cold.

"Not so fast," someone said, calm and menacing. I turned to see a man pressing a gun to Boris's temple.

Fuck.

Big Al, the loan shark, walked into the workshop, followed by another of his enforcers. The sneers on their faces made my blood boil.

"Did you think I wouldn't come for my compensation?" Big Al drawled, his tone laced with mockery. "Thought it was all over just because you paid that stupid fuck Adam Carruthers a bit of cash?" He chuckled darkly. "It doesn't work that way, son. That fuck owes me a fortune, with interest. And that quarter of a mill he tried to skip town with? Barely scratched the surface. So, you see, that little girl,"—he pointed lazily toward Emily—"she's mine. Payment in kind."

Like hell!

"You don't get to buy and sell kids, you disgusting fuck!" I snarled, every muscle in my body tensing as I prepared to lunge at the Cockney bastard and tear that smug grin off his face.

The man holding the gun to Boris tutted, the barrel pressed harder against his skull.

"You really don't want to do that," the thug said, his smirk dripping with malice. "Unless you're into redecorating with your mate's brains on the walls."

"Personally, I think it'd give the place a little something extra, but I'm no designer. Not like that pretty lady in there," Big Al said, nodding toward Sara, who was clutching her daughters, her eyes wide with fear.

"Now, let's get this over with. Hand the girl over, and we'll be on our way. You can all go back to whatever miserable lives you were living before."

"Over my dead body!" My fists clenched and fury boiled inside me. I was going to fucking end him.

Big Al smirked while the thug beside him let out a low laugh.

"That can be arranged," the man with the gun muttered.

"Hand her over now, before the price goes up and I start asking for the woman… maybe even the other little one, too."

Before I could retort, Boris muttered something in Russian, a string of words we couldn't understand. But the intent was clear.

Big Al turned his gaze to him. "Russian?" he sneered,

then shouted toward the back. "Adam, get your fucking arse out here now."

Carruthers came out of the office, looking like a trembling mess. I shifted, positioning myself in front of the door, with the girls and Sara still behind me in the office.

"Adam, what the fuck is this? A Russian? You'd better not have dragged me into something with the fucking Bratva, or I'll bloody kill you," Big Al snarled.

"I… well, I… No, of course not!" Carruthers stuttered, stumbling over his words.

"I am Bratva, we both are," Boris said, a grin spreading over his face. "And now you've made enemies of us."

The men exchanged uneasy glances.

Big Al was furious. "You stupid fuck!" he yelled at Carruthers.

"I didn't know, Big Al. All I knew was this guy," he gestured to me, "has got Russian friends, businessmen with money. That's how I knew he was good for the quarter of a mill even after he paid the one fifty. But I had no idea they were Bratva, I swear," Adam said, shaking his head as he took a step back.

"That's not true. You knew exactly who you were dealing with," I said, rounding on Carruthers.

Big Al gestured to the guy with the gun, and without hesitation, the thug turned and pulled the trigger, shooting Carruthers in the head.

I flinched, not at the situation, but at the gasps from inside the room. I was glad my body still blocked their view, but I knew the sound would have terrified them.

Before Carruthers' body even hit the floor, Boris lunged at the shooter, tackling him to the ground. I saw my chance and flew at Big Al's other enforcer.

Launching myself at him, I tackled him to the floor as all

the fury I'd been holding at bay came flooding out. I grabbed his head, slamming it hard against the floor, again and again, bashing his brains in.

As I stood, the sounds of Boris still grappling with the other man barely registered, drowned out by the pounding in my head. The scent of blood was thick in the air, hot and metallic, but I couldn't afford to be distracted. I snapped my attention to Big Al, my heart thundering as adrenaline surged, the need to end this fight consuming me.

His eyes blazed with fury as he looked at the dead man. "Come on then you fucker," he sneered as he reached for another weapon. I didn't give him the chance. Drawing my knife, I flicked it open and drove it into his chest in one swift movement. His eyes widened as he staggered back. I smirked, following him, pulling the knife out and driving it into his heart. He fell to the ground, clutching the wound. He started to say something, but no words came. Instead, with a final, choking breath, he went limp as the life drained from him. I twisted the blade and pulled it free.

Boris stood, the fucker who'd held a gun to his head now lying dead beside the others.

Breathing heavily, I scanned the room for something to clean up with. I needed to see Sara and the girls—but not covered in blood. I grabbed some scraps of fabric from a nearby box and wiped down the weapon, then my hands. Tossing another scrap to Boris, I turned toward the doorway.

Sara stood there, the girls cowering behind her.

"It's over," I said, my voice low as I approached, my heart heavy with everything that had just happened.

Emily took a tentative step forward, and I held my breath. They'd all seen what I'd done. Would they hate me now? The thought of losing them made my chest ache, but I'd do it all again—sacrifice everything if it meant keeping them safe.

She met my gaze, her expression raw but softening. Something shifted in her eyes—a mix of vulnerability and trust.

"I love you," she whispered, so quietly I almost didn't hear it.

My chest tightened, a lump forming in my throat. I swallowed it down and met her gaze, feeling Sara's watchful eyes on us as I whispered back, "I love you too, sweetheart."

She grinned, jumping into my arms. I hugged her tight, and Lily clamped her little arms around my waist. I dropped a hand to her head, pulling her into the embrace as well.

"I love you too, Trigger," she said, voice trembling with a sniff.

Sara wrapped her arms around us, and I could feel the tears of relief and joy welling up in her eyes as they spilled over. We were all together. Safe.

EPILOGUE

TRIGGER

SEVERAL MONTHS LATER

After cleaning up from the fight with Big Al and his men, Boris had contacted Miki, who'd sent over the Bratva cleanup crew. I stayed in the office with Sara and the girls until the bodies had been removed and the place cleaned up before finally heading home.

Miki arranged for Adam Carruthers' death to be reported as an accident—a car crash. The girls would get the insurance money, placed into a trust for their future.

Things had been difficult for them in the weeks following their father's death. It was only natural they'd be affected by everything that had happened, but I'd arranged for appointments with the child psychologist. Both girls had shown vast improvement since then.

So, for now, the nightmares were over. The healing could finally begin. And I would be there with them for every step of it.

Strangely, I hadn't had an attack of my own. It was as if I'd finally accepted that Vlad had been right. I had survived for a reason and that reason I now believed was Sara and the girls.

"Hurry, they're coming!" Emily called, her excited voice pulling me from my thoughts.

Smiling, I moved over to her side, and we hid behind the lion's enclosure just as planned. Lily was bouncing on her toes, her lips pressed tightly together in an attempt to contain the squeals of excitement threatening to spill out. I chuckled, even as nerves twisted in my gut.

Lola and Cammy were bringing Sara here under the pretext of a casual afternoon at the zoo. She had no idea what I had planned.

I took a deep breath, trying to calm my racing heart. This moment felt like it had been a long time coming. More than just a proposal, it was a symbol of everything we had fought for—everything I had been lucky enough to find in them, in Sara.

The distant sound of footsteps reached us, and my pulse kicked up a notch as I adjusted the ring box in my pocket. Emily and Lily grinned at me, excitement written across their faces. This was it. The moment I would ask Sara to marry me.

As Sara appeared with Lola and Cammy, a smile tugged at my lips. She looked at me with that familiar warmth in her eyes, the same warmth that had drawn me in from the start. Her hair fluttered in the breeze, the setting sun casting a golden glow over her. She looked perfect.

"Hey, love," I said, my voice steady despite the rush of emotions coursing through me. "Got a surprise for you."

Sara tilted her head, her eyes narrowing with curiosity. The girls stood behind me, whispering to each other.

I stepped forward, taking her hands in mine. "I don't have the right words to tell you how much you mean to me, but every day that I've spent with you and the girls, it's been like a dream come true. I never thought I'd get this lucky, but here I am, standing in front of the woman I want to spend the rest of my life with."

I dropped to one knee, pulling the small velvet box from my pocket. The ring inside glinted in the light, a perfect symbol of everything we'd been through together.

Sara's breath caught, her hands trembling slightly in mine. The girls watched with wide eyes, their faces lighting up with joy.

"Sara," I continued, my heart pounding. "Will you marry me?"

There was a long pause, and it felt like the whole world was holding its breath. Finally, Sara's eyes softened, and a tear slipped down her cheek as she nodded. "Yes, Hugh. Yes!"

She jumped to her feet and into my arms. Lily let out a squeal, rushing forward to hug both of us at once, and Emily joined in. Lola and Cammy beamed at us, and even Tom, the lion keeper who had been standing off to the side, gave me a thumbs-up.

I slid the ring onto Sara's finger, and we shared a kiss—gentle and full of promise.

The zoo, our place, had seen so many firsts for us. And today, it was witnessing our future. It was the start of something beautiful. Together. Always.

SARA

I glanced at the ring on my finger. It sparkled in the afternoon light, the three diamonds catching the sun just perfectly.

"It's beautiful, Hugh," I said, my voice trembling slightly

with emotion as the girls oohed and aahed over it, their faces lighting up with excitement.

"There are three diamonds," he said, his voice thick with pride, "one to represent each of my girls."

I smiled, my heart swelling. "Oh, Hugh, I had no idea you were quite so romantic. That's lovely." I leaned in, brushing my lips against his, a soft kiss that carried all the love I felt for him.

"And you girls knew all about this and didn't tell me?" I said, feigning mock offense, my eyes sparkling with playful accusation.

They giggled in response, their joy infectious.

"Oh, Mummy, it was soooo hard to keep it a secret, but I did it," Lily said, her eyes shining with pride. She bounced on her toes, the excitement in her voice so pure, so genuine, that it tugged at my heart.

"You did so well. I'm very proud of you. Both of you," Trigger said, his voice warm with affection. He pulled them into an embrace, squeezing them tight. He ruffled Lily's hair, the tenderness of the moment almost overwhelming.

My smile couldn't get any wider, this moment, this proposal, had made this the best day of my life. For a long time, I'd never dared to imagine a future like this. A future with him, with the girls. And now, with the ring on my finger, everything felt like it was falling into place.

I didn't think it could get any better, but then I should have known. Where Trigger was involved, not only could it get better—it would always defy all my expectations.

"Now that we have the first important part of my plan out of the way," he said, drawing in a breath, "I have another thing, just as important, to do."

I looked at him, confused but intrigued. My heart skipped a beat as he turned to face the girls and me.

He dropped to one knee in front of us, and I felt a shiver of surprise run through me as he pulled another two boxes out of his pocket. He opened them to reveal two little rings, gold with a small diamond of their own.

"Sara," he started, his voice steady, "I've been thinking about this for a while now. You've already given me more than I ever expected. You, the girls… you've made me the happiest man alive. And now, I want to make you all my family."

I blinked, trying to process his words, but he wasn't finished. He turned his head towards the girls and spoke directly to them.

"Emily, Lily. By marrying your mother, I will become your step-dad. But I'd like very much to be more." His gaze flicked to me, and I read the vulnerability there and nodded, encouraging him to continue. "If you'll have me, I want to be there for every part of your lives, just like I'll be there for your mother. I want to adopt you girls and be your father, in every sense of the word."

I felt my breath catch, tears welling up in my eyes as I looked from Trigger to the girls. Lily's face lit up, and Emily was trying to hide a smile behind her hands.

Trigger wanted to be their father. My heart broke in the best way possible. I couldn't believe how blessed I was to have met him and how lucky we were to have him in our lives.

Lily was the first to speak, her voice a little choked, but full of happiness. "I want that. I want you to be my daddy."

Emily nodded, her eyes shining. "Me too," she whispered, her voice soft but firm. "You're already like a dad to us."

Trigger beamed, and I heard sniffles from Lola and Cammy as he put a ring on each of the girls fingers. As he did, he made them a vow. "Girls, these rings are my promise to be there for you no matter what you need, whenever you need me, and for the rest of my life."

The three embraced, and I saw Trigger blink back a tear. Lily squealed again in delight as a silent tear slid down Emily's face.

Tears streamed down my own face, and I bent to hug both, them, wrapping all three of them in my arms.

"I'm so proud of you all and so very happy," I whispered, my heart full, my chest tight with emotion.

Trigger stood, pulling me into his arms, his love surrounding me.

"Let's see those rings, girls," Lolita said, winking at us as she drew the girls away to give us a moment of privacy.

While they chattered and showed off the rings, I couldn't stop the tears, couldn't stop the overwhelming joy that surged through me. "We're a family now," he murmured against my ear, his voice low and full of promise. "Always."

And I knew, in that moment, that nothing would ever be the same again.

It was the beginning of our forever.

ABOUT THE AUTHOR

Jax Knight is a fledgling author who finally gave in to the voices in her head, letting them come to life in her first dark contemporary romance series.

Jax lives in Scotland with her husband and son. She enjoys martial arts, reading and coffee and can often be found hiding away in a corner, glued to her Kindle or with her head buried in a book while sipping a Mocha.

A sucker for sexy, protective villains with morals and feisty, fun females, all her books have them aplenty and a guaranteed happy-ever-after!

Ash is her debut novel and the first of six books in her Bratva Blood Brothers Series.

If you'd like to keep up with all of her new releases and more, please come and join her newsletter or follow her on social media to stay up to date!

ALSO BY JAX KNIGHT

Bratva Blood Brothers

Ash

Romi

Miki

Marko

Luca

Anton

Bratva Bodyguards

Trigger